Nancy Jackson

It TAKES *an* ANGEL

OTHER BOOKS BY DAN YATES

Angels Don't Knock!

Just Call Me an Angel

Angels to the Rescue

An Angel in the Family

It TAKES *an* ANGEL

a novel

DAN YATES

Covenant Communications, Inc.

Cover images ® copyright 1999 PhotoDisc, Inc.

Published by Covenant Communications, Inc.
American Fork, Utah

Printed in the United States of America
First Printing: March 1999

06 05 04 03 02 01 00 99   10 9 8 7 6 5 4 3 2 1

ISBN 1-57734-471-5

This book is dedicated to my best friend. Her name is Jean, and without her, none of my stories would have been possible. She's always there with her special brand of love and support. She's my number one editor. She gives me encouragement when things aren't going as smoothly as I think they should; she always has that special word I can't find anywhere else that's exactly what I need; and she never complains because of the hours I spend in front of my computer. I've been married to her for forty-three years, and plan on staying with her at least until the end of forever. Yes, we are covered by one of those special contracts mentioned so many times in my stories. And by the way, if you've read my stories you should know her. She has short blond hair, eyes the color of a summer sky, a feisty spirit always ready to see the good in any situation, a will to conquer any problem placed in her path, and the charm of a lady princess. I try to capture everything about her as I weave her into each of my stories. I don't use her real name, of course. In my books you've come to know her as—Samantha.

PROLOGUE

For ten long years Brad Douglas had called a tiny island in the Caribbean Sea home. Brad had come to the island, along with his sister, Shannon, and niece, Tanielle, to escape James Baxter. James was Shannon's abusive husband who relentlessly kept her life in turmoil.

Brad had only been on the island a short time when he discovered something very strange about the place; it was haunted by the three-hundred-year-old ghost of a sea captain named Horatio Symington Blake. Once the captain came to realize he couldn't frighten Brad off his island, the two became fast friends.

Life on the island might have gone on even longer if James Baxter hadn't discovered Shannon's whereabouts. He showed up on the island with the intention of kidnapping Shannon and taking her back to San Francisco, where he could make her pay for running away from him all those years before. What Baxter didn't reckon on was the involvement of a couple of special angels who were there to straighten out some kinks that had managed to occur in a few destinies.

These angels were Jason and Samantha Hackett, who had married after a most unusual courtship. Because of a mix-up in his destiny, Jason was born thirty years too soon and found himself on the far side of forever by the time Samantha was old enough for him to court her. But that same destiny which had brought him to this world too soon had also chosen Samantha as his forever sweetheart. Thus, Jason ended up courting Samantha as an angel. A little awkward, but not an impossible feat. With the authorization of the higher authorities, Samantha simply stepped across the line and became an angel herself. Thus, she and Jason became forever partners in a marriage made in heaven—literally.

Once Samantha took on her new role as angel, she set right to work playing matchmaker to friends and family still on this side of mortality, a role she dearly loved. And that's how she happened to cross paths with Mr. James Baxter.

When Baxter met his death in an explosion, there was no longer a reason for Brad, Shannon, and Tanielle to remain on the island, especially since a massive storm completely destroyed everything Brad and Shannon had built there.

This story begins with their return home—Shannon and Tanielle to a new life, and Brad to . . . Well, Brad didn't know for sure what he would be returning to, since Lori—the one love of his life—was now married to another man.

But was she? The surprising answer to this question, and many more, lay just ahead for Brad. Decisions lay ahead, too. Decisions that would affect the rest of Brad's life, as well as his forever.

Fate had dealt Brad a tremendous blow in his past. Now, fate would need a hand in overcoming the damage done by that blow. Where would this help come from? Well, if you read on, you will see that for this particular brand of help—it takes an angel.

CHAPTER 1

Lori stood on the forward deck of Howard Placard's magnificent yacht, her long blond hair flowing delicately to the rhythm of the brisk sea breeze brushing over her face. There, she contemplated the possibility of a future with the only man she had ever loved. Tears that might have moistened her eyes were quickly dried by the wind. Howard stood just behind her. Good old Howard. How many times had she wished she'd never met this man or even so much as heard his name? But she did meet him. That chapter of her life was well behind her now—as were so many of her dreams. She felt Howard's hand on her shoulder as he carefully pulled her around to face him.

"It's over for you and him, Lori," Howard said, a pleading look in his eyes. "Can't you see that now? Give me the chance to make you as happy as I know I can."

Before Lori knew what was happening, Howard took her left hand in his and slid a diamond band on her finger. "You know how I feel about you," he continued. "Take this ring, say 'yes,' and make me the happiest man in the world."

Lori stared at the ring. Apprehension filled every corner of her mind as the fullness of Howard's intentions became vividly clear. Here, in the shadow of all that had happened these last few days, he was asking her to marry him. He was offering her yachts, a beach house, fine cars, life in the fast lane—he was even willing to accept the fact that she didn't love him. "You could learn to love me," he contended.

Instinctively, Lori's right hand moved to the gold chain around her neck. The chain Brad had given her so long ago. The chain that held a secret known only to Lori, and to none else.

"I'm waiting for your answer," Howard pressed impatiently. "What will it be? A life of lonely nights thinking about him, or the life of lights and laughter that comes with a 'yes' to my offer?"

Lori looked deeply into Howard's eyes. There, with his ring on her left hand and the feel of Brad's gold chain against her neck—her decision was clear. A slight smile crossed her lips as she prepared to give Howard his answer.

* * *

Brad took his seat in the chopper and secured his shoulder harness. A thumbs-up to his friend and pilot Bob Rivers signaled he was ready to go. Bob shoved the accelerator forward, and the overhead chopper blades bit noisily into the air. With a sudden jerk upward, they were on their way.

With mixed emotions, Brad watched the houses, people, and cars on Saint Thomas Island grow smaller and smaller as the chopper ascended into the cloudless blue Caribbean sky. More than ten years had slipped by since the day he first set eyes on the island through the window of an Air Force cargo plane that brought him here, along with his sister, Shannon, and niece, Tanielle. Tanielle was only five at the time. Brad had to admit it had been fun watching her grow into a lovely fifteen-year-old young woman. He was the closest thing to a father she had known, and even though it was only an honorary title, it gave him a feeling of great accomplishment.

"Would you like to make one last pass over the old homestead before we head for the mainland?" Bob asked as he headed the chopper out over the Caribbean.

"Yeah," Brad said with a smile. "I'd like that—although there's probably not much left of the place after the granddaddy of all storms hit it last month."

"A month?" Bob asked. "Has it really been that long? Boy, how time flies. So how are Shannon and Tanielle doing now? Are they settling into life back in the States?"

Brad nodded yes. "They're doing great. I contacted my old friend Tom Reddings, who's an Air Force pilot, and he set the girls up with a flight home. He even helped them move into an apartment in the same complex where he lives. They're in good hands with Tom. Tom's the guy I thought Shannon should have married in the first place, instead of that worthless James Baxter. Oh well, with Baxter out of the picture now, I hope Shannon can find herself a good man. And as for Tanielle, well, she can start a brand new wonderful life with new friends, new places to see, the works. It's great, Bob. I'm really happy for them both."

"Uh huh," Bob responded. "I can see you're happy for Shannon and Tanielle. But what about Brad Douglas? How do you feel about going home to pick up the pieces?"

Brad grew silent. What would going home be like for him? He could never work as a motion picture director again—Howard Placard would see to that. Not that he would be too bad off financially. He had enough money from the sale of his boat to get by for a while, and he could always fall back on his impressionist routine. Plus, there were the gold coins Captain Blake had given him as a parting gift on the day Brad left the island. If worse came to worse, he could look for a buyer for the coins. They should bring in a few dollars at least.

The biggest question concerning Brad's return home was not financial, however. The biggest question was Lori. What if he should run into her again? How would he react? He shuddered at the thought of seeing her with another man, but the fact was, she belonged to another now.

"I don't know how I'll feel about picking up the pieces, Bob," he said at length. "I'll just have to take it one day at a time and see where the trail may lead."

Bob smiled. "Well, you know I wish you the best, Brad. And from the looks of the island down there, I'd say you have nothing left to worry about leaving on this end."

Brad had been so deep in thought that he failed to notice they were over the tiny island he and the girls had called home for ten years. As Bob called it to his attention, he glanced out the window to see for himself. "You're right, Bob," he said in astonishment at the sight. "The old place really took a beating, didn't it? You have no idea how hard it is to let this all go, Bob. I put a lot of blood and sweat into building that house and everything that goes with it. From the looks of it now, it would take a lot more blood and sweat to make the place livable again."

"Maybe it's better this way," Bob said reassuringly. "With the strings cut to the past, the future may be a little easier to reach for."

"Yeah," Brad acknowledged with an insincere laugh. "This isn't the first time I've watched my efforts turn to dust, Bob. I had a marriage once. I put a lot of effort into building that, too. But in the end, the marriage came tumbling down just like this house. Sort of makes me wonder if it's even worth reaching for another future. Nothing I do seems to last more than a few years at best."

"Just as I thought," Bob said, shaking his head. "You're still thinking about Lori. I swear, Brad, I don't think I've ever seen a guy have a harder time forgetting a woman than you've had with Lori. Give it up, friend. Get on with your life. You'll find someone else if you put your mind to it. Just relax and learn to live again. Okay, buddy?"

Brad managed a smile. "I'll give it my best shot."

As Bob turned the chopper toward Key West, where his passenger was to catch a plane bound for home, Brad strained for one last look at the tiny island. He knew every rock, tree, and cove on the place. This would be his final good-bye to them all, so he strained for the last possible glimpse as it became a tiny dot on the water and soon disappeared altogether.

* * *

Unknown to either Brad or Bob, two extra passengers were listening in on their conversation from the back seat. "Well, my cute little ghost," Samantha said to Jason. "Our boy is on his way home. Now comes the big question—how do we handle the next part? We had better come up with a plan pretty quick, since the higher authorities have decreed we have to have the job done in less than a month. Any suggestions where we can start, Jason?"

"What's this?" Jason teased. "You're asking me to come up with a plan to get Cupid's arrow in the bow? Now there's a twist for the record book."

"What can I say, Jason?" Samantha retorted. "I mean, it took a lot out of me getting my brother and Jenice Anderson together. And besides, you're my partner in this Special Conditions Coordinator thing we've just inherited. It's only fair you should pull your share of the load. So what about it? Any ideas?"

"You're Cupid's helper in the family," Jason argued. "Not to mention this SCC thing was your doing and not mine. Ask me to come up with a new dessert, or a better way to serve stuffed squash—that I can do. But ask me to think of a way to solve Brad Douglas' ten-year-old romance problems . . . ? Forget it, Sam. It's not my area of expertise."

"Jason Hackett, I don't know what I'm going to do with you," Samantha scolded. "All you ever think of is cooking. In fact, isn't that what sent you from your mortal dimension into this one twenty-some odd years ago—tasting some of your own cooking and choking on that chicken bone? Forget about food for a minute, and help me out here with more important matters. Surely you can think of something."

"How about this?" Jason suggested, tongue in cheek. "We'll contact Arline Vincent and have her invite everyone involved to her talk show. They can all hash out the problem in front of a television audience. We can even have Captain Blake make an appearance. Everyone loves seeing dirty laundry displayed on a television talk show, and just think how the ghost of a three-hundred-year-old dead sea captain would boost Arline's ratings."

Samantha leaned over and gave Jason a quick kiss. "I love it!" she cried. "I don't know why I didn't think of it myself. You're a genius, my handsome little husband. And you tell me I'm the only one in the family capable of dreaming up romantic schemes."

Jason was flabbergasted. "What?" he gasped. "You like the idea of airing the problem in front of a television audience?"

"No," Samantha scowled as she elbowed Jason in the ribs. "We're not going to put Brad on television, but we are going to use Arline and Bruce's influence in bringing this case to a quick resolution. They're perfect for the job, and neither of them will have the slightest problem accepting us as angels, which takes care of the problem of who we can appear to and ask for help. They'll even accept the captain when they realize he's one of us."

Jason laughed. "Bruce Vincent and Captain Blake together. Now there's a pair if ever I thought of one. Talk about complete opposites! They'll hate each other, Sam."

"They won't hate each other, Jason," Samantha reassured him. "You're judging Bruce by the man he used to be. Admit it, Bruce is a different man now that Arline's helped him discover who he really is. You're not still jealous of the man, are you, Jason? Just because I was engaged to him before I met you?"

"No I'm not still jealous of Bruce. I never was jealous of Bruce. Well—maybe just a little, but not that much. And I have to admit, he has changed. But he's still Bruce Vincent, a highly polished individual who likes being around other highly polished individuals. And I don't think even you can give the captain higher than a two on a scale of ten when it comes to being polished."

Samantha laughed. "You are still jealous of Bruce. Tell you what, I'll wager my apology against yours that Bruce and Captain Blake will hit it off as great friends. I'll even apologize in front of anyone you choose if I lose."

"Okay, Sam, you're on. When this is over, I'll invite Gus and his wife, along with Maggie and her husband, to our place for dinner. Maggie and Gus have been after me to have them over ever since we replaced them as Special Conditions Coordinators. I'll fix up a big feast, and whichever one of us loses can apologize in front of the whole group. And you can bet, I intend to make you grovel, my cocky little wife."

"Oh? You plan on making me grovel, do you?" Samantha smiled calmly. "Well, Jason Hackett, what do you say we get this show on the road so we can see who makes who grovel all the sooner? What do you say we pay Bruce and Arline a visit?"

CHAPTER 2

Arline Vincent stared listlessly through the large picture window revealing the majestic forest view of Henderson Mountain. She loved living in this mountain lodge. She loved doing her new television talk show that originated from one of the lodge's conference rooms. Most of all, she loved being Mrs. Bruce Vincent. Releasing a deep sigh, Arline thought about how perfect her life was. How could it be any better?

So engrossed in the beauty of the mountain had she become, that she failed to hear Bruce stepping up from behind, until she felt his strong arms around her waist. "Hi," he said. "How did your show go this morning?"

Arline rested her hands on his and lay her head back against his shoulder. "Hi to you, too," she purred. "The show went great. How are things with you, big guy? Is managing a lodge proving to be mentally challenging enough to suit you after all your years as a psychologist?"

"Oh yes," Bruce nodded. "It's keeping both my mind and my muscles occupied. Other than moving my couch once in a while, I got almost no exercise in the old occupation. This job is great. I feel better than I have in years, and I'm loving every minute of it." Bruce kissed her on the cheek. "And it's all your doing, beautiful lady. In all the years I spent as a psychologist, I never managed to turn any of my clients around like you've turned me around. I remember how Jason Hackett used to call me a wimp. He was right, you know. I was a wimp."

"Umm," Arline said, snuggling closer to Bruce. "If Jason were here now, he wouldn't call you a wimp, you can be sure of that, *darling*."

"Darling?" Bruce laughed. "There you go, mocking my old habits again. I've been trying to give up using the word, you know. Some old habits are hard to break."

Arline turned in his arms and kissed him. "You can call me darling anytime you want, Bruce Vincent. Just don't you ever let me catch you using the term on any other woman, you hear?"

Suddenly Arline became aware of two other individuals standing only a few feet away. A closer look gave her the shock of her life. "Sam? Jason?" she gasped. "Am I seeing things or is it really you?"

"It's us, Arline," Jason spoke up. "And the lady's right, Bruce. I'd never call you a wimp now. You're proving to be an all-right guy in my book. Who knows, I might even be able to teach you the art of cooking for your resort dining room if I have the time."

Samantha moved forward and pulled Arline into a hug. "Wow!" Arline cried out, jubilantly. "What's changed since I last saw you, Sam? We couldn't hug back then, remember?" As Arline looked on in amazement, Jason walked to Bruce and offered his hand. Bruce, obviously surprised by the gesture, reached out and accepted the hand. "I agree with Arline," he exclaimed. "Something has changed since I saw you on Howard Placard's beach the day I proposed to Arline. I can feel your hand."

It was Samantha who explained. "You two have to understand, being in the angel business means that Jason and I can sometimes be full of surprises. This time it's because we've been promoted a rung higher on the ladder. You might call us second-level angels now. And second-level angels can do things first-level angels can't. Like give hugs and shake hands."

Arline squeezed Samantha tighter. "I like this second-level thing," she declared. "You'll never know how badly I've missed your hugs, Sam. This is super."

"You look wonderful, Sam," Bruce acknowledged. "Life with this Jason fellow must suit you pretty well."

"Oh yes," Samantha said, reaching out and ruffling Jason's hair. "Life with this Jason fellow is what you might call 'out of this world.'"

"Oh, ouch," Bruce grinned. "I sort of asked for that one, didn't I?"

Samantha reached out and pinched Bruce's cheek. "You're looking pretty good yourself, Bruce. I'd say life with this Arline lady must suit you pretty well. Aren't you glad I got the two of you together?"

Bruce looked at Arline with deep love in his eyes. "Yes, Sam, I'm very glad you got us together. It's funny, considering all the time I knew Arline, and I had no idea she was the right one for me until you brought us together. I hope the time comes when I can repay you somehow."

"Oh, I think you'll get your wish on that one, Bruce," Jason laughingly observed. "When you learn why we're here, I'm pretty sure you'll know what I mean."

"Why are you here, Sam?" Arline asked. "I'm sure you wouldn't just drop in without a pretty good reason."

"You got that right, Arline," Jason agreed. "This wife of mine can't seem to get enough of meddling in people's lives on this side. Wait until you hear what she got me into this time. Thanks to her, the two of us now share the title 'Special Conditions Coordinator.'"

"Special Conditions Coordinator?" Arline echoed. "Isn't that the title you gave Gus when you introduced me to him way back when?"

"Oh yes, Gus was the Special Conditions Coordinator back then. But he's moved on to greater things now, and guess who took his place?"

Arline looked back and forth between Samantha and Jason. "You and Sam share the title now?" she asked.

"Yep. That's why you could feel Sam's hug. We were moved up a notch in the chain of progression in order to qualify for the position. Personally I was perfectly happy as head chef in the finest restaurant of our galaxy, but Sam managed to finagle us into this position."

"So, you're not just regular angels now?" Arline ventured. "You're special somehow?"

Samantha laughed. "No, Arline, we're no more special than we ever were. We've just taken on some added responsibilities is all. I'm sure Jason explained how Gus was responsible for bringing the two of us together, and even though you probably never knew it—he was also responsible for bringing you and Bruce together. I just sort of helped him out on that little item."

"Uh huh," Arline laughed. "And now the two of you are responsible for getting someone else together, right? And you're here to ask either Bruce or me to help? Am I getting warm, Sam?"

"You always could see right through me, Arline," Samantha responded. "And the answer to both questions is yes. Except we want both yours and Bruce's help with this one. And don't pay any attention to Jason's grumbling. It's all an act. He loves every minute of being an SCC. This way he gets to spend more time with me, instead of those stuffy cooks at the Paradise Palace."

Arline nodded. "I remember the first time you came to me asking for my help, Jason," she said. "Tell me the truth. Did you honestly believe Jenice Anderson was right for Bruce, or were you just putting me on all along?"

Jason shifted his weight nervously from one leg to the other. "I, uh . . ."

Arline winked at him. "Never mind," she said. "I get the picture, and it all worked out fine in the end." Then another thought came to Arline's mind. "Hey, correct me if I'm wrong. You're here this time asking our help to get Jenice married off to some poor unsuspecting guy. Am I close, or what?"

"No," Samantha laughed. "Not this time. Not that Jenice wasn't one of our projects, but we already have her set up with Mr. Right." Samantha released a long sigh. "I'll bet you can't guess who her Mr. Right turned out to be, Arline."

Arline thought a moment. "No, I really can't come up with even a wild guess. Who is the poor fellow? Anyone I know?"

"Oh yes, you know him all right. I used to set you up with him every chance I got when we were all teenagers."

Arline's mouth fell open. "No, Sam, tell me it isn't true! You didn't set your brother, Michael, up with Jenice Anderson, did you?"

Samantha smiled and nodded yes. "After you get to know Jenice," she explained, "she's really quite a lady. We both misjudged her, Arline."

"Misjudged her!" Arline half shouted. "After the way that hussy dumped Bruce, how can you call her a lady?"

"Uh, Arline," Samantha pressed. "If you think about it, I 'dumped' Bruce, too. Does that make me a hussy in your eyes?"

"Well, no. But that's different. You're my best friend, and you had Jason there to sway you away from Bruce. The two of you were destined for each other, remember?"

"That's true. But it's also true that Jenice had Michael there to sway her away from Bruce. Neither of you knows this, but Michael and Jenice were in love before Bruce and Jenice met. Take my word for it, Arline. Jenice is the right one for Michael, and I'll count it an honor having her as my sister when the big day arrives. I'm sure you and Bruce will be invited to the wedding."

Arline shook her head. "I'll take your word for it, Sam. I remember how protective you always were of your brother. If Jenice has proved herself to you, then who am I to argue? So if it isn't Jenice you need our help with, then who?"

"You don't know him," Samantha explained. "His name is Brad Douglas, and we're faced with a unique problem in securing his destiny. It's going to take a lot of work on your part, a lot of work on our part, and a lot of work on the part of a very colorful fellow you've yet to meet—Captain Horatio Symington Blake."

"Captain who?" Bruce chortled.

Jason grinned. "Long name, eh, Bruce? Wait 'til you meet the fellow. I think you'll agree the name fits him like a glove. An old, worn-out glove that's pulled one too many barracuda from the net."

"Pay no mind to him, Bruce," Samantha said, stepping between the two of them. "Captain Blake is indeed a colorful fellow. You'll love him, I'm sure."

Now it was Arline's turn to laugh. "You know," she said with a wink in Jason's direction. "The last time you came looking for my help I ended up getting kidnapped. I'll never forget that awful feeling of being locked in a safe. I hope you have things under better control this time."

"Not to worry, Arline," Samantha explained. "I'm in charge of this operation. You're in good hands, kid. No kidnapping this time, I promise."

Arline hesitated. "You know I'm locked into being here for my morning talk show, don't you? What you have in mind won't interfere with this, will it?"

"Not at all," Samantha assured her. "In fact, your TV show is a big part of our overall plan. Not only do you get the chance to help us— I guarantee your ratings will skyrocket because of it. Are the two of you game for this?"

Bruce and Arline exchanged glances. "We're game," Bruce answered for them both. "After what you did for us, I'd say we owe you immensely. What would you like us to do?"

"Thanks, Bruce. I knew I could depend on you guys. The first thing we need to do is fill you in on what we're up against here. How would you two like a little history lesson?"

"History lesson?" Arline asked dubiously. "You're sending us back to school?"

"No, Arline. I'm sending you to the movies. I know how much you love a good romance on the big screen; I've sat through enough of them with you over the years. And the sort of movie I have in mind beats anything you've ever seen. It's called a 'selected event shown by holographically enhanced regeneration.'"

"A what?" Arline asked in shock.

"Don't let the tricky name fool you, Arline. It's like having history reenacted with you right there in the middle of it. You can even feel what the people in the holograph were feeling at the time the event took place. You're going to love it, lady. It's the next best thing to chocolate."

Arline grinned. "It sounds interesting enough. You say it's a romance? You know me. Should I grab a box of tissue?"

Samantha laughed. "Yeah, knowing you, I'd say a couple of boxes wouldn't hurt."

"What about popcorn? You know I can't enjoy a movie without my popcorn."

Jason spoke up. "Now you're talking my language, Arline. While you're getting ready to watch the replay, I'll make a quick trip to the Paradise Palace and whip up a batch of popcorn like you've never tasted. What the heck, I should be entitled to a little fun on these assignments. I'll be back before you have time to dim the lights."

Samantha watched as Jason suddenly vanished from their ranks. "I don't know what I'm going to do with him," she said. "Try as I might, I can't tear him away from his chef's job." She shook her head. "Now, we need a room where we can have some privacy. Where would you suggest?"

"How about my study?" Bruce suggested. "It's just down the hall, and we'll have all the privacy we need there."

"Talk about nostalgia," Samantha observed as they stepped into Bruce's study. "This room looks exactly like your old office, Bruce. Furniture and all. Back when you were a psychologist, I mean."

Bruce shrugged. "I had to hang onto something from the old me," he explained. "Arline agreed I could keep my office, at least."

"It was a small price to pay," Arline grinned. "And I sort of like having a reminder of the old Bruce around once in a while, too. It helps me appreciate just how much I love and respect the new improved model."

"Oh well," Samantha chuckled. "Let's get started. Grab a seat on the sofa, you two, and get comfortable. First stop is the airport."

"The airport?" Arline questioned. "You're going to bring the airport right here to Bruce's study?"

"Hey, it's no big deal. Being an SCC makes me somewhat of a big shot on my side of the line. This sort of thing is child's play, believe me. I'm not only going to bring the airport to Bruce's study, I'm going to take you back ten years while I'm at it. You're about to meet a younger version of Brad and Lori Douglas, who happen to be the stars of this production. And for you, Bruce, you're about to see one face you'll recognize right off—Howard Placard."

"Howard Placard?" Bruce asked. "Howard's part of the reason you need our help?"

"Oh yes, Howard is part of the reason. In fact, Howard is the cause of the problem in the first place. I know you two are friends, but you're about to learn some things about the man that may surprise you, Bruce."

"I wouldn't exactly refer to Howard as a friend, Sam," Bruce explained. "He used to refer clients to me once in a while when I was a practicing psychologist. Howard deals with lots of actors and actresses who sometimes become quite eccentric."

"Maybe the guy should have recommended himself to you, Bruce," Samantha retorted. "He probably needed more help than those he recommended did. Just watch the show, and you'll see what I mean."

By the time Arline and Bruce were comfortable in their seats, Jason was back with the popcorn. "Here you go, Arline," he smiled. "Enjoy."

Arline took a taste. "Wow!" she exclaimed. "You can take me to the movies anytime, Jason, as long as you furnish the popcorn. This stuff is fantastic."

CHAPTER 3

The sound of the loud speaker announcing the final boarding call for Flight 1377 bound for Acapulco, Mexico, sent cold chills running down Lori's spine. It wasn't as though this were the first film ever to take her husband to some faraway location, but this time something was different. Even though Lori didn't know exactly what the difference was, she did know it was real. A voice inside kept calling out for her to ask him not to go, but that would be absurd. Brad was a director. It was his job, and where the job took him was where he had to be. She assured herself everything would be fine. After all, it would only be for three months or so.

Brad pulled Lori into his arms and kissed her. She felt so secure in his arms, and his lips were warm and assuring. For some reason it reminded her of the first time he had kissed her on a moonlight hayride when they were freshmen in high school. For days afterward all she could think of was his kiss. From that time on, she had known that Brad was the one she wanted to marry someday.

Brad picked up his carry-on bag and stood smiling at her a few more seconds. "Call you tonight, babe," he said.

Lori placed a gentle hand against the side of his face. "You'd better," she replied, brushing a tear from her eye with the other hand. "And you'd better keep your distance from all those girls in beach bikinis."

"Deal," he said, his smile deepening. "I'll keep my distance."

One last quick kiss, and Brad stepped to the loading gate where he handed his boarding pass to the attendant. "Don't forget to miss me," he called back to Lori.

"I won't forget . . . ," she said, raising her hand in a shoulder-high wave as she watched him vanish into the tunnel leading to the airliner.

For what seemed an eternity, she stared after him wishing somehow he would reappear, saying he had decided against the trip.

She would probably have stood there longer if it hadn't been for the feel of a hand on her shoulder. Glancing back to see who had touched her, she was surprised to see Howard Placard, the producer of the film that was taking Brad away.

"Morning, Lori," Howard said. "I take it you're here to see Brad off to Acapulco?"

"Oh, yes, Mr. Placard, I am. Brad just this instant walked through the loading gate."

Lori was caught off guard by the sudden appearance of a man as busy as Howard Placard always seemed to be. She had no idea what he could be doing here at the airport. The thought that he might have come to see Brad off never occurred to her.

"Don't look so startled to see me here, Lori," Howard smiled. "I do find the time to get a little personal with my people once in a while. I was on this side of town for an early morning business meeting and the thought hit me, as long as I was this close, why not drop by to see Brad off. You know, wish him luck. That sort of thing."

"Oh," Lori smiled. "I'm so sorry. You just missed him. I know he would have appreciated seeing you here."

"Too bad," Howard shrugged. "That's the price one often pays for holding such tight schedules." Howard glanced at his watch. "Would you look at this?" he laughed lightly. "It's nearly noon. I'm starved. How about you, Lori? May I offer you some lunch?"

Lori glanced back to the loading gate one last time. "Thank you, Mr. Placard. But really, I shouldn't. I have my car here at the airport, and the parking meter is running, you know."

Howard smiled. "That's no problem. We can take your car, and I'll have my driver pick me up later at the restaurant. I won't take no for an answer. What are you in the mood for? Chinese? Mexican? Or how about a steak?"

Lori had to admit, she was a little hungry. She had fixed a big breakfast for Brad—with him leaving for Acapulco and all—but she hadn't eaten. The offer was tempting. Still . . . something about having lunch with Howard Placard didn't seem right under the circumstances. If Brad were with them, it would be one thing. But Brad was aboard a departing plane.

Howard pressed his point. "The Hunter's Cottage is only a short distance from here. I can call ahead for reservations, using my cellular phone. The restaurant has a lovely lakeside patio, and the food there is out of this world."

Lori took one last look at Brad's plane through the large glass window overlooking the docking station. She was torn whether or not to accept Mr. Placard's invitation. After all, Mr. Placard did provide a lot of work for Brad. She wouldn't dare do anything to offend the man. She tried one last time. "I appreciate the offer," she said, smiling warmly. "But I have some things needing to be done, and—"

"Nonsense," Howard pressured. "I insist you let me take you to lunch. Which way to your car?"

* * *

"What is going on here, Sam?" Arline broke in. "Is this guy trying to hit on Lori, or what?"

"Just keep watching," Sam replied. "And remember, everything you're seeing here is ten-year-old history. There's nothing you can do to change it now. But there is something you can do to help mold what's still in the future. The future is what we need your help with and the future is why I'm asking you to watch this now, even if it doesn't make for the most pleasant afternoon."

Arline glared at the holograph still playing out in front of her. "So this is the infamous Howard Placard?" she mused aloud. "It was on his private beach where you parachuted down from the sky to propose to me, Bruce, remember?"

"Certainly I remember, Arline. Howard gave me unlimited access to his beach as a perk for accepting the clients he sent my way."

"Look at him," Arline scowled. "He has shifty eyes. I never trust a man with shifty eyes. I'll lay you odds he's up to no good."

Samantha looked at her a moment and said, "You got that right, Arline. In fact, you'll soon see just how right you are. Just keep watching, okay?"

Helping herself to another handful of popcorn, Arline turned back to the replay with heightened interest.

* * *

"This is Brad's car?" Howard asked Lori as they approached a two-tone brown Pontiac Grand Prix. "I'm surprised. Most film directors drive something a little . . . wilder. I somehow pictured Brad in a racy sports car."

Lori laughed. "Like a candy apple red Porsche 911?" she asked.

Howard nodded. "Yeah, a Porsche—or something of that nature. Certainly not an old man's car like this Pontiac."

Lori sighed. "Believe me, Mr. Placard. I've tried to talk Brad into buying a Porsche. Oh how I've tried, but you have to understand the way Brad thinks. To him, everything has to be practical. That's the biggest rule in his life: if it's not practical, we don't do it."

Lori stepped to the passenger side door, and took her keys from her purse with the intention of unlocking the door. To her surprise, Howard reached out and took the keys from her. "Here," he said. "Let me do that. Where I come from it's the man's place to open doors for the lady, not the other way around."

Lori stood out of the way while Howard opened the door and motioned her inside. "You might as well let me drive while we're at it," he smiled. "I know where we're going, and it would be easier for me to drive than try to give you instructions."

With a shrug, Lori slid into the passenger seat. Howard closed the door, then rounded the car to the driver's side. As he settled himself in his seat, he looked at the key ring she had handed him. A curious medallion was fastened to the ring; it was a little larger than a silver dollar and engraved with what appeared to be a family crest of some sort. In the middle of the medallion was a large dent.

"This is an interesting charm," he observed. "It almost looks as if it stopped a bullet at some time. Is there a story behind it?"

Lori glanced at the medallion. "Yes," she responded with a soft smile. "It does have a story behind it. My father gave it to me, and it was passed down from generation to generation. It belonged to my great-grandfather, Amos William Parker. Amos was only fourteen years old when he and his older sister were victims of a stage holdup. They probably would have been killed if it hadn't been for a mysterious stranger who happened along just then."

"A mysterious stranger who happened onto a stage holdup?" Howard remarked with keen interest. "I'd like to hear the whole story sometime. Being a motion picture producer, I'm always on the look-out for an interesting story. So how did this stranger save their lives?"

Lori shook her head. "I'm sort of sketchy on all the details, Mr. Placard. But apparently one of the stage robbers shot at the stranger. The medallion you're looking at stopped the bullet and saved his life. He was able to apprehend the robbers, and later gave the medallion to my great-grandfather. That's about all I know."

"That's quite a story," Howard said as he slid the key into the ignition and started the engine. "Now, how about if we drop the Mr. Placard thing? I keep thinking you're talking to my father. Call me, Howard, please."

Lori nodded, then stared as Howard pulled some sort of a portable phone from his briefcase. With the phone in one hand, he backed out of the parking space. As he headed the car toward the exit, he dialed his chauffeur, Don Harrison, with instructions to drive to the Hunter's Cottage and wait there. Lori remembered that Howard had referred to a cellular phone earlier, but she hadn't understood what he meant.

"Wow, that's a neat gadget," she commented as he completed his call. "I've never seen one like it. Can you call from anywhere with it?"

"Oh this?" Howard said, holding the phone up so she could get a closer look. "It's the newest thing in phones. It's called a 'cellular.' There are only a few on the market now, and it cost me a bundle. And yes, you can call and receive calls from almost anywhere. They say in the next few years there'll be thousands of these phones in use. Who knows, maybe they're right. It's a pretty handy device, for sure. Watch this, and you'll see what I mean."

As Lori looked on in amazement, Howard placed a second call. This time it was to the Hunter's Cottage, where he made reservations for two. "I can't believe this," Lori laughed. "What will science come up with next?"

Howard grinned, obviously pleased with himself for impressing Lori. "Science already has come up with some unbelievable things, Lori. I should know—I can afford them all. If you're ever around me much, you'll get to see some pretty amazing things. If Brad weren't so practical, as you claim he is, he could afford to show you some exciting things himself. I should know; I pay the biggest part of his salary. And believe me, he doesn't come cheap."

When they reached the restaurant, Howard gave Lori's keys to the parking valet, which was a first for her. She had to admit, being with Howard was sort of exciting.

When they went inside, they were seated immediately at a table on the veranda overlooking a small lake.

"This is nice," she said to Howard. "I wish I could talk Brad into bringing me here sometime."

"If you think it's nice now, you should see it at night," Howard declared. "The view is breathtaking, and they have live music. I'm surprised Brad has never brought you here."

"Brad never brings me to places like this," Lori sighed. "He's more . . ."

"Practical?" Howard broke in, finishing Lori's sentence for her.

"Yeah," Lori agreed. "Practical." She smiled and drew in a deep breath. "I love that guy but . . ."

"You wish he weren't so practical," Howard continued her thought for her. "You were raised differently than that, weren't you, Lori?"

Lori nodded. "My parents weren't wealthy, but they did know how to relax and enjoy themselves. With Brad, I don't know . . . it's not that he's cheap—he's just—Brad. He's been that way ever since I met him back in the ninth grade."

Howard looked surprised. "You met him in the ninth grade? You were more or less childhood sweethearts, then?"

"You could say that. Brad was the only guy I ever dated seriously, and I was the only one for him. We just sort of grew up together." She paused. "Brad's always been very practical, but just once I'd like to have him do something spontaneous, something romantic, like surprising me with a trip to Hawaii or some place. I'd even settle for an evening at a place like this once in a while."

The corners of Howard's mouth twisted into a sly grin. "I think I see what you mean," he said. "You'd like a little more excitement in your life than Brad thinks is necessary."

Lori looked out at the small lake where a couple of swans floated gracefully amid the lily pads. "Yes, I would," she agreed with a smile and a sigh.

"Can I get you something to drink?" asked a young waitress who had quietly approached the table. Howard looked at Lori to see what her order would be, before ordering his own.

"I'll have a 7-Up," Lori said.

"Make that two," Howard responded. "And you can take the rest of our order now if you'd like. I'll have the house filet, well done, salad with blue cheese dressing, and load my baked potato with the works."

The waitress wrote the order, then turned to Lori. "And you, ma'am?" she asked.

Lori's eyes caught Howard's. "I'm not hungry enough for a steak," she said. "What I'd really like is a grilled tuna on sourdough bread. And maybe some barbeque chips."

Howard shrugged. "Give the lady what she wants," he said to the waitress.

"So what do you plan on doing to entertain yourself while Brad's away having the time of his life in Acapulco?" Howard asked when the waitress had left them.

His question brought a beaming smile to Lori's face. "I'm going to work," she answered, excitedly. "Not permanently, though. It will just be while Brad's away in Acapulco. I'm hoping to get some experience so I can start my own business in interior decorating someday."

"Interior decorating?" Howard asked. "I remember Brad mentioned you majored in interior decorating in college. He never mentioned your wanting to start your own business, though."

"Brad came up with this idea," Lori explained. "He knows I've always wanted to do something like this, and he figured with him being away it would give me something to occupy my time. He even found the job for me. I'll be working as an instructor for Sanderson's College; the college is run by a Miss Betty Sanderson. She's very good. Her work has been featured in all the major interior design magazines."

Howard appeared thoughtful as the waitress placed their drinks on the table. As she walked away, he asked Lori bluntly, "Are you any good? At interior decorating, I mean."

His question caught Lori by surprise. She really didn't know how to answer him. Howard noticed instantly.

"Come now. Forget about modesty," he pressed. "You know whether you're good or not. Just tell me."

"Yes," Lori said, through a bright red blush. "I am good. Very good, in fact."

"I'd love to see some samples of your work. Do you have anything you could show me?"

"Well, yes. I have a portfolio filled with pictures of my work. But why would you want to see it?" Lori asked curiously.

Howard fingered his straw and began swirling it through his drink. "I'm a movie producer, Lori," he responded. "I'm always looking for people with talent. If you're as good as I think you might be, I could possibly use you as a set designer. I have an opening right here at our local studio where we record some of our television productions. I venture to say I'd pay better than Sanderson's College, and I'll bet the job would be a lot more exciting than teaching a bunch of wannabe's. What do you say? Can I take a look at some of your work?"

Lori's heart was pounding. Imagine someone like Howard Placard wanting to see her work, with the possible idea of hiring her as a studio set designer. "Yes, Mr. Placard. I'd love to show you some of my work."

Howard waggled a finger at her. "What did we say about that Mr. Placard thing?"

"I—I'm sorry, Howard," Lori stammered. "When would you like to see the samples of my work? Shall I stop by your office sometime?"

Howard shook his head. "Forget the office. Too stuffy. I'll send my chauffeur to pick you up for dinner tomorrow night. You can bring along some samples of your best work, and we can discuss it in a more relaxed atmosphere."

* * *

"Oooh!" Arline grumbled. "I don't like that man. What a pompous jerk he is, taking advantage of Lori's youth and inexperience. I'd love to get that man on my talk show sometime. I'd give him what for, you can bet on it."

"Who knows?" Samantha smiled. "You might get the chance. Just keep watching. The scene's about to change."

Arline leaned back and watched as the scene shifted to an airliner in flight. Snuggling a little closer to Bruce, she told herself that no Howard Placard could ever sway her thinking. As she watched, she realized the replay had switched to Brad Douglas. It was amazing how accurate Samantha's description of this experience was. Arline could actually feel what Brad was feeling. A scary thought, but a true one nevertheless.

* * *

Brad marked his place and closed the script he had been trying to read. Laying it on the empty seat next to him, he glanced out the window at the billowy clouds beneath the plane. Thoughts of Lori filled his mind. He had wanted her to come with him for this filming, but he realized that three months was a long time to live in a hotel. Especially when he couldn't be with her other than a short while in the evenings, and on Sundays. As usual, he'd be glued to the set between twelve and fourteen hours for six days every week. For that reason he had suggested she take the job as an instructor at Sanderson's College.

Three months. How could he ever survive that long without her? Oh well, three months would go by fast. And after all—he and Lori did have the rest of forever together. He released the latch on the seat and leaned back as far as possible. In a couple of minutes, he was fast asleep. Dreaming of Lori, of course.

CHAPTER 4

The scene on the holographic screen shifted again, back to Lori as she sat at her kitchen table. She had spent most of the day sorting through the samples in her portfolio. A mixture of excitement and guilt raced through her mind as she rehearsed for the hundredth time the events that had transpired since seeing Brad off at the airport yesterday morning. But despite her excitement that Howard Placard would consider her as a set designer for the studio, she was filled with guilt as well. What tormented her most was that she had agreed to have dinner with Howard while her husband was two thousand miles away.

Lori hadn't mentioned Howard when Brad called last night to tell her his flight had gone well and his hotel room felt lonely without her there. It wasn't that she felt she had anything to hide. She had just convinced herself there would be plenty of time to tell Brad the good news if she actually did get the job. She knew he would be thrilled for her.

The door chime sounded, and Lori glanced at the clock on the mantel. Seven-thirty, the exact time Howard had indicated his chauffeur would be there to pick her up. Brad always said Howard Placard was the most prompt man he had ever run across and that he demanded the same of all his employees.

Picking up the portfolio, Lori started for the front door, all the while feeling a little ashamed for hoping Brad wouldn't call tonight. Under any other circumstances, she would have camped by the phone anticipating his call. As fate would have it, her only choice was to meet Howard for a late dinner, or forget the whole thing. She couldn't help it if Howard kept such a tight schedule that he couldn't squeeze her in any earlier in the day. If Brad called, she'd just have to find some excuse for being gone. After all, he had called only last night. And it wasn't like she was going to make a habit of being away in the evenings. It would just be this once.

Lori opened the door to see Don Harrison looking precisely how a dutiful chauffeur should look. He stood straight and tall, and wore the whole uniform right down to the navy blue blazer and matching leather-billed cap. Glancing over his shoulder, she spotted the longest, shiniest, white stretch limo she had ever seen. For a moment, it took her breath away.

Lori was glad the sun had already set. She hoped that in the darkness none of the neighbors would notice her driving away in a limousine. If that should get back to Brad, it could take more explaining than she was prepared for.

As they made their way through the city streets toward the downtown area, Lori had an amusing thought—one that actually brought a smile to her face. *I'll bet Brad's never even ridden in a limo like this one. For once in my life, I'm a step ahead of him. Who knows, maybe someday the two of us can ride in one of these limos to the Academy Awards where Brad will win an Oscar for best director and I'll win one for best set designer. It could happen.*

After a fifteen-minute drive, Don pulled the limo into the circular entry of the Thunderbird Hotel. Lori thought it a little odd that Howard would pick a hotel restaurant for their meeting. Of course, she wasn't used to dealing with important men like Howard Placard. Maybe this is the way they all do business. She shrugged it off.

The hotel attendant opened her door. "Ms. Douglas, I presume?" he said as she stepped out.

"I'm Mrs. Douglas, yes," she corrected, a little surprised at hearing the attendant use her name.

"Yes, of course. Mrs. Douglas it is. Mr. Placard is awaiting your arrival. If you'll be so kind, I'll show you the way."

As they entered the lobby, Lori could see the doors leading to the dining area at one end of the room. When the attendant went in the opposite direction, she became very confused. "Wait," she said to the attendant. "There must be a mistake. I'm supposed to meet Mr. Placard in the dining room."

"Oh no, ma'am," the attendant quickly explained. "Mr. Placard never uses our dining room. He keeps a suite reserved; he prefers dining in a more secluded setting."

Lori stopped dead in her tracks. *A suite?* she gasped to herself. *He expects me to meet with him alone in a hotel suite?*

The attendant seemed taken aback at Lori's hesitation. "The suite is this way, ma'am," he said, motioning for her to follow. "I'm sure you'll find everything to your liking."

Everything to my liking? Lori thought nervously to herself. *I don't think so. I'm a married woman. I don't go around meeting men in hotel suites. I've got to get out of here. But how? How did I get myself into this? I had no idea the man expected me to be alone with him in a hotel suite.*

"If you'll be so kind, ma'am, we'll need to take the elevator. Mr. Placard's suite is on the seventh floor."

Lori's stomach twisted in knots. What was she to do? She couldn't just walk away from Howard Placard. Not with Brad having such a great working relationship with him, she couldn't. If she did anything to damage their relationship, there was no telling what the repercussions might be. And, too, she desperately wanted to pursue the chance he had offered her for a fabulous career of her own. Swallowing hard, she accompanied the attendant to the elevator. On the seventh floor, the attendant led her to a door near the end of the hall. He tapped lightly on the door. Seconds later Howard opened it.

"Oh, Lori, good. Come on in, dinner is waiting. I hope you like Alaskan crab; they prepare it to perfection here. Afterward, we can look over your samples. I see you brought them along."

Lori froze at the door, staring inside the room at the table prepared elegantly for two. It was the sort of setting she would die for if it were with Brad—except for one thing, that is. Near the table was placed an ice bucket that contained what appeared to be an unopened bottle of champagne. Lori prided herself on never using alcoholic drinks of any sort. What was she to do? So much seemed at stake on her sharing dinner with this powerful man, but it went against her every instinct. As she stood, frozen, Howard himself came unexpectedly to her rescue.

"I'm sorry, Lori. I see by your hesitation that something is bothering you. Is it because I have dinner prepared for the two of us in my private suite? Yes, of course it is. How thoughtless of me. I'm not used to dealing with women of your character. Let me grab my coat, and we'll go downstairs to the dining room."

Lori breathed a thankful sigh of relief as Howard instructed the waiting attendant. "Get us a good table, will you? Somewhere in the corner of the room where we can have some privacy. Then you can grab my chauffeur and the two of you can enjoy the crab dinner. No sense in letting it go to waste."

"Yes sir," the attendant smiled as he hurriedly headed for the door. "I'll get right on it."

Howard slipped into his dinner jacket and offered Lori his arm. Together, they stepped into the hall, and he closed the door behind them.

"I—I'm terribly sorry, Mr. Pla—uh—that is, Howard. I just don't feel comfortable . . . You do understand, don't you?"

"Of course I understand, my dear," Howard assured her. "I should have been more thoughtful of my arrangements. Sometimes I get so tied up in my business affairs I tend to forget the human side of things."

Once they were in a room full of people, Lori found she actually enjoyed sharing dinner with this man. After all, she was only here to discuss a business deal.

The Alaskan crab was wonderful, and to her relief, there was no mention of champagne.

After dinner, Howard asked the waitress to clear the table so he could examine Lori's samples. "Well, let's see what we have here," he said, thumbing through the pages of her portfolio. "Hum, these look good. I'm impressed, Lori. It's evident that Brad doesn't horde all the talent in your family. I can definitely use you at the studio, if you're interested."

Containing her elation was impossible. "Yes!" she exclaimed, clapping her hands excitedly. "I am interested. I'd love the chance to work on designing your studio sets."

Howard smiled and removed an envelope from his inside jacket pocket. "I anticipated your work would be good. And I anticipated your reaction to my offering you the job. So—I took the liberty of having a contract drawn up. Here," he said, handing her the envelope. "Look this over and see what you think."

Lori stared at the envelope in Howard's hand. Slowly, she reached out and accepted it. Removing the papers from the envelope, she carefully read the three-page document. Her heart did a flip when she read the amount of money Howard was offering for her services. She bit her tongue to keep from crying out in excitement. Taking a deep breath, she fought to remain calm as she spoke. "This is a very generous offer, Howard. I'd have to be a fool to turn it down. When do I start?"

"I was hoping you'd say that," Howard said with a slap to the tabletop. "Stop by my office tomorrow morning, and my secretary will take care of all the necessary paperwork. Tax forms, and that sort of thing, you know." Reaching across the table, he took her hand and drew it over to his lips where he kissed it. "I'm looking forward to a long and prosperous relationship between us, Lori. You'll never be sorry for your decision, I promise."

Howard reached into his inside coat pocket for his wallet with the intention of leaving a tip. As he did, his hand brushed against something he had forgotten about for the moment. It was the medallion that had been on Lori's key ring. When he had used her keys to drive her car to the Hunter's Cottage, the medallion had somehow fallen off in his pocket. He hadn't noticed until later that night. He decided he'd simply return the medallion to Lori the next time he saw her. But now that the time had come when he should return the medallion, he found himself having second thoughts. Lori hadn't mentioned missing it. He made a decision to let it go for the time being. For some reason, having the medallion made him feel good. It was nice having something of Lori's that he could keep near his heart to remind him of her. He could always return it later, if the subject ever came up.

* * *

It was after eleven when the white limousine dropped Lori off at her home. With high anticipation she checked her phone messages. Sure enough, Brad had called. Four times, in fact. Lori felt ill. His message said to call whenever she got home, regardless of the time. According to her calculations, it was after two a.m. in Acapulco. What should she do? What could she tell him. Certainly not that she had been to dinner with Howard Placard. Nervously, she reached for the phone and dialed the number for Brad's hotel in Acapulco. On the third ring, a voice answered in Spanish.

"Uh—please," she said slowly. "Could you ring room 420."

"Ah, sí señora. Un momento, por favor."

After what seemed an almost unbearable wait, Brad's voice came on the line. "Lori! Is that you?"

"Yes, Brad, it's me. I'm sorry to wake you, but you said to call regardless of what time I came home."

"You didn't wake me. I couldn't sleep for worrying about you. Is everything okay there?"

"Everything's fine, Brad. I just . . . uh . . . went to a show with my friend Stacy. We stopped off for hamburgers on the way home." A surge of guilt shot through Lori as the lie crossed her lips. This was Brad she was talking to. There were no lies between her and Brad. There never had been, but how could she tell him about Howard? True, she had done nothing wrong in meeting Howard and accepting his offer for a new job. But—would Brad understand? Or would he make something more of her meeting with Howard than a simple business dinner? She just couldn't take that chance. "I'm sorry, Brad. I just never thought about you worrying. I didn't expect you to call tonight when you'd called last night."

"I'm sorry too, Lori. I should have known everything was all right. I'm just a worrier by nature. So what movie did you see?"

"The movie? It was . . ." Lori tried desperately to think of a movie that was playing at the theater now. She was in deep trouble, and she knew it. Quickly, she formulated a plan. "Oh, no. I've left the front door standing open. Excuse me a minute, Brad, while I close it." Not giving Brad the chance to respond, she dropped the phone and head-ed straight where she had left the newspaper laying on the family room coffee table. Frantically she tore through the pages until she found the entertainment section. There she spotted the title to a movie. Returning to the phone, she tried her best to sound composed. "Okay, Brad, the door is closed now. What was it you asked? Oh, yes. The movie. We saw *Field of Dreams*. It was a movie about baseball."

"Yeah, I know. I heard it was good. Kevin Costner and James Earl Jones, right?"

"Uh, yes, yes, that's right. Kevin Costner and James Earl Jones."

"Are you sure you're all right, Lori? For some reason you don't sound like yourself tonight."

"I'm just sleepy, Brad. I didn't sleep well last night either. I miss you too, you know."

"You'd better miss me, Mrs. Douglas. And I'd better let you get some sleep. That goes for me, too. I have to get up in less than three hours from now. I've got a hunch this is going to be a very long day."

Lori couldn't help herself. She started to cry. "I love you, Brad. I'm so sorry I caused you to miss your night's sleep. Please be careful tomorrow."

"I'll be all right. But you'd better be resting up yourself. When you start teaching on Monday, you'll need all the energy you can get. I'll bet you can't wait, can you?"

She was crying even harder now. "No, I can't wait. You know how excited I am about the job."

"Knock 'em dead, baby. Knowing you, how could you do anything else? I'm going to go now, okay? Maybe we both can get some much needed sleep."

"I hope so."

"Love ya."

"I love you too, Brad."

"Night, sweetheart."

"Brad, wait!"

"I'm here. What is it, Lori?"

"Call me tomorrow, okay?"

"I'll call. You can count on it."

"Good night, Brad. I love you."

"Love you too, baby. Talk to you tomorrow."

For several minutes after hearing the click of Brad's receiver, Lori remained listening to the silence on the line. At last, she placed the phone on the hook. "I love you, Brad," she managed to say through her sobs. "I love you so much." It was deep into the early morning hours before she finally managed to cry herself to sleep.

CHAPTER 5

While Lori shed tears from out of the past, Arline wept fresh tears of her own. Wiping her eyes dry with a clean tissue, she added it to the growing pile of used ones on the coffee table. Samantha couldn't help but smile.

"I'll never understand how you can be such a successful talk show hostess, Arline," she observed. "I can't remember ever going to a movie with you when you didn't cry. I think you even cried through clips of the Three Stooges. How do you ever manage to turn off your sensitivity when your guests share their heart rending problems?"

"I only do this at movies!" Arline shot back in her own defense. "At movies, and when I read a mushy novel. My television show is reality, and reality is different. Reality I can handle just fine."

"Uh huh," Samantha responded with a chuckle. "For your information, Arline, this holograph is reality, not some Hollywood clip. It happens to be history being reenacted exactly as it originally happened."

"Well I can't help it. It looks like a movie to me, and I can even feel Lori's emotion. Don't get the idea I can't stay in control when I meet the lady for real. It's just that this looks like a movie, that's all."

"I'll take your word for it," Samantha conceded. "But keep that box of tissue close. You're about to meet two more players in the drama. The next scene takes place at the same point in time as the one you've been watching, except this time we shift the location to San Francisco, California, and a different problem all together."

"No more low-life home wreckers, I hope," Arline proclaimed. "One of those per scenario is all I can handle."

"Well, Arline," Samantha explained. "This problem does deal with a low-life home wrecker, but of a different sort than Howard Placard. This home wrecker targets his own marriage, not another man's. His name is James Baxter and I can assure you, you'll like him even less than you like Howard. Eat some more popcorn, and I'll have Jason whip up some really great celestial fruit punch to wash it down with."

Jason smiled. "Gotcha, Sam," he said with a wink. "I'm on my way. Be back in a flash with the refreshments."

Arline turned her attention back to the holograph. She saw a woman at the wheel of a car with a young girl in the seat next to her. While she had noticed the woman and girl, however, Bruce was drawn by something altogether different.

"Hey, would you look at this?" he exclaimed excitedly. "They're in a Lexus, like the one you talked me into selling, Arline. This one's a little older than mine, but it's the same model exactly. I'd forgotten how much I missed that car until seeing this."

Arline scowled at Bruce. "Bruce Vincent, don't you dare start slipping back to your old ways on me. I've worked hard to turn you into a Mustang convertible man, and I happen to love you this way."

Bruce leaned over and kissed Arline on the lips. "Don't worry, darling. The car has never been built that would tempt me into doing anything to make you think I'm slipping back to my old ways— although I have been thinking about trading up to a Thunderbird convertible. You know, to make it a little easier on long trips and that kind of thing."

"Watch the movie, Bruce," Arline declared. "We'll stick with the Mustang."

* * *

It was Tanielle's fifth birthday. Shannon, Tanielle's mother, wanted to do something to make the day special, so she bought tickets and treated her daughter to an afternoon at the circus. It was now early evening, and they were just returning home. The last rays of a sinking sun still lingered against the edge of the sky as Shannon pulled the black Lexus into the three-car garage between James' speedboat and his Jaguar. She pressed the button on the remote, closing the door. Then loosening the strap on Tanielle's seat belt, she lifted the child to the floor and led her into the house.

"Shhhh," Shannon said to Tanielle, with a finger to her lips. "We don't want to disturb Daddy, do we?" Shannon lifted Tanielle in her arms and tiptoed past James' study where she knew he was in conference with some of his business associates. Shannon knew perfectly well that James Baxter was not a man to be disturbed when he was busy. That was especially true of *her* disturbing him.

Time and again she had asked herself why she'd ever married him in the first place. She had to admit, she was never really in love with him. If Shannon had ever been in love with anyone, it was Tom Reddings. Tom had even proposed to her, and she had been tempted to say "yes"— but at that immature time in her life, being in love had not been a high priority. Finding someone with the means to give her the finer things she craved had topped the list in those days. And so, when she met James Baxter, she made the decision that would break Tom's heart. What wouldn't she give now for a second chance at making that decision?

James Baxter was a rich and powerful man. No question about it, he was a man who could give her all the fun and desires she had conjured up in her youthful mind. Shannon learned too late that when James gave something, it always came with a price tag.

It wasn't as though she had entered the marriage blindly. Her brother, Brad, had talked his face purple, attempting to discourage the marriage. He had pressed for her to marry Tom instead, right up to the very minute she said her "I will's" and sealed her fate as Mrs. James Baxter.

It didn't take long for Shannon to realize the mistake she had made, but she refused to give up hope that her marriage could be turned into a pleasant one. She convinced herself that when children came into the marriage, things would change. When she became pregnant with Tanielle, she discovered that things did change. Unfortunately, they changed in the wrong direction. From the start, James had insisted on an abortion. When Shannon refused, he became more violent than ever. The very night Tanielle was born, Shannon's face was bruised and swollen from an encounter with James' rage. As usual, she covered for him. This time it was supposed to have been a shoe box falling from the top of her closet, striking her on the face.

But that was five years ago, and this was now. She desperately wanted to make it to her room without James knowing she was home. Holding her breath, she swiftly moved past his open study door and hoped for a miracle. It wasn't to be. "Shannon, is that you?!" James called out rudely.

Shannon stopped dead in her tracks, swallowed hard, and forced out what was meant to sound like a cheerful answer. "It's me, James. Tanielle and I are just returning from the circus. I didn't think you'd mind since we wouldn't be here to bother your business affairs that way."

Before Shannon realized what was happening, Tanielle slipped free and ran giggling into her father's office, stopping suddenly just inside the door when she made eye contact with three crass-looking strangers who had been talking to James. "No, baby," Shannon cried out, rushing to retrieve the child.

"Get that kid out of here!" James bellowed, pounding his fist on his desk. "You know better than to let her interrupt when I'm attending to business!"

Shannon scooped Tanielle into her arms and hastily retreated from the room, closing the door behind herself. James was furious, and she knew it. Trembling violently, she clung to Tanielle, and tried to think of something, anything she could do to save herself from the punishment she knew was imminent.

Earlier that day Shannon had made a birthday cake for Tanielle, and invited a few friends over for cake and ice cream. James had become irritated with the noise. Bursting into the kitchen, he immediately sent the visiting children home. When Tanielle cried, he had slapped her angrily across the face. It was the first time James had struck his daughter, and Shannon refused to let it go unchallenged. Snatching up the child, she started for the door with the intention of getting out of the house at least for the day, but James couldn't let it go at that. Grabbing up a slice of cake and rushing after Shannon, he shoved it violently into her face.

That's when Shannon had left the house, taking Tanielle with her. Over and over, she told herself not to return, but where could she go if she didn't come home to James? She bought circus tickets, and spent the early evening trying to forget. Now, however, with James furious over Tanielle's interruption in his office, Shannon knew the time had come to face the problem head on. Otherwise, she would be little more than a doormat to the man for the rest of her life. Gathering more courage than she thought possible, she rushed upstairs and threw a few necessities together. She knew James wouldn't leave his important meeting for anything so insignificant as checking on her whereabouts. Especially since he was so certain she would never leave him. Hurrying back to her car, she backed it out of the garage and headed north on Highway 101, putting San Francisco behind her as fast as the speed limit allowed. She had gone nearly a hundred miles before pulling over at a roadside rest stop. There, she sat crying for several minutes while Tanielle slept peacefully in the seat next to her. It was no use. She couldn't do it. How could she ever leave her husband? What would become of her? How could she support herself, and Tanielle? Even though she was a certified teacher, she had given it up when she married James. She had written three novels, but fearing his wrath she had never submitted any of them to a publisher. She was at his mercy, and nothing in the world could change that fact. With knots in her stomach the size of baseballs, she turned the car around and started for home, if anyone could call it home. She knew what was waiting when she faced James. But, after all, it was her fault. She should never have tried to leave him. Next time she'd just have to try harder not to upset him. Maybe then, James would change, too.

* * *

There was no need for tissues as Arline watched this segment of the replay unfold in all its ugly vehemence. She was furious. "I hate it when a woman has so little self-esteem that she thinks she has to put up with a jerk like James Baxter," she bellowed. "And as for Baxter, who does he think he is, anyway? Just give me the chance to get his story on my television show, Sam. I'll see to it the man is taken down a peg or two."

Samantha laughed. "You're a little late, Arline. You have to remember what you're watching here is ten-year-old history. James Baxter met his fate in a dingy cave on a tiny island in the Caribbean Sea a few months back. Believe me, he's not pushing anyone around

where he is now. If you can get your blood pressure back down a
notch, we'll get back to Lori's part of the story."

Arline was still fuming. "Personally I'd rather see the part where
James Baxter got what was coming to him—but this is your show,
Sam. Go ahead. You certainly have my attention. And by the way,
Jason, this celestial fruit punch is really something to brag about. Pass
some more popcorn, will you, Bruce?"

* * *

Oh what tangled webs we weave, when first we practice to deceive.
Never had these time-honored words been more meaningful to Lori
than during the first weeks on her new job. Not that she didn't love
the job, and not that she didn't want to tell Brad about it. It was just
that—she couldn't find the right way to tell him. Not that she had
really done anything wrong—she hadn't done anything a dedicated
wife shouldn't do; it only appeared that way. Somehow she'd have to
find a way to convince Brad that her dealings with Howard Placard
were strictly business, and not personal—but how? True, she and
Howard did spend a lot of time together. They even shared lunch
most days, but it was all for professional reasons. And after a long day
at work, Lori made it a point to be home every evening between the
hours of six to eight when she knew Brad might call.

Lori did have to admit she enjoyed working with Howard. There
was something about him—something she really couldn't pin down—
but whatever it was it set him apart from any man she had ever met
before. He had a certain charisma, and he was so . . . spontaneous. Yes,
that was the word that best described him. He was spontaneous. Lori
never knew what to expect from him next. Like the time she and the
film's director were in the middle of a dispute over the design of a particular set. Howard suddenly called a halt to work and had the entire
crew transported to his private beach where they all spent the remainder of the day. Lori got to ride with Howard in his limo. She loved it.
At the beach, she kicked off her shoes and walked barefoot through the
shallow surf. When Howard joined her she thought it was funny, seeing
a man as powerful as Howard traipsing along the wet sand in his bare
feet. The next morning they all returned to work, with everyone in a

great mood. This time the set came together without a hitch. At times like these, Lori found herself wishing Brad could be more like Howard.

It was at lunch, about a week following the day at the beach, when Howard dropped another little surprise in Lori's lap. "I think you know by now how impressed I am with your work, Lori," Howard explained as the two of them shared a table in the studio cafeteria. "I'd like to make you an offer."

"An offer?" Lori asked with cautious excitement. "What kind of offer?"

"I'm working on a special film in Carmel. It's the story of a wealthy family who moved there from the East in the late 1800s. I'll be overseeing this one myself, and I could sure use your expertise on it. Carmel is one of the most beautiful sea villages you'll find anywhere, and it would only be for a couple of weeks. Will you consider coming with me?"

A cold shiver passed through Lori at the significance of what Howard was proposing. "Oh, Howard," she stammered. "I'd love the chance you describe, but—"

What Howard said next caught Lori by complete surprise. "You're worried about Brad, aren't you?" he asked.

Lori stared at him. "What did you say?" she gasped.

"You've never told him about your job at the studio, have you, Lori?"

Lori's chin dropped and her eyes opened three sizes. "Hey," Howard affirmed, "I have no problem with you not telling him. And believe me, I understand why you haven't. I know Brad a little better than you think I do, and I know he could have a tendency to be a little on the jealous side. Even of a good friend like me. Your work can be our little secret as long as you want it to be. You see, Lori, I'm in a position where I can pull strings. If and when I might need your services in the future, all I have to do is find a place to ship Brad off on a directing assignment. Believe me, it's no big deal. And if you're worried about him calling at night and not finding you at home, I have that base covered, too. There's a fairly new gadget on the market these days called a cellular phone. You saw me use it once, remember?"

"Yes," she meekly responded. "The day we met at the airport when Brad left for Acapulco. You called ahead for dinner reservations."

"That's right, Lori. It's a phone you can take anywhere. It works by way of a satellite. I can give you a little telephone that you can carry in your purse, and any call that comes to your house will be automatically forwarded to it. So you see, when Brad calls—you can take your calls from home no matter where you are. And think about this, Brad is enjoying his day in the sun in fabulous Acapulco. Why shouldn't you enjoy a little time in Carmel by the Sea? What do you say? Will you do it? Oh, by the way, it'll be worth a healthy bonus if you do—say, in the neighborhood of ten grand."

Lori couldn't believe what she was hearing. Howard knew her secret. He had known it from the beginning. She suddenly felt very embarrassed. "I—don't know what to say," she stammered.

"It's simple," Howard responded. "Just say you'll go to Carmel with me. What Brad doesn't know won't hurt him. Tell you what, don't give me an answer right now. Go home and think it over. But just remember, if you want to get ahead in this business—you can't do it turning down offers like this one."

Never had Lori had so much to think about in so little time. Accepting Howard's offer to accompany him to Carmel by the Sea would come with some pretty heavy consequences. Turning down his offer would bring consequences of a different kind. With all this in mind, she hoped Brad wouldn't call that evening, but he did.

For the first time she realized how much easier lying to him had become, and she realized how tied down she had come to feel for having to be near the phone every night just in case he did call. The cellular phone Howard had proposed would have its points. With a phone like that in her purse, she could take Brad's calls anywhere, anytime, and he would be none the wiser.

"Listen, Brad," she said after they had talked just a few minutes, "I really should hang up now. I have a lot of things to take care of tonight. For my teaching job at Sanderson's College, I mean."

"Yeah, okay," Brad replied, disappointment hanging heavy in his voice. "I know how important your job is. At least, things are getting close to winding up here. I'll be home before you know it. I miss you, baby."

Brad's words hit Lori's ears like daggers. Under other circumstances those same words would have filled her veins with tingling excitement. How could she ever face him? How would she explain away all her lies? But then, why should she have to make excuses when she'd done nothing wrong?

"You'll be coming home? When?" she asked.

"I don't know for sure. I'd guess another three weeks at the most."

Three weeks, she thought. *That will give me plenty of time to accompany Howard to Carmel, if I decide to go.* "That's wonderful, Brad. It'll be great having you home."

"It'll be great, huh? For some reason you don't sound all that enthused. Is there something wrong that you haven't told me about?"

"No, Brad. Of course there's nothing wrong. I'm just tired, that's all. And I have a lot to do tonight."

There was a pause before Brad spoke again. "All right," he eventually said. "If you have that much to do I'll let you go. Not because I want to, I love hearing your voice. I miss you, baby. And I love you."

"I miss you too, Brad."

There was another pause. "You miss me, and you love me, right?"

"Yes, Brad," she said almost angrily. "I miss you and I love you. You know I love you. Why would you say such a foolish thing?"

By the next morning, Lori had made up her mind. She would go to Carmel with Howard. That would give her one week to set things in order before Brad came home. She could find a way, she just knew it. After Carmel, there would be no more lies.

CHAPTER 6

"Cut! That's a take, and that's a wrap." Brad breathed a sigh of relief as the sound of his own words marked the end of this film project. The final few scenes, shot on the open beach, were now captured on film and ready for the cutting room crew. The movie had threatened to slip past the projected target date, but it was finished now, giving way to thoughts of home—and of Lori.

He shoved a handful of papers into his briefcase and snapped it closed. As he did, he noticed Hank Stoner walking in his direction with his distinctive limp. Hank was a special effects man who had managed to blow away much of his left leg with an explosive device that accidentally detonated too soon. Hank had gained two things from this accident: a prosthetic limb from the knee down on his left side, and a respect for his craft that actually worked to make him one of the best special effects men in the business. Where some men would have turned tail and run to a more practical profession, Hank bit the bullet and drove himself even harder into the work. That's the sort of man Hank was. It was that trait that attracted Brad to him in what many called a friendship of misfits. Even though the two men liked and respected each other, they seldom agreed on anything more important than whether it was raining or not.

From the look on Hank's face, Brad knew what was coming even before he spoke. The first words out of Hank's mouth confirmed his suspicions.

"Hey, man, let's party!" And, with a slap on Brad's back, he added, "Talk about a dream come true: here we are in Acapulco on our own time. I'd say we've died and gone to heaven, pal, how about you?"

Brad laughed, and as usual shook off Hank's rhetorical offer. "You know me better than that, my friend. I have a gorgeous woman waiting at home whom I haven't seen in more than three months. What makes you think I'd waste my time hanging around here with an ugly old goat like you?"

Hank threw up his hands. "Get real, pal. Your old lady will be there anytime. Take a look around you, man. Nothing but babes in bikinis. Take it from one who knows, pal, these chicks are dying to spend some time with rich movie titans like us."

"Rich movie titans?" Brad chortled. "Us? Get real, Hank."

"Hey, pal. If these chicks want to think of me as rich—as well as a great-looking dude—who am I to disillusion them? Loosen up! Let's go hit a few joints. You can crawl back to Mama after you sober up."

"No sale, my impulsive friend. I wouldn't trade one of Lori's smiles for anything Acapulco has to offer."

"You know what your problem is, pal? You take life too seriously. Cut me an inch of slack here. What could one woman possibly have that would entice a man away from all this?" Hank waved his hand toward the city for emphasis.

"Well, let me tell ya, pilgrim," Brad came back using his best John Wayne impersonation. "There aren't many things better than a good woman at home to care for the aches and pains of a hard day's ride. That's something you'd do well to learn, partner. You might just come to know there's more to life than can be found in a smoke-filled saloon."

Hank rubbed the back of his neck and stared at Brad. "How do you do that, man? You're always making your voice sound like someone else's."

"Doing voice impressions is how I got my start in entertainment, Hank. I threw together a few stand-up comic routines and spiced them up with voice impressions. My audiences ate it up."

Hank tried to appear unimpressed. "Big deal. Anyone can do John Wayne. I could probably even sound like the Duke if I tried. Who else can you do?"

Brad grinned. "You ask who I can do, man? I can do this pesky little special effects dude who hangs around here givin' me one hard time after another. Get what I mean, pal?"

Hank narrowed one eye to a squint. "That was supposed to be me, I take it?"

"I'll be darned. And they call you 'slow,' Hank. You picked up on that one quicker than a speeding tortoise."

"Always has to be a wise guy in every crowd," Hank grumbled. "So let me rephrase myself. Is there anyone's voice you can't imitate?"

"Yeah," Brad laughed. "Barbara Streisand. I nearly blew a tonsil the one time I tried her. Come on, Hank, the studio trolley is about to pull out for the hotel. Let's catch it before we find ourselves waiting an hour for the next one."

Brad grabbed the hand rail and pulled himself up to the open car trolley where he took the first available seat. Hank followed suit, taking the seat next to Brad. In only a moment, they were on their way back toward town.

"So give it to me straight, pal," Hank said as they rode. "What is it about this little gal of yours that draws you home like iron to a magnet?"

Brad leaned back and stared up at the open sky. "Lori and I grew up together," he replied dreamily. "She's the only girl I ever dated, Hank. I've loved her since she was a freckle-faced ninth-grader with the cutest little pony tail you've ever seen."

"Big deal. That's great when you're at home. But this is Acapulco, man. What's so bad about taking an apple off another tree once in a while? I mean, that's what the good life's all about."

"Good life?" Brad echoed. "Hank Stoner, you wouldn't know the good life if it reached out and grabbed you by the nose. All this stuff you're trying to tempt me with is like a coat of bright paint over a surface of rust. Give it up, Hank. Go home to Blanch where you belong. She's the one who can offer you a real dose of the good life."

Hank shook his head in disgust. "Now there's an oxymoron if ever I heard one," he grunted. "Good life, in the same breath as marriage. You're talking to one who knows. I spent five years with my first old lady before I wised up and dumped her."

"Loretta dumped you, Hank. I was there, remember? And she wasn't an old lady. She was a very attractive young woman whom you completely failed to appreciate."

"Yeah, whatever," Hank shrugged. "A split is a split, and after five years it was time. I've been with Blanch a year now, and I'm about ready to ship her off to the farm as well."

Brad shook his head in disbelief. "Blanch is too good for you, Hank. But then, any woman is too good for you, now that I think about it."

Hank arched his eyebrows. "Can I take it then that I'm to be partying without the pleasure of your company, Mr. Stuffed Shirt-stay-at-home-duller-than-dirt Brad Douglas?"

Brad shook his head again and leaned back in his seat as he looked up at the cloudless sky overhead. "Yeah, Hank. I guess that's the way you can take it, pal. And I'll lay you odds my head feels better in the morning than yours will. But then, as you always say—that's what they make aspirin for, isn't it?"

Back at the hotel, Brad wasted no time calling the airline for reservations on the next flight home. The first flight out was at seven that evening, Acapulco time. That would put him home about nine in the evening, Lori's time. That would be perfect. He wouldn't even call to warn her he was coming. He laughed thinking how surprised she'd be when he walked in unannounced.

* * *

Howard had been right, Carmel was the most beautiful seaside village Lori had ever seen. It was a wonderful experience. The studio had rented a quaint old home not far from the ocean where most of the inside filming took place. Working on eighteenth century settings in the rustic old place allowed Lori to explore parts of her imagination never before tapped. It was a breathtaking experience. But the best part of the two-week extravaganza came in the evenings after the day's filming was over. This was time she spent with Howard. They dined in the finest restaurants, they walked barefoot on beaches with sand nearly as white as new fallen snow, they fed the seagulls, and laughed at the antics of the seals. It was all so wonderful, right down to being able to take Brad's phone calls whenever and wherever she happened to be at the time. Once he called while they were dining in a restaurant with live music, but she simply ran to the ladies room before answering. It was a little embarrassing since her conversation was overheard by the others in the room, but she survived it.

The two weeks had flown by so quickly, she could hardly believe they were over. By the time she reached home again, she was faced with an even greater dilemma of how to face Brad. Without question, her two weeks in Carmel would be the hardest to explain. "But," she sighed, "it was worth it."

Carmel had been like adding icing to the cake on an exciting new adventure. Somehow she had never considered what she must have missed by never dating anyone other than Brad. Now that she had learned there were other things out there to enjoy, she wanted to grab every minute possible of the dream. All too soon the alarm would sound and she would awaken to the drab but secure world where she really belonged. True, her adventure had meant bending some of the values she had always lived by. But then, she hadn't really broken any rules; she had only allowed them to bend a little. Brad would have to be faced, but by now she knew it was all worth it. She still had a week or so to get ready for his return. *Tomorrow,* she vowed. *Today I'll go to my job at the studio as if it were mine forever, and tomorrow I'll decide how to put things back where they belong.*

Lori started for the door on her way to the studio when she was caught short by the sound of the phone. Rushing to the kitchen, she took the call on the wall phone there. "Hello?"

"Hi, Lori. It's me, Howard. I have a big favor to ask, and I refuse to take 'no' for an answer, so don't even try using the word on me."

Lori laughed, and marveled at how excited she felt hearing Howard's voice. "What sort of favor?" she asked.

"Don't come to the studio today. Just enjoy the day off, and I'll have Don pick you up in the limo around seven. Wear something fancy. I have an evening planned that will knock your socks off."

"What are you talking about, you have an evening planned? Don't you think you should tell me what you have in mind? I might just be inclined to turn you down, you know."

"Trust me this time, okay? I give you my word you won't be sorry."

Lori hung up the phone and thought about his strange request. Trust me, he said. She was almost ashamed to admit how much she did trust Howard Placard. More than she had ever trusted any man—except Brad, of course. In a way she felt a little let down at the thought of not going to the studio on the day she decided would be her last. But—she could enjoy the day shopping and wondering what sort of evening this newfound knight in shining armor had planned. And that's exactly what she did.

Just as expected, Don was there in the limo at precisely seven o'clock, not so much as thirty seconds late. Having seen him through the front window, Lori locked the house and walked to the limo before Don even had time to get out. "Thought I'd save you a trip to the door," she laughed.

Don opened the back door of the limo. "Hey, who am I to argue at saving a step or two?"

Lori brushed past him and took her seat. "So what's this big mystery all about, Don?" she asked. "Where are you taking me?"

"Uh uh," he said, with the wave of a finger. "It's a secret. If I spill the beans, I die. Just sit back and relax, listen to some Mozart or something on the tape deck. You're in for an hour's drive so you might as well enjoy it."

"An hour's drive? That's all you're going to tell me?"

"That's all I'm going to tell you," he affirmed, closing the door and returning to the driver's seat.

They had traveled only a few blocks when Lori realized she didn't have the cellular phone with her. She had left it on the seat of the old Pontiac, which she had taken shopping that morning. What if Brad was to call? She thought about asking Don to go back for the phone, but realizing what a stickler he was for staying on a schedule, she shrugged off the idea. If Brad did call and find her away, it would be just one more thing she would have to explain.

* * *

Brad glanced at his watch. It was seven o'clock Lori's time. He had been in the air for three hours and had another hour to go before touchdown on good old U.S.A. soil. He wondered what Lori was doing right about now. She was probably home watching television or preparing herself a late dinner. Brad smacked his lips at the thought of Lori's cooking. Living out of restaurants just didn't cut it in his book. It felt great to be going home. Poor Hank. The guy didn't have a clue what life was all about.

* * *

Lori couldn't believe it when Don brought the limo to a stop near a lakefront lodge. "Where are we?" she asked. "I've never seen this place before."

"Not many people have seen this place," Don explained. "It's a private lodge that Howard owns. Other than the caretakers and a few invited guests now and then, no one but Howard ever comes here."

Lori did a double take of the lodge. It was huge. "Howard owns this lodge?" she asked.

"Howard owns everything you see here, including the lake," Don further explained. "It's all part of his very elaborate estate."

The immensity of what Don said was just sinking in, when the door to Lori's side of the limo suddenly opened. She glanced out and saw Howard's smiling face looking back at her. He was wearing a black tuxedo. It was the first time she had ever seen him in one, and he looked fabulous. He offered his hand, which she accepted as she stepped from the limo.

"You look stunning, Lori," he said, eyeing her closely. After seeing how he was dressed, she was glad she had picked up a new gown for the evening. She had almost worn that old red dress Brad had given her before he left for Acapulco. Not that it was that old—she had only worn it once, and that was to see him off at the airport. But since Howard had seen her in the dress, it sort of made it old. In her mind, at least.

"What are you up to, Howard?" she asked, looking him straight in the eye. "Why have you brought me here to your private lodge?"

"We're not going to the lodge," he teased. "I have something far better in mind. Step right this way."

Howard led Lori toward a nearby boat dock, and her confusion grew even stronger when Howard pointed at the sleek red speed boat waiting there. "You're taking me for a boat ride?" she asked. "Somehow I got the idea tonight had to do with my work at the studio. When you asked me to dress for the part, I just assumed there would be people involved in whatever you were up to."

"Please, Lori, trust me just this once. What I have planned for this evening is of the utmost importance to me. It's not like we're strangers anymore. We're two responsible adults, and there's no reason we can't act like responsible adults whether or not we're in the presence of a crowd."

Howard stepped into the boat and offered Lori his hand. When she hesitated, he reached out and took hold of her arm and gently pulled her into the boat. Somewhat reluctantly, she took a seat next to him. Tossing aside the securing line, Howard started the engine and piloted the boat out onto the lake. "What you're about to see," he explained as they picked up speed, "is something very few people ever see. It's the biggest pride and joy of my life. There's an old saying that 'no man is an island,' and that may well be true. But there are a few men who *own* an island." Howard threw out his chest in a gesture of pride. "I'm one of them, Lori. I own this lake and everything that goes with it. That includes two islands, one of which I've had transformed into a little piece of paradise, all my own."

By now, Lori felt a growing alarm. All at once she wished she had searched out Howard's intentions a little further before allowing herself to be so easily swayed. She had assumed what he had in mind for tonight was a party of some sort, one that included the whole studio crew. A party where she would have simply been one of the guests. Well, maybe a little more than simply one of the guests, but she certainly didn't expect anything so intimate as this evening seemed to indicate. Whatever gave Howard the idea she would approve of such a thing?

The question prompted Lori to conduct a quick examination of her recent activities. Beginning with their chance meeting at the airport, she did a mind's eye, moment-by-moment review of the past three months. As she did, something happened. A faint glow penetrated the veneer of glamor Howard had managed to paint, and Lori was left with a stinging reality that came like a cold slap in the face. Why wouldn't Howard think she would approve of this? What single thing had she done to make him suppose otherwise? In her eagerness to enjoy all the newfound freedom Howard had offered, she may well have given him the wrong impression. Or was it the wrong impression? Had she inwardly wanted Howard to develop feelings for her? Had she inwardly wanted to let her own feelings for him develop to this point?

Suddenly her thoughts turned to Brad. What if he could somehow see her at this very moment? Clutching her purse tightly in both hands, she thought of the missing cellular phone. At that moment another thought came to mind—she had left the package of photographs laying on the front seat, next to the phone. The ones she had picked up from the developer only this morning. They were photos taken in Carmel when she and Howard were there. Several were of her and Howard together, snapped by some stranger here and there that Howard had entrusted the camera to. How could she have ever been so foolish as to allow those pictures to be taken? And furthermore, how could she have ever been so foolish as to put herself in a compromising situation like the one in Carmel?

"This island we're headed for," she asked nervously. "Will there be other people there?"

Howard laughed. "Are you still anxious about being alone with me after all this time?"

"Well I . . ."

"Lori, Lori, Lori, what am I to do with you? Don't worry about it, the caterers will be there. I sent them ahead to prepare our dinner."

The caterers, Lori thought. *That's it? I'll be on an island in the middle of this lake with Howard, and the only others there will be the caterers, who will have been instructed by Howard not to disturb his privacy. How did you allow yourself to get into this situation, Lori Douglas? You have some things that need turning around in your life, woman. And you're going to start first thing tomorrow morning. No, not in the morning. You're going to start tonight. Those pictures are headed for the trash can before you go to bed, and all ties with Howard Placard are going in there with them. Wake up, woman. Howard brought new excitement to your life, but it's a forbidden excitement for you, lady. Why is it the forbidden always seems so desirable? And why does playing on the borders of the forbidden always come with such staggering consequences?*

* * *

The flight home was uneventful. After claiming his luggage, Brad caught a taxi. One stop at the florist for a dozen red roses, and then it was straight home. It was nearly nine o'clock when he paid the cab driver and walked to the house.

Setting his suitcases on the porch he inserted the key as quietly as possible, opened the door, and slipped inside with the roses behind his back. The house was strangely quiet as he crept into the family room. He paused a minute or two when he didn't see her, then called her name.

"Lori? Are you here?"

There was no answer. He searched the house, but Lori was nowhere to be found.

Pulling a vase from one of the kitchen cupboards, he put the roses in water and set them on the counter top. Next, he checked the garage to see if the car was there. It was.

"This is really strange," he said to himself. "She must have gone to the show with a girlfriend, or something. Oh well, she's a big girl. She can take care of herself."

He smiled. "But won't she be surprised to find me here when she does come home?"

Brad retrieved his suitcases from where he had left them on the front porch and proceeded to unpack and put everything away. After that, he sat on the sofa and glanced at his watch. It was now a quarter past nine. His eyes felt very heavy. His biological clock was still on Acapulco time where it was just past midnight. Raising his feet, he lay full length on the sofa, and in no time at all fell fast asleep.

* * *

Lori couldn't believe her eyes as she stepped from the boat. Howard had called his island a little piece of paradise, and he wasn't kidding. It staggered her imagination. There were palm trees, the scent of flowers, and even piped-in background music. Off to the right, she made out what appeared to be a golf course, and to the left stood a huge house. Howard slid his arm through hers and led her toward the house, which was only a short walk from the boat dock. The closer they came to the two-story structure, the more Lori realized that calling the place a house failed to do it justice. "Mansion" seemed much more appropriate.

Inside the house proved to be even more stunning. The entire floor was covered with white carpet. The furnishings were so elegant, it took Lori's breath away. Even with her gift for interior design, she couldn't have created a more perfect decor.

In the center of the entry hall stood a massive circular staircase that led to a large and very elegant overhanging balcony on the upper floor. To the left of the staircase, double doors opened to another spacious room she assumed was used for entertaining. Howard ushered her to this room, where a wall-size window revealed a spectacular view of the island with the lake in the background. Soft music filled the room, and the only light came from candles in silver candelabrums situated throughout the room. Near the window, a small table had been prepared for two.

Taking Lori's coat and purse, Howard lay them on a sofa and walked to the table where he pulled out a chair for her. Lori stared first at the chair, then at Howard. "I really don't feel comfortable with this," she said, with a sternness in her voice never before used for Howard's benefit.

"Nonsense," Howard objected. "What's to feel uncomfortable about? Sit down, Lori. You're about to taste a shrimp cocktail prepared so exquisitely, it'll drive your taste buds wild. After that, it's swordfish, sautéed to perfection by the finest chef this side of Paris."

Cautiously, Lori walked to the chair and sat down. Howard quickly moved around the table and took his own seat. Reaching for the wine glass in front of Lori, he dipped it in the ice bucket, swirling it a few times before dumping the ice back in the bucket. Next he lifted the bottle of wine and painstakingly untwisted the wire seal until the cork popped out with a loud bang. He then filled the glass and handed it to Lori. She didn't take it.

"You know I never touch wine, Howard. Why even offer it to me?"

"Lori, I'm offering you much more than a glass of the finest wine the grape can produce. I'm offering you a whole new life. Take this glass. Try one sip. When you do, I guarantee your palate will never say 'no' again. And the wine will enhance your taste for the food that follows. Relax, Lori. Let me teach you how to enjoy life's richest offerings."

Lori stood abruptly, knocking over her chair in the process. "No, Howard," she bluntly declared. "I won't taste your wine. And suddenly I'm not very hungry either. I'd like you to take me home."

Howard released a long, lingering sigh and set the glass back to the table. He stood to face Lori. "Please," he said. "Not just yet. We'll forget dinner for now if you like; maybe we can come back to it a little later on. I'd like you to go for a walk with me around the island. There are some things I want to say to you."

"I'd really rather go home now, Howard," Lori repeated.

"All I ask is that you hear me out, Lori. Just walk with me while I explain some things to you. Then, if you still want to go home—we can go.

Lori glanced through the glass windows at the lovely evening. A full moon reflected its splendor off the calm surface of the lake. A walk along the lakeshore was tempting. Still . . .

"I'm wearing high heels, Howard. Walking in the sand would be a little difficult."

"There's no need to walk in the sand. I have a concrete sidewalk that spans the whole island. You're dressed perfectly for a walk next to my lake, Lori."

"All right. We'll walk and I'll listen to whatever it is you have to tell me. But that's it. I want to go home."

Howard smiled. "I'm hoping you'll change your mind when you hear what I have to say."

For several minutes they walked along the edge of the lake with neither of them speaking. The only sounds heard were from a distant cricket and the gentle lapping of water against the shoreline. They were out of earshot of the music on this part of the island. At last, Howard stopped and leaned against the white iron rail that paralleled the walkway on the lake side. Standing back some distance from Howard, Lori folded her arms and waited for him to speak.

"You remember the day at the airport?" Howard began. "The day we met by chance while seeing Brad off to Acapulco?"

"I remember," Lori affirmed coolly.

"It wasn't by chance that we met, Lori. It was by design. I planned it that way."

Lori didn't know what to say, so she responded with only a slight nod of her head.

"I planned it all, Lori," Howard confessed. "Even to the point of hiring Brad to direct the movie in Acapulco. I wanted him out of the picture for a while, and that seemed like the perfect way."

Lori dropped her hands to her sides and stared at Howard. "Let me get this straight," she said sharply. "You hired Brad to do the film in Acapulco because of me?"

Howard turned to face her. "The truth is, I'm in love with you, Lori. I've been in love with you from the first time I laid eyes on you at my father's ranch. You were with a group of high school girls who came to the ranch for a field trip into the mountains on horseback. That's when I first saw you, Lori, and I couldn't keep my eyes off you. You were the most beautiful woman I had ever seen. You didn't know, of course, but I saddled my own horse and followed you into the mountains that day. I watched you all day, staying just far enough away that you wouldn't notice."

Lori was horrified. "This is insane, Howard. You can't possibly be in love with me."

"I am in love with you, Lori," Howard insisted. "I would have stepped forward to introduce myself that day at my father's ranch, except my parents already had my future wife picked out for me. They were set on me marrying a girl named Betty Wilson, because she was socially acceptable in their minds. You'll never know how much I wish I could live my life over from that point. If only I had been brave enough to go with my instincts right then, I would have given Brad Douglas a real fight for your hand, Lori. But I didn't. It wasn't until years later that I managed to bolster my courage enough to oppose my parents. I never did marry Betty Wilson, but by the time I made that choice you were already married to Brad. I do love you, Lori. I love you enough to do whatever it takes to win you away from Brad. I thought if you saw all the exciting things I have to offer, you might be tempted to leave him for me. I know you've enjoyed these last months. You can't deny that, Lori."

Lori was stunned beyond belief. "I—I'm not denying that I've enjoyed the time we've spent together. And I admit, I may have inadvertently done some things to encourage you. But . . ."

Before Lori could stop him, Howard stepped forward and kissed her. Instantly, she pulled away. "Stop that, Howard! You have no right. I'm a married woman."

"Yes, you are a married woman, Lori. But tell me you love Brad now that you've had a taste of how life can be with a man like me. Go ahead, tell me you love him. You can't, can you?"

All of a sudden the fog in her mind lifted and Lori saw herself more clearly than she had for a very long time. "Yes!" she shouted in Howard's face. "I do love Brad Douglas. I don't know how I'm going to face him again, but I do love him. I'm sorry if I led you to believe there could ever be something between us, Howard, but I'm telling you now—there can't be. Now I'm begging you, please take me home."

* * *

Arline pressed her head into her hands and muttered, "Help me out here, Sam. Tell me this isn't headed where it appears. Lori's going to find a way to get rid of those pictures before Brad sees them, right? She'll come clean with the truth, and Brad will understand, won't he? Come on, Sam, set my mind at ease, will you?"

"Can't do that, Arline. History is history. Even a talented coordinator like myself can't change history."

"Why are you showing me this? I was having such a great day, and now you've gone and ruined it for me. What is it you have in mind? Surely you don't expect me to come up against a man as powerful as Howard Placard? It would be futile to try to protect my television show from that guy. He could cancel me with one stroke of his pen."

Samantha laughed. "Not to worry, Arline. No one is going to cancel your television show. I'll be sure you keep it safely tucked out of Howard's reach. But to answer your question, yes, I do expect you and Bruce to lock horns with our illustrious Howard. And when you do, you'll have Jason, Sam, and the good Captain Horatio Symington Blake right behind you. I think you'll find Howard's not quite as powerful as you suppose. Not when he has three angels like us to contend with, he's not."

"That's the second time you've mentioned this Blake fellow," Arline pointed out. "When do we meet him?"

Samantha smiled. "All in due time, Arline. Now sit down and watch the next part of the show, will you?"

CHAPTER 7

It was midnight when the limo pulled up in front of the Douglas home. Like Cinderella, Lori's night at the ball was over. Only with Lori, there would be no glass slipper. There would only be the unpleasant job of cleaning up her shattered pumpkin and finding a way of convincing Brad he was the only Prince Charming she would ever need again. At least now she knew how to face him. She would face him with something she had put off all too long—the truth. But not on his first day home. Oh no, she wouldn't have him come home to that bombshell. She'd make his homecoming one fit for the prince he had become in her eyes. Then, after a day or so to prove her love for him—she'd bite the bullet and admit her mistake. Brad would be hurt; he might even be angry. But he would forgive her, and she would find a way to make it up to him, somehow. How grateful she was that through it all she had at least kept the most solemn of all vows. If she had fallen into that trap, forgiveness might well be out of reach forever—Brad's forgiveness, as well as the forgiveness that came from within her own heart.

"You will be at the studio tomorrow, won't you, Lori?"

Howard hadn't spoken for most of the ride home and now that he did, his words came like a voice out of a dense morning fog. Lori's voice was icy as she answered.

"I'm not sure, Howard. Probably not tomorrow, and maybe never. I'll have to let you know. Right now I have some pieces of my life to get back in place." She opened her own door and stepped out. "Don't bother seeing me to the door. I can find my way just fine."

Howard quickly exited the limo and circled to Lori's side. "I won't hear of it, not at this time of night. I'll see you safely inside without further argument."

Lori would rather he didn't, but at this point all she wanted was to get inside where she could be alone to think. If letting Howard walk her to the door would hurry this along, then so be it.

She was still digging through her purse looking for her key when Howard tried the door. It opened. "I don't understand," Lori remarked. "I distinctly remember locking this door when I left."

Howard pushed the door open and looked inside. The hall light was on, making it possible to see clearly into the front part of the house.

"That's something else strange," she said. "I never leave that light on."

Howard stepped inside where he could get a better look around. "Everything looks okay," he observed. "But maybe I should check the rest of the house before I leave, just to be on the safe side."

"No, Howard," Lori quickly responded. "I'm sure everything is fine. I must have forgotten to lock the door and left the light on in my rush to leave."

Catching Lori by complete surprise, Howard pulled her into a second kiss. Even before she could manage to push him away, she caught a glimpse of someone standing in the hallway watching them. It took less than a second to realize who.

"BRAD?!" Lori cried, tearing herself free from Howard's hold. "What—?"

"What am I doing home?" he asked, his voice shaking noticeably. "From what I've just seen, it's obvious you weren't expecting me."

"No, Brad! You've got it all wrong. It's not the way this must look. I can explain."

"I think you already have explained," Brad replied. "I've always known I'm not the exciting man you'd like me to be, but I had no idea it would ever come to this."

Fire blazed in Brad's eyes as they moved to Howard. "Is this why you hire me for so many 'on location' films, Howard? So you can have a free hand at home with my wife?"

Howard drew in a deep breath, and let it out slowly. "I assure you, Brad, what you just saw was much more my fault than Lori's. She had no idea I intended to kiss her. Believe me, my friend, Lori is all yours. Not that I haven't given my best shot at taking her away from you, because I have. Take my word for it. She is all yours."

"'Friend'?" You have the gall to call me 'friend' after what I've just seen? Tell me, Lori, how long has this been going on? No, never mind. I really don't want to know. I guess I must be quite the laughingstock in your new circle of friends, right?"

By now Lori's face was soaked from her tears. "Brad, please believe me. Nothing has been going on. I made some mistakes, but I can explain if you'll only let me."

Lori searched Brad's eyes, longing to find them filled with understanding and forgiveness; instead she saw only bitter hurt and a fury she never suspected him capable of. They were almost like the eyes of a total stranger. As she looked on in horror, Brad shot forward gripping Howard with such force it sent him crashing against the open door frame. Like a scene in slow motion, Lori watched Brad's free arm draw back as his hand rolled into a tight fist.

"No, Brad!" Lori cried frantically. "Don't!"

The unheeded words had scarcely escaped her lips when Brad's blow sent Howard tumbling out the door where he fell to a crumpled heap on the edge of the lawn. Laying a hand to his jaw, Howard stared glassy-eyed up at Brad. "That was a mistake," he growled spitefully. "No one lays a hand on Howard Placard and fails to regret it. I lied to you when I said Lori didn't expect me to kiss her. She's grown to appreciate being kissed by a real man. I'm taking her away from you, Brad. Lori deserves a better life than you can ever afford, and I'll see to it she has that life. As for you, your career is over. You'll never work another day in the motion picture business as long as you live. You have my word on it, Brad Douglas."

Lori covered both ears in a desperate attempt to block out the horrible exchange between the two men, knowing that she herself had brought it on with her own foolish judgment. In her worst nightmares she had never expected things to turn out this badly.

"STOP IT, BOTH OF YOU!!" she screamed at the top of her voice. "NO MORE LIES! NO MORE VIOLENCE! I CAN'T STAND THIS ONE SECOND LONGER!" But it was no use. Like a runaway locomotive, the two men were set on a course so tempestuous there was no stopping them.

Grabbing Howard with both hands, Brad pulled him to his feet. "Don't worry about me ever working for you again," he spat out. "There's not enough money in your bank account to pay for one more minute of my time. Now get off my property before I decide to add real fuel to your threats."

Through gushing tears Lori watched as Brad dragged Howard down the walk where he viciously shoved him into the side of the waiting limo. Don opened the door and stepped out, as if to intervene on behalf of his employer. "Hold it right there, fellow!" Brad warned in a loud voice. "This is not your fight! Just stay back, all right?!"

Don raised both hands face high and nodded his intention to let well enough alone. Brad returned his nod and stormed back into the house.

All of this was just too much for Lori. Something inside snapped and she ran sobbing to her bedroom where she slammed and locked the door. Then, falling helplessly across her bed, she cried out her very soul.

After a moment, she heard Brad at the door. He tried once to open it, but after discovering it was locked, he made no further attempt. Instead, he asked the most cutting question Lori could ever remember hearing. "Why, Lori? What did I do that was so wrong?"

Lori wanted to answer, but words refused to penetrate her uncontrollable sobbing. She wanted to go to him, but her body refused to stop shaking long enough to even stand. There was a long pause from the other side of the door, then came Brad's final remark. "Why didn't you just plunge a knife through my heart? It would have been more merciful."

The next sound she heard was the garage door opening, and she knew Brad was leaving in the Pontiac. Now she was alone. More alone than she had ever been in her short lifetime. And filled with more pain than she had ever imagined possible.

* * *

Howard opened his own door and staggered into the back seat of the limo where he gingerly rubbed his painful jaw. "So help me, Don, if one word of this ever gets out . . ."

"Don't worry, sir," Don replied. "I won't breathe a word of it to your friends. No sir, not me. Of course that leaves a lot of people I can tell, since you have so few friends."

Taking off his chauffeur's cap, Don tossed it onto the seat. "If there's one thing I dislike more than anything else in this world, it's a worm who has nothing better to do than break up another man's marriage. You can mail me whatever I have coming, Howard. I don't work for you anymore." Having said this, Don closed the door and walked off into the night.

"Go on, you fool," Howard mumbled, while moving to the driver's seat. "You're just lucky I have bigger things on my mind right now." He started the engine and took one more look at the closed door to Lori's house. "You may have closed the door on me tonight, Lori," he vowed. "But I'm not giving up. I'll be back, and one day you'll say 'yes' to the life I can offer. I swear that day will come, if it takes half my life." He put the car in gear and drove away.

* * *

For a very long time Brad had stared at the locked door that stood between him and the only woman he had ever loved. His mind raced in torturous thought, trying desperately to come to grips with the unexpected twist thrown into his life in the last ten minutes. As a teenager, he had had the habit of working out a problem by getting behind the wheel of a car and just driving around. So it was only natural that his old habit should resurface now. On the way to the garage, he noticed the roses bought earlier that last evening for Lori. They were so beautiful, just like the life he shared with Lori had been. The roses would fade and die in a short time. Is it possible his dreams of spending forever with Lori would do the same?

He was just sliding behind the wheel of the Pontiac when something caught his eye. He immediately recognized it as a cellular phone. He had seen one or two of these phones before. Several of the wealthy producers owned them, including Howard Placard. This one still had the power cord plugged into the car lighter. Then, he noticed something else. It was an envelope of pictures. Picking up the envelope, he opened it. His stomach turned sour as he thumbed through picture after picture of Lori's smiling face with Howard next to her.

Brad slammed a clenched fist against the dashboard. "How long has this been going on?" he grimaced. "If she's in love with another man, why didn't she tell me? I could never stand in the way of her happiness—even if it meant losing my own."

Brad dropped the pictures to the seat, hit the switch on the remote garage door opener, and started the engine. Backing out, he deliberately turned the car in the opposite direction he had seen Howard take when driving away. And then, he drove. For hours he drove, going nowhere in particular. As he drove, he rehearsed the problem over and over in his tormented mind. How could this have happened? The answer always came up the same. He was the only man Lori had ever seriously dated. She had married him without ever having compared him to anyone else. When a man like Howard Placard came along, it was only natural for her to find him glamorous and exciting. Brad had seen them kissing. And he saw the photos. It didn't take a rocket scientist to figure out their relationship had developed into a close one.

Brad knew he was now the odd person out. There was little question that Lori would be leaving him for Howard. Choked with a hurt so heavy it felt as if he would crumble under its weight, Brad vowed to step aside and give Lori her freedom. But what was to become of him? There was no way he could stay in this area, where he would be forced to see the woman he loved now living in another man's world. What was he to do? It was a question with seemingly no answer.

As the sun came up, Brad realized he was driving on a lonely mountain road several miles from town. For the first time he glanced at the fuel gauge and realized it was below the one-quarter mark. The only gas stations open at this time of day were along the freeway back near town. He headed the car in that direction.

Suddenly, he was startled by the ringing of the cellular phone on the seat next to him. For several seconds he stared at the phone, not knowing if he should answer it. It might be Howard, and he was in no mood for that man or anything associated with him right now. On the fourth ring, he gave in and picked it up. "Hello?"

"Brad! Good, I was hoping I would catch you at home. I need your help, buddy. It seems we have a problem. A big problem."

Brad recognized the voice as that of Tom Reddings. Tom had been Brad's friend since high school. In fact Tom had dated Brad's sister, Shannon, for some time. Brad always thought Shannon should have married Tom instead of that jerk James Baxter. Tom had been pretty broken up when Shannon didn't marry him. He had remained a bachelor, and made a career for himself in the U.S. Air Force.

Brad was confused. How was it possible that Tom knew the number to this cell phone unless . . . ?

"Tom, you might think me crazy for asking, but did you just dial my home phone number, by chance?"

"Yeah, buddy, I dialed your number. How else was I supposed to reach you?"

So that's how she did it, Brad concluded. *All our home calls are forwarded to this cellular phone. If Lori wasn't home to answer the phone there, she could use this phone to answer wherever she might be. So when I called at night thinking she was at home . . .*

"Listen to me, Brad," Tom came back. "We have a problem. It's your sister, Shannon."

"My sister? What's wrong with my sister, Tom? Is it her husband again?"

"Bingo, you nailed it. Shannon left him this time, about a week ago. She came to me for help, Brad. She was pretty beat up this time, you know—bruises, a black eye . . . nothing broken fortunately. She finally got up the nerve to leave the jerk when he started venting his wrath on Tanielle."

"That monster hurt my little niece?!" Brad shouted into the phone. "What did he do to her?!"

"He slapped her on her birthday. Then last week he hit her again. This time it was hard enough to leave black and blue marks. Shannon left that night, after Baxter was in bed."

Brad saw red. "I'm telling you, Tom. Shannon had better stay away from that man this time or so help me . . ."

"Listen to me, Brad," Tom broke in. "I'm trying to tell you we have a big problem here. Shannon left the man, but he's evidently been looking for her and I'm afraid he's found her. I arranged for Shannon and Tanielle to move into an apartment across the hall from mine, and when I stepped out to get my paper this morning I heard voices inside, Brad. Male voices. From some of the things they were saying, I figure they're Baxter's henchmen. We've got to get Shannon out of there before they take her back to him. What should I do, Brad? If I call the police they'll take Shannon in protective custody just long enough for Baxter to get his high-powered lawyers involved. She'll be back in his hands before the sun goes down. She's managed to leave him this time, Brad. She may never get this much courage again."

"You're right," Brad quickly agreed. "Listen, Tom, I'm in my car right now. I'm talking to you on a cell phone, and I'm at least half an hour from your place. But I have a plan. Can you give me the phone number to Shannon's apartment?"

"Of course," Tom replied. "Where did you get a cell phone?"

"I'll tell you about the phone later. For now, here's what I have in mind. I know James Baxter's voice better than I know my own. I'll convince those guys I'm him, and set a trap for them. They'll think Baxter is giving instructions for them to leave the girls in the apartment while they break into your car for some legal documents. Naturally I'll convince them the car belongs to her. I'm sure these guys are so dumb they'll take the bait hook, line, and sinker. In the meantime, you can alert the police and they can catch them in the act. And we can get the girls out of there fast."

"That's right," Tom mused aloud. "You do voice impressions. Can you do Baxter good enough to fool these guys?"

"You're darn right I can. Are you still driving that same Chrysler convertible?"

"Yeah, but is it a good idea to use my own car? Right now James Baxter has no way of tying me in with Shannon. Maybe we should try to keep it that way. I'm looking out the window at the parking lot now. I see a green Honda, license number GVB 707. How about we substitute it for my Chrysler?"

"Good thought," Brad agreed. "The owner of the Honda might not like it, but Shannon's life could be at stake here." Brad jotted down the license number on the back of the envelope containing the photographs of Lori and Howard. "I'll need Shannon's phone number, Tom. And maybe you'd better give me yours while we're at it."

As Tom gave him the phone numbers, Brad wrote them under the license number. "One more thing, did you happen to catch the name of either one of Baxter's cronies?"

"Yeah I did. I heard one of them call the other Marty."

"Good. You contact the police, Tom. I'll take care of the rest. And I'm on my way to your place now."

Brad cleared the phone, then dialed Shannon's number. Just as he suspected, a man answered. "Yeah, who is this?" came the gruff male voice.

Brad spoke in a perfect imitation of James Baxter's voice. "Marty, is that you?"

"No, boss, this is Sarge. You want Marty?"

"No, Sarge, you'll do fine. Look, I've learned that Shannon has some legal papers locked up in the glove compartment of her car. I've got to have those papers at all costs. You can forget about Shannon and the brat. What I want are those papers."

"Forget about Shannon and the brat?" Sarge asked. "I'm confused here, boss. I thought . . ."

"Never mind what you thought, Sarge! Something's happened to change the game. Leave Shannon and the kid where they are. Just get to her car and get me those papers. It's a green Honda, license number GVB 707. It should be parked somewhere in the apartment building lot. If you fail to get me those papers I'm not going to be happy, Sarge. You know what it means when I'm not happy, don't you?"

"Yeah, boss. We'll get the papers. Don't you worry about that."

"And one more thing. I want Shannon and the kid unharmed. I want to deal with them myself."

"Leave the woman and kid alone, get the papers. Gotcha, boss."

Brad abruptly shut off the cellular phone and pushed the Pontiac to its limit as he drove toward town. The problem of Lori and Howard was still there, like a spike through his heart, but now he had another problem. This problem he could do something about.

By the time Brad reached the apartment building, his plan was well under way. The police were there arresting the two stupefied culprits. Brad wasted no time getting his car parked. Hurrying inside the building, he took one look at the elevator and decided the stairs would be faster. Reaching the fifth floor he went straight to Tom's apartment. Not bothering to knock, he entered the room to find Shannon and Tanielle already there. Shannon was crying.

"Brad," she cried at first sight of him. "Thank goodness you're here. Tom explained how you got rid of those awful men. They were going to kidnap Tanielle and me. Our lives wouldn't be worth a nickel if James got us back in his power. What am I going to do? I know James will only try again once he realizes this plan failed."

"I have a suggestion," Tom broke in. "But it's pretty drastic."

Brad's eyes shifted to Tom. "What suggestion?" he asked.

Tom explained his idea. "As an Air Force pilot, I fly cargo planes all over the world, you know. I have a flight scheduled this afternoon to the island of Saint Thomas in the Caribbean Sea. I have enough connections there to get Shannon and Tanielle set up with a place to stay, for a while at least. Baxter would have a hard time finding her there."

"An island in the Caribbean?" Brad asked. "You're right, that is a drastic plan. But it might just be a good one. What do you think, Shannon?"

Shannon was sitting on the sofa holding a sleeping Tanielle in her lap. She looked down at the child's face. "I . . . don't know," she said hesitantly. "Tanielle will be starting school soon. Do they have schools on this island you mentioned?"

"Sure they have schools," Tom responded. "But you're a teacher, Shannon. A darn good one. You could home school her for a while if you had to."

Shannon lay her cheek against Tanielle's. "I'm so frightened," she admitted. "I know your idea is a good one, Tom. But I'm not a strong woman. I've never done anything like this. Not on my own."

"You won't be alone, Shannon," Tom assured her. "Like I say, I have friends on the island. I'll make sure you're taken care of."

As Tom and Shannon talked, their attention strayed from Brad for the moment. Had they paid closer attention they would have certainly noticed the pain etched across his face. The reality of losing Lori had grown quite strong by this time. This, added to the precarious nature of his sister's situation, was almost more than he could stand. He quickly worked out a plan in his mind, and ran it over and over again to be sure it was the right thing to do. At last, he spoke up.

"Listen, Shannon. I have some bad news of my own, it seems. Lori is—that is our marriage—what I'm trying to say is things are all wrong at home."

The surprise in both Tom and Shannon's eyes couldn't have been more evident. "You and Lori are having problems?" Shannon asked numbly.

Brad swallowed hard. "Yeah. She's found someone else."

"Oh no," Shannon gasped. "I don't believe you. Not Lori."

Brad tried to force a smile that refused to come. "I have a hard time believing it myself, sis. But I can't erase what I've seen with my own eyes. Anyway, I was thinking. Maybe I'll go with you to the Caribbean. I can help you get established and—"

"Isn't there a chance you and Lori can work things out?" Shannon protested.

Brad closed his eyes and shook his head. "Not after what I saw. And I have evidence it's been going on for some time. I'm telling you, sis, going to the Caribbean might be as good for me as it is for you. I can't stand the thought of being here where I can see her with another man. There is room on your cargo plane for one more passenger, isn't there, Tom?"

Tom nodded a sober yes. "There's plenty of room, Brad."

Brad stood and walked to the window. The early morning sun was still low in the eastern sky on this, the worst day of his life. He wondered if the sun would ever rise on another happy day again. "Then it's settled," he said. "There are some things you and I need to talk about, Tom. And I'd like to leave a note for Lori. Do you have some paper I can use?"

* * *

Lori stared at herself in the bathroom mirror. Her eyes were red and swollen from a night of crying. She hadn't slept. The horror of what she had caused with her foolish actions haunted her now with a vengeance. How could she ever face Brad again? She had gotten up sometime during the early morning hours after the sound of the phone had brought her out of her painful stupor. She hadn't answered the phone for fear it might be Howard. She definitely did not want to talk with Howard right now. Maybe never again. Only after the phone had stopped ringing did she remember the cell phone in the Pontiac. This thought sent another wave of fear through her mind. Brad must have discovered the phone. If not before it rang, then certainly he would have discovered it once it did. And, those pictures she had left in the car. Oh no!! Brad must have seen them, too. If things weren't bad enough that Brad had seen Howard kissing her, that phone and those pictures would send his suspicions through the roof. How could she ever explain the truth to him now?

She checked the house on the faint hope he might have quietly returned home during the night. No such luck. He was gone and so was the car. It was then she first noticed the dozen beautiful roses on the family room coffee table. Roses bought by a loving, caring husband— but meant for a happier occasion than the one they now celebrated.

Lori washed her face with cold water. Just as she was reaching for a towel, she heard what sounded like the garage door opening. Listening more closely, she learned she was right. The familiar sound of the Pontiac engine came to her ears, and she knew Brad had returned. Her heart pounded within her. How she wished she could rush to his side and smother him with warm kisses. But remembering the hard lines of Brad's face, she knew that was out of the question. She heard the door open and the sound of his steps as he moved closer.

There was no way she could face him now. Quickly, she moved back to the bedroom where she fell to the bed and feigned a deep sleep.

* * *

Brad glanced at his watch. It was just after seven. That meant it had been seven hours since his world had first started to crumble. The house was quiet. He wondered if perhaps Howard had returned for Lori sometime during the night. The thought stabbed painfully at his heart. He looked around. Where would be the best place to leave the letter he had written to her? Then he noticed the roses. He could leave the letter there. Crossing the room, he leaned the envelope against the vase. He drew a breath, and looked at the bedroom door that had been locked the last time he was here. This time, it was ajar. Did she leave it that way when she left with Howard? He just had to know. Quietly, he slipped up to the door and looked inside. Lori was on the bed, apparently in a deep sleep. She was still wearing the gown, the same gown she had worn when he saw her kissing Howard. It was a fancy gown, all right. Fancier than any she had ever worn for him.

He wanted to leave, but felt drawn like a magnet to her side. Ever so quietly he moved to the bedside and looked lovingly down at the most beautiful face in the world. "Oh, Lori," he said in a whisper. "I love you so much. I always have and I always will. Please think of me once in a while. And have a wonderful life."

Kneeling down, he leaned over and placed a gentle kiss on her cheek. Then, he quickly stood and hurried out of the house to a waiting taxi.

* * *

When Lori heard the front door close, she realized Brad must be leaving. She couldn't let that happen. Leaping from the bed, she ran to the front door and flung it open just in time to see a taxi pull away. "No!" she cried. "All I've done now is make it worse. Why didn't I throw my arms around him when he kissed me?"

Closing the door, she leaned against it and cried. Minutes passed before she could even move. When finally she did make her way back through the house, she spotted the envelope near the roses. It had her name on it. Quickly she grabbed it and tore it open. It was a letter from Brad.

Lori,

I couldn't go without at least leaving you this note. After last night it's obvious that we have no future together. I ran into another problem during the night, too. It's my sister, Shannon. You know about James Baxter. Well, she left him. Or at least she tried to. He's a dangerous man, Lori. Shannon has to find a place where she can be free from him once and for all. I've decided it might be best if I go with her to that place. You see, I love you too much to bear the thought of you with another man. Maybe if I'm so far away that I can't see it, it might be a little easier.

I want you to know, if there's anything to forgive, then I do forgive you. I know I could never be as exciting or romantic as Howard Placard. I guess you and I just married a little too soon, before you had the chance to learn there were more interesting men out there than me, huh? I'm sorry I lost my temper and hit him. Tell him for me, will you?

The house and car are yours. I won't need them where I'm going, anyway. I've given my Power of Attorney to Tom Reddings and instructed him to be sure that everything is transferred over to you. I won't contest the divorce. I've made sure Tom knows that.

This much I want you to know. I love you. I have always loved you, and I always will. I give you your freedom. I wish you all the happiness in the world. And if by chance we ever meet again, please save one of your smiles for me. Be good, and be happy.

Love, Brad

Lori clutched the letter to her heart. "What have I done?" she gasped. "What have I done?"

CHAPTER 8

As the final scene of the holographic replay faded into darkness, Arline was searching the empty Kleenex box for just one more tissue. "Here, use this," Bruce said, handing her a handkerchief from his pocket.

"This is a terrible story, Sam," Arline sniffed, wiping one eye and then the other. "What happened to Brad? Did he end up somewhere in the Caribbean? And how about Lori? She didn't marry Howard, I hope. And if all this took place ten years ago—what could you possibly expect Bruce and me to do about it now?"

Samantha broke out laughing. "Same old Arline. Patience was never one of your virtues was it?"

"Stop that, Sam! I don't need a big sister lecture. Whoever said patience was a virtue, anyway? No one in my business, that's for sure. You don't hesitate when you have a hot story on the grill or you end up seeing it on Oprah Winfrey." Arline stopped long enough to glare at Samantha. "Come to think of it, I don't remember you being any Rock of Gibraltar yourself when it comes to patience, Samantha Hackett. Now are you going to tell me what's going on here, or do I have to drag it out of you?"

Samantha was laughing so hard she had to borrow Jason's hanky to wipe her own eyes. "All right, already, I'll explain. Brad did go to the Caribbean. He and the girls settled on a small island near Saint Thomas, where they lived until about a month ago when James Baxter finally found out where they were hiding. Baxter came to the island with the idea of taking Shannon back to San Francisco. That's when Jason and I first got involved. Baxter never knew what hit him, and with him out of the picture there was no longer a reason for our friends to remain on the island. So, with a little help from our side, they decided to come home and pick up their lives. Shannon and Tanielle came home right away, while Brad stayed behind on Saint Thomas to wrap up a few loose ends. He's on his way here now, even as we speak."

What about Lori? Did she marry Howard, or not?"

"You can set your mind at ease, Arline. Lori never married Howard. Not that the man didn't keep trying, mind you. A year after Brad vanished, Howard got his high-powered lawyers involved to handle Lori's divorce, and he's pressured her to marry him ever since. A man like Howard can't handle rejection. His life has never been the same since Lori turned him down, and he'll never rest until he convinces her to change her mind."

Bruce entered the conversation with a question of his own. "What about Brad?" he asked. "Does he know that Lori and Howard never married? From what I've seen so far, I assume he doesn't know."

"Still thinking like a psychologist, eh, Bruce?" Samantha laughed. "You hit it on the head. Brad is certain Lori married Howard before the ink was dry on her divorce papers."

"Am I to assume you want Arline and me to play the matchmaker game, like in getting Brad and Lori back together after all these years?"

Samantha arched her eyebrows. "You have something against playing matchmaker, Bruce?"

Bruce flatly denied this. "No, Sam. I have nothing against playing matchmaker. At least not in this case where the players were already married at one time. I've helped save plenty of marriages as a psychologist. Let me ask you this. Did Lori have the good sense to quit her job at Howard's studio after her fiasco with the man? I would hope she did."

"Yes, Bruce. Lori did a dumb thing letting Howard draw her into his trap, but once she woke up she kept enough distance to ensure it wouldn't happen again. She never went back to the studio. Instead, she opened a small interior design business of her own and has been making a moderate living at it ever since. Howard did his best to talk her out of leaving the studio, but she refused to let him sway her."

"I don't like that man," Arline bluntly said. "I hope you have big plans for him, and I hope I'm there when those plans come down around his overstuffed head. Which brings up the point—what exactly do you want Bruce and me to do?"

"The first thing I want you to do," Samantha smiled, "is to meet the one who will be working with you on the assignment. Arline, Bruce, let me present the honorable Captain Horatio Symington Blake. Who, by the way, happens to be an angel on the level of Jason when you worked with him before, Arline."

As Arline watched in amazement, the figure of a black-bearded crusty-looking seaman suddenly stood in the midst of the group. "Glad to be meetin' ye, lad and lassie," Blake said with a huge grin. "It'll be me pleasure workin' with ye, says I."

"Happy to make your acquaintance, Captain," Bruce responded. "May I assume you're the sort of angel who can't shake my hand?"

"Aye, laddie. That be the case. But I tips me hat to the lady and ye." The captain removed his hat and bowed, first to Arline, then to Bruce.

Arline's eyes opened wide in amazement as she turned to Samantha. "He'll be working with Bruce and me together? I don't understand. When I worked with Jason, I was the only one who could see him."

Samantha nodded, understanding Arline's confusion. "It's a general rule that an angel be seen by only one person at a time," she explained. "But Jason and I have decided in this case it would be better to give the captain a little freer hand. We petitioned the higher authorities with the idea of Blake having near total visibility. They agreed, and so here he is for most everyone involved to see. I might even get it cleared for you to interview him on your television show if you can talk him into it, Arline. In fact, you could interview Captain Blake and Brad together. They are great friends, you know. I mean, they should be after spending ten long years together on a tiny island in the Caribbean. Think about it. An interview with those two would be great entertainment for your viewers."

Arline's eyes lit up as she contemplated the possibilities of what her friend was saying. "You really know how to tempt a girl, don't you, Sam?" she laughed.

Samantha grinned back at Arline. "I've been known to throw out a tasty morsel of bait at times. So how about it? Are you in?"

With a sigh, Arline nodded. "You know I can't resist you when you put on the pressure, Sam. By the way, where is our boy Brad now? You mentioned he was flying home, didn't you?"

Samantha's lips curled into a satisfying smile. "He's just about to disembark from the plane as we speak, Arline. Within the next few minutes, he'll be back on the sidewalks of home for the first time in a decade."

* * *

Brad's flight home from Saint Thomas Island was much different from the flight that had taken him to the island more than ten years before. The first leg, from Saint Thomas to Key West was in Bob's chopper. At Key West, he caught an airline for the last leg of the journey. It was a long flight, one that gave plenty of time for thinking about what lay ahead. The only conclusion he could find was that he was walking into the biggest question mark of his life. Oh well, every question has an answer. He'd just have to play things by ear until he found the answer to this one.

Touch down was smooth, and disembarking from the plane was relatively easy due to the light passenger load. As Brad stepped from the tunnel into the airport terminal, he was surprised to see how little it had changed since the last time he was here. Strangely enough, it was the same terminal he had used when he departed for Acapulco all those years ago. Moisture filled his eyes as his mind pictured again what was to be his and Lori's final good-bye. From out of the past he heard the announcer give the final boarding call for Flight 1377 bound for Acapulco, Mexico. Brad could almost feel the warmth of Lori's lips against his as he drew her to him in a good-bye kiss. "Call you tonight, babe," he had said.

He remembered Lori placing her hand against his cheek as she replied, "You'd better. And you'd better keep your distance from all those girls in beach bikinis."

"Deal," he had told her. "I'll keep my distance."

Then came the last kiss. It was a quick one, but one that would have to last a lifetime for Brad. There would never be another.

"Don't forget to miss me," he had called back to Lori as he headed for his flight.

Her answer rang in his mind clearly now. "I won't forget . . . ," she said, raising her hand in a good-bye wave. Brad wondered now how she could have acted so cool, so natural, as if there was nothing wrong between them. She must have been in love with Howard even then. Brad's greatest hope was that she had found the happiness with Howard that had eluded her when she was his wife. As for him ever seeing her again—well, maybe that was an idea better left forgotten.

Brad didn't have to bother with the baggage claim; everything he owned was in his carry-on satchel. Throwing the strap over his shoulder, he started for the exit but was distracted by the sound of his own name being spoken from someone behind him. Turning to look, he discovered it was Tom Reddings.

"Over here," Tom said with a wave.

Brad hadn't expected anyone to meet him, but the sight of his old friend was a welcome one. He hurried over to Tom.

"Wow, this is a surprise," Brad said, as the two men shook hands and exchanged back slaps. "I had no idea you'd be here to meet me."

"I almost wasn't here; you never told me you were coming. If my buddy Bob Rivers hadn't called, I'd never have known."

"Bob called you?"

"He called me from Key West, right after dropping you off. If you'd told me your plans, I'd have personally flown to Saint Thomas to pick you up. You know how I hate airports. Why didn't you say something, man?"

"I didn't want to put you out, Tom."

"Put me out? How could an old buddy like you put me out? And besides, I have to stay on your good side since we may be brothers-in-law in the near future."

"Shannon's agreed to marry you?!" Brad asked excitedly.

Tom shrugged. "Well—she didn't say no this time. I think she'll come around soon enough. Tanielle's on my side. She's pressuring her mom pretty hard."

"Hey, I'm best man—and don't you forget it!"

"You got it, pal. Now what do you say we get you home."

Brad's smile faded. "I—uh—don't exactly know where home will be. I was figuring on getting a room somewhere."

"Getting a room! What for? You have a house, you know."

"I what? Are you talking about the old place where Lori and I . . ."

"Yeah, that's what I'm talking about. You have your house, your old brown Pontiac, and you even have your bank account. Lori refused to take one thing from you, Brad. You still have it all. I'd have told you a long time ago if you hadn't made me swear never to contact you for fear that James Baxter would pick up on something."

Tom's words came with staggering impact. "Lori refused the house?" he gasped.

"Like I said, she refused the whole package."

Brad rubbed the back of his neck as he thought about this unexpected development. "I suppose that's not such a strange thing at that," he concluded. "Considering she's married to someone as rich and powerful as Howard Placard. What possible use could she have for anything I may have left her?"

"All I know is I had a message on my answering machine about a month after you and the girls left for the Caribbean," Tom said. "It was a message from Lori, telling me she had vacated the house. When I checked the place, I found a note telling me where everything was. I thought she might seek me out for help in looking for you, but she never did. In fact, I never saw or heard from her after she moved out of the place. But then, as an Air Force pilot, I'm gone most of the time. Even when I'm here, I don't run in the same circles as movie tycoons like Howard Placard."

"Yeah, I see what you mean, Tom."

"So, anyway, I personally took care of the old place for you. I figured you'd come home someday." Tom pushed open the door leading from the airport terminal to the outside. "My car's across the street in the parking lot," he said. "You can spend a few days at my place if you like. At least until we get your car running again."

Brad drew in a deep breath allowing the sweet smell of home to fill his nostrils. It felt good. Like rediscovering an old familiar friend long after giving up ever seeing him again. "Thanks for the offer, Tom. But if the old house is there, I'd really like to see it. As for my car—I've got nothing better to do. I might as well get started making it roadworthy again."

"Suit yourself, Brad," Tom shrugged. "But the offer is there if you should change your mind. The old place is bound to be filled with ghosts, you know."

Brad cracked a smile. He knew Tom's use of the word "ghosts" was linked to the memories the old place would hold, but after ten years with Captain Blake the word had a deeper meaning for him. Good old Captain Blake. Darned if he didn't miss the old fellow.

They reached Tom's car, and as Tom was unlocking the door he paused to take a long look at Brad. "You know," he remarked with a sly grin. "If Shannon hadn't warned me about your beard, I would never have recognized you in that thing. What's it supposed to be, a new image or something?"

Brad reached up and rubbed the beard. "Nah, it's anything but new. I've been wearing it for the past ten years. The last time I shaved, in fact, was the night I caught Lori with Howard. After that, I didn't have any real reason to shave, so I just gave it up."

"Yeah, well, if I were you I'd think about picking up the habit again. I hate to be the one to tell you this, but you do look pretty raunchy in the thing. Like some 1960s flower child from San Francisco. My advice would be to either shave it off, or trade your Pontiac in for a Volkswagen van. By the way, the key to your house and car are in my glove compartment."

Brad ignored Tom's remark about his beard. Sliding into the car, he opened the glove box and took out an envelope with his name on it. "Is this what you're talking about?" he asked.

"That's it. The keys are inside along with your bank statement. Ten years interest hasn't hurt your balance, pal. There should be enough there to tide you over until you get back on your feet."

Brad opened the envelope and glanced at the balance. He almost choked. "Wow, this will help a sore toe, all right. Lori must have never spent a dime out of this account."

Tom started the car and pulled out of the parking lot onto the roadway. "Did Shannon tell you she got a job teaching?" he asked.

"No," Brad answered. "She didn't. Where's she teaching?"

"She had to take a job in a pre-school. Her credentials are too far out of date to teach high school. She can get them renewed by taking some night classes, but that will have to come in time. Still, she's in pretty good shape what with the royalties on her books, and all. She turned into a pretty good mystery writer in the last ten years. I've been working on reading her books ever since I learned about them. Tanielle is enrolled as a high school sophomore and loving every minute of it. The boys are falling all over themselves trying to impress her. New girl on the block, you know."

"Good for her," Brad smiled. "She gave up a lot living on that island. She deserves her moment in the sun."

The drive home proved to be a real trip down nostalgia lane for Brad. Everywhere he looked, a memory jumped out at him. No question about it, this was home. It was hard to realize that Lori wouldn't be waiting at the old place. But her not being there was just something he would have to get used to.

At last the moment came. Tom turned the corner, and the house came into view. Some things about the place looked the same, but others looked almost out of place. Like the tangerine tree in the front yard, for instance. Lori had planted that tree a week after they moved into the place. It certainly wasn't the mere twig she had spent so much time nurturing back then. Now it was huge, covering most of the front yard with its shade.

The blue and white trim was the same as when Brad had painted it, though it had definitely dimmed with age. One thing was obvious. The house had been well cared for through it all. "From the looks of the place I'd say I could be in real trouble when I get your bill," Brad laughed. "You did a fantastic job keeping it up."

"You don't owe me a thing, Brad. I'm a bachelor, remember. I had plenty of time on my hands to tinker with the place. I have several nieces and nephews who thought that doing the yard work was a great way to earn a buck, and I didn't think you'd mind that I let my folks use the place for a summer home three or four times. I made out fine on the deal, friend."

Brad stepped from the car and leaned in the open window. "Thanks, Tom. For everything. I'd have been in a mess without your help. Tell Shannon I'll drop by to see her and Tanielle as soon as I get settled in."

"You got it, Brad," Tom grinned. "And if things are too rough after you see the inside of the place, give me a holler. The offer to stay at my place still goes."

Brad watched as Tom pulled away, then picking up his satchel, he walked to the house and unlocked the door. His first glimpse inside brought painful memories, since it was here—next to the front door—where he had seen Lori kissing Howard. He quickly passed this point and checked the rest of the house. The furniture was unchanged, the kitchen cabinets held the old dishes, and perhaps the greatest shock of all came when he discovered all his old clothes still hanging on his side of the closet. Tom was right; the house was filled with ghosts. It took several nights of sleeping on the sofa before Brad could bring himself to use the bedroom.

For the first few days, Brad either walked or used a taxi to get around. At last, he got up the nerve to face the next obstacle, the old Pontiac. Of all things he found one photograph that Lori had evidently missed when she cleaned her things out of the car. It was a picture of her and Howard standing barefoot on a beach. Brad studied the picture closely. She was so beautiful, but it hurt knowing her smile was meant for Howard, and not him. He tore up the picture.

The car itself proved to be in great shape. A new set of tires, a battery, an oil change, and a trip to the car wash, and it was ready for the road again. By now it was an old car, but with so few miles on it, it was like new—to Brad's practical mind, at least.

Brad knew he would have to do something about finding work soon. His savings wouldn't hold out forever. It didn't take long for him to learn that Howard's promise that Brad would never again work in the movie industry was one cast in stone. Even after all this time Howard's threat hung over him like a black cloud. Everyone he checked with had the same story to tell. *It's great to see you back, Brad, but I can't give you work. Howard Placard has made it clear what will happen if I do.*

These were all friends of Brad, and he pointed no blame in their direction for not hiring him. He knew and understood how Howard worked. It seemed that Howard had not only stolen Brad's wife, he had also stolen his career—just one thing more for Brad to shrug off in his effort to get on with his life. He could always fall back on his comic impressionist act. He checked with a few of the old spots and found that most wanted to use him. True, it wouldn't pay much, but at least it was work, and Brad soon found it was enough to get him by.

* * *

Howard Placard slammed down the phone and sat staring at it for several minutes. At last he picked it up again and dialed the number for Myro Finderman, the man he always turned to when the need for a private detective came up. "Finderman's Detective Agency" came a voice from the other end of the line. "How may I help you?" It was Marge, Myro's secretary.

"Hi, Marge. It's me, Howard. Is Myro in? I need to talk with him, if he is."

Marge laughed. "Myro happens to be out, sir—to everyone but you, that is. I'm sure he'll take your call. Let me put you on hold a second or two, all right?"

"All right, Marge, but make it quick. I'm in a hurry to get him on the job."

Howard was on hold only a few seconds when Myro came on the line. "Howard, my man. Good to hear from you. What's up, good buddy?"

"It's happened, Myro. Brad Douglas is back. After all these years, the man has come back. I just received a call from the studio; he was there looking for work. I want you to put a tail on him right away. If he even thinks about going near Lori, I want to know about it immediately. You got that?"

"Yeah, I got it. Did your source say anything about where the man is staying?"

"He's in the same old house where he lived before. I have no idea how, but he managed to get the place back. You can't know how this upsets me, Myro. I was hoping he would never show his face in these parts again."

"Yeah, well, you just never know. I'll get a tail on him right away, Howard."

"You do that. And mark my words, I want to know if he goes near Lori. Call me day or night if you see any likelihood of it, Myro. Do you hear?"

Howard replaced the phone on the hook. Slowly he reached into his inside coat pocket and removed a small round medallion. The one he had acquired from Lori more than ten years before. Rubbing the medallion between his fingers and thumb, he remembered the wonderful times he had spent with Lori back then. He had kept the medallion all these years because it reminded him of those times.

"So help me, Brad Douglas," he growled through clenched teeth. "You'll never have her back. She belongs to me, and me alone. You should have stayed gone, old enemy of mine. But no matter. I'll be rid of you again soon enough. You have my word on it."

CHAPTER 9

It was a warm Friday morning just under a month since Brad's return home, when the thought came to him that he was beginning to settle into his new life with at least some degree of comfort. Things could be better, but they could be worse, too. He was working several nights a week, and things were pretty much at a stage he could now consider normal. Or so he thought until Shannon showed up one morning with all the makings for breakfast. "What are you doing, sis?" Brad jokingly asked as he watched her walk in and take over his kitchen.

"What does it look like? I'm fixing you a decent breakfast for once. I've seen the contents of your cupboards, and I know what your eating habits have deteriorated to, Brad Douglas. Without a woman around to look after you, you're sinking to an all-time low, and I think it's time I do something about it."

Brad didn't argue. Not when he got a whiff of what she was cooking up. Eggs, bacon, biscuits with gravy, even a stack of hot cakes. "You're going to spoil me, sis," Brad said as he sat down to the meal. "I could get used to this in a hurry."

Shannon poured two glasses of orange juice and fixed herself a plate. "That's my point in being here, Brad," she told him. "I've decided you need a woman in your life."

Brad nearly choked on a bite of egg. "You've decided what?"

"I have my hands full taking care of Tanielle and earning a living. And besides, you need more than a sister. It's time you found yourself a new wife, brother dear."

"I don't want a wife," Brad grumbled. "If you'll recall, my first marriage didn't do much for my lifestyle."

Shannon took a bite of pancake and ignored Brad's protest. "I've set you up with a date tonight," she said nonchalantly.

Brad dropped his fork. "You've done what?!" he gasped loudly.

"Stop shouting," Shannon scolded. "I'm sitting right here, and I hear you fine."

"What do you mean you set me up with a date? I don't want a date. I'm perfectly happy with things the way they are. Good grief, Shannon, what were you thinking?"

"Don't argue with me Brad, I know what's best for you. It's time you got a little feminine companionship back in your life. You'll be picking her up at seven."

"I'll be picking . . . ? NO! I won't do it!"

"Oh yes you will. I've already made reservations for you at the Longhorn Steakhouse, and Loretta is expecting you."

"Loretta? Loretta who?"

"You probably remember her as Loretta Stapleton. She was my best friend back in my high school days."

"Loretta Stapleton? You're darn right I remember Loretta. How could I ever forget? She spent so much time at our house, I thought she was my adopted sister. She ended up marrying Hank Stoner, the special effects guy with the prosthetic leg I used to worked with way back when."

Shannon glared at her brother. "And you hold that against her? How was she to know what a jerk Hank would turn out to be. It didn't take her long to leave him when she woke up to his playboy antics, did it? And give her a little credit. She did better the second time around. She was married to Chuck Bradbury for nine good years."

"Loretta married again?" Brad asked, surprised. "I didn't know."

"Neither did I until we came home from the island. She married Chuck about the time we went to the Caribbean. Then he was killed in an auto accident last December. On Christmas Eve, of all things," Shannon sighed and shook her head, before adding, "Loretta is a very sweet lady, Brad."

"I'm not saying she's not a sweet lady, sis. I'm only saying . . ."

"You're saying you're too darned stubborn to do anything about your lonesomeness. Don't be so selfish, Brad. Loretta is lonesome, too, you know."

"Lonesome? Me? What makes you think I'm lonesome?"

Shannon rolled her eyes. "Don't give me that line, mister. I'm your sister, remember?"

Brad squirmed nervously in his chair. "So maybe I do get a little lonesome. That doesn't mean I need to get married. I have a much better idea. Let me take Tanielle somewhere for a weekend once in a while."

"Tanielle has better things to do with her time than chase around with her uncle. She stays pretty busy these days in the company of young men her own age. And as for you, Brad, you'll pick Loretta up at seven. Are you listening to me?"

Brad took a bite of bacon and thought for a moment. Dropping his fork again, he pointed a finger at Shannon. "I'll bet you one thing," he said, adding to his argument. "I'll bet Loretta's as thrilled over the idea of this date as I am. Tell the truth, Shannon. Am I right?"

Shannon shrugged. "She's a little—apprehensive. But you're the first guy she's dated since losing Chuck."

"Hey! I haven't dated anyone since losing Lori either, you know."

"You think I don't know that, Brad? You never dated anyone *before* Lori. It's been over between the two of you for more than ten years. Get a life, brother of mine. You're still a young man. Don't throw away the years you have left."

Brad poked a fork at his pancakes as he pondered this conversation a little more deeply. "There's something you should understand, Shannon," he said at last. "After what Lori did to me, I could never trust another woman with my heart. Much as I loved Lori, I couldn't trust her again if the chance ever presented itself. Nothing has ever hurt me as badly as what she did. I could never take the chance of being hurt like that again."

Shannon was quiet for a moment but she refused to back down. "Take Loretta to dinner tonight, Brad," she urged. "Maybe the two of you won't hit it off, but it will at least break the ice for both of you. I'm not looking for an overnight miracle, but I think in time you can find someone you're willing to trust your heart to again. Do this for ME, Brad. And finish your breakfast before it gets too cold to enjoy."

CHAPTER 10

Brad pulled the Pontiac to a stop in front of Loretta Bradbury's home and glanced at his watch. Ten to seven. He was early. What should he do? Drive around the block? Sit here in front of the place and wait out the ten minutes? Ah, heck with it. He'd just go to the door and hope she'd be one to appreciate promptness.

With a sigh, he exited the car and made the long walk to the front porch, where he stared at the door bell switch for what seemed an eternity before gathering the courage to press it. The door opened and there he was, face to face with a young, very attractive woman. He had to admit, Loretta was even more attractive than he remembered. She was smiling, but somehow her smile didn't reach her eyes.

"Hi," Brad said, forcing a smile of his own. "I think you remember me, don't you? Brad Douglas, Shannon's brother."

"I remember you, Brad," Loretta responded with a soft feminine voice. "All except for the beard, that is."

"Oh, yeah, that's right. I used to go clean shaven, didn't I?"

"I didn't mean—that is—the beard looks nice."

Brad raised a hand and stroked the beard nervously. "I'm sorry," he said trying not to look directly at Loretta. "I'm a bit rusty at this sort of thing. It's been a few years since I . . . ."

"I understand perfectly," she broke in. "It's been a long time since I've dated, too."

"I have reservations at the Longhorn Steakhouse. Is that all right with you?"

"Oh, yes. It sounds nice. Just let me get my coat."

Brad waited nervously until she returned, then led the way to his car. It was a twenty-minute ride to the steak house, but it seemed much longer as the conversation grew more and more awkward. Inside the restaurant it was more of the same. They talked of the weather, how the price of sugar was soaring, the way there was nothing good left on television, and who did they think would win the next election for state governor. As they began to eat, Brad asked, "Is your steak all right, Loretta?"

Loretta glanced down at the steak on her plate. "My steak? Oh, yes, it's perfect, Brad. The steaks are always good in this place."

"You've been here before, then?"

"Yes," she sighed, her eyes glistening even in the dim light. "Chuck and I came here often. It was one of our favorite restaurants."

Brad stared at the morsel of steak on the end of his fork. "This place stirs a few memories for me, too, Loretta. Lori and I used to come here. Of course that was a very long time ago."

Loretta looked up at the same time as Brad, and for the first time they allowed their eyes to hold contact more than a split second. "You loved her very much, didn't you, Brad?" Loretta ventured to ask. "Lori, I mean."

"Yes, Loretta," Brad readily admitted. "I did love Lori. Losing her was the hardest thing I've ever endured. I—uh—know it's the same with you. Losing Chuck."

Loretta brushed away a tear with the corner of her napkin. "Chuck and I had nine wonderful years together," she replied. "There are times now when I think I can't go on living. Everyone keeps telling me the sun will shine again—but I don't know when that will be. Life is so empty without him."

"I'm sorry," Brad said. "I didn't mean . . ."

Loretta reached across the table and squeezed Brad's hand. "It's all right," she answered, somehow managing a smile. "At least I know that Chuck still loves me, and I'm sure he misses me as much as I miss him. I'm just as sure that the two of us will be together again when the time comes. You don't even have that much to hold to with Lori."

"Would you look at us?" Brad said suddenly. "Here we are, just two lonely people trying to find comfort in each other's company, and we end up with four people at our table. I mean, we can't see Chuck and Lori—but they are here, aren't they?"

This time Loretta's smile was genuine. "You're right, Brad. There are four of us here. Do you feel as awkward with this as I do?"

"You're a beautiful woman, Loretta, and I'm flattered you came with me tonight, but—"

"I know exactly what you mean, Brad. You're a fine man but I'm not ready for this, not yet anyway. Right now I'm not sure I ever will be ready for it."

"Well," Brad suggested. "Now that we have that out of the way, how about we finish our dinner and at least take in a movie?"

"Would you mind terribly if I decline the movie? I'd really much rather just finish dinner and let it go at that. Don't get me wrong, Brad. It's not your fault. But I just have this guilty feeling, you know—like I'm still a married woman and shouldn't be out with another man."

"I understand perfectly," Brad agreed. "It's been well over ten years in my case, and I still feel the same way. I, uh, hope you'll overlook my sister's helpfulness. Shannon means well . . ."

"I understand perfectly, Brad," Loretta assured him. "You're Shannon's brother, and I'm a friend from way back. It's only natural she would want to help us."

Brad took another bite of steak, and then decided to press his luck with a question of a different nature. "I guess you know, Loretta, that your first husband, Hank Stoner, and I were once pretty good friends, don't you? In fact, we worked together during the last movie I ever did."

"I know," Loretta smiled. "I also know you were ten times the man Hank was back in those days, Brad. I never did understand why the two of you hit it off like you did."

"Yeah," Brad returned, with a smile of his own. "I used to try convincing Hank how good married life could be. I guess he ended up having the last laugh on me, didn't he? I mean with me losing Lori, and all."

Loretta stared at Brad several seconds before answering his remark. "You don't know what happened to Hank, do you, Brad?" she asked.

Brad was surprised at her question. "Hank and I have been out of touch many years now," he admitted. "What happened to him?"

"It happened not long after you and Lori split up. Hank swears he was visited by an angel while he was on his way to a party."

"What?" Brad questioned in shock. "Hank says he saw an angel?"

"So help me, Brad. That's what the man claims. He even gives his angel a name, Gus something-or-other. Hank describes him as a very laid-back angel with a way of tearing up the English language like no one else he ever knew."

Brad scratched his head. "Okay, so Hank saw an angel. I imagine the guy saw a lot worse than that on some of his lost weekends."

"That's probably true, Brad. But when Hank saw this angel he was cold sober. Gus apparently told Hank that he and Blanch had some sort of angelic contract tying their destinies together. If Hank didn't shape up, that contract would be null and void. The way Hank puts it, Gus told him to either start treating Blanch right or he'd end up on Gus' side of the line tuning violin strings for Johann Sebastian Bach's celestial orchestra."

Brad couldn't believe his ears. "Are you saying this angel was asking Hank to be faithful to Blanch and no one else? Wow! What a concept. So, what happened to Hank? Did he die?"

"Oh, he's very much alive and kicking. That's the good part, Brad. Hank gave up the movie business, and went back to school to become a psychologist."

"A psychologist?" Brad gasped. "Hank Stoner? Come on, Loretta, you're kidding me, right?"

Loretta shook her head firmly. "I am not kidding you, Brad. Hank is now a marriage counselor. He's saved dozens of marriages. And if that's not enough, he brings flowers home to Blanch almost every night. He takes her to movies, out to eat, and even goes shopping with her. I've never seen such a turnaround in all my life. He even gave the eulogy at my husband's funeral. He couldn't have done a better job. "

All Brad could do was shake his head in amazement. "Hank Stoner a marriage counselor. I'm telling you, Loretta, angels must be pretty powerful creatures to pull off something as big as turning Hank around." *And they must be a lot more powerful than three-hundred-year dead ghosts of old sea captains, too,* he added to himself.

Back at Loretta's front door, Brad glanced at his watch again. "An hour and a half," he chuckled. "This may well be one of the shortest dates in history, Loretta. Who knows, we may even make the *Guinness Book of World Records.*

"Maybe so," Loretta smiled. "Thanks for dinner, Brad. Believe it or not, I really did enjoy getting out of the house for an evening."

"Yeah, me too," Brad agreed. "I'm glad we did this. It felt good talking to someone who understands how I feel. Good night, Loretta."

"Good night, Brad."

* * *

Lori set her pencil aside and picked up the drawing she had been working on. As she looked it over in detail, she gave a satisfied sigh. "Yes," she said to herself. "This will do. I think even the stuffy Mrs. Vandersteen will be satisfied with her living room in this arrangement. It should give her plenty to show off when she has all those socialites over for her new housewarming. Or should I say mansion warming? How could any one person possibly need as much house as she'll be moving into? I wonder if she's a distant relative of Howard Placard. The place looks like something he'd want to live in."

Glancing at the clock on her office wall, she gasped. "My heavens! It's nearly eight-thirty. I had no idea it was this late." Lori stood and stretched. Lori hated driving home alone after dark, which frequently happened when she got absorbed in her work.

She set the project aside, and retrieving her purse from under her desk, she walked to the front door of her office. After one last look around, she turned out the light and stepped through the door onto the outside patio of the Marble Fountains Suites where her office was located. As she did, something caught her eye. The light was still on in one of the office spaces directly across the patio from hers. That in itself wasn't so strange. The strange thing was what had happened to the office space since she saw it at lunch time earlier that day. At that time, it had been vacant. Now, it was completely decked out as—of all things—an ice cream parlor.

"That doesn't make any sense," Lori said to herself. "Why would someone put an ice cream parlor in an office complex like this one? It's completely out of place." But the "Open" sign was lit and flashing.

Lori would have ignored the place and gone straight to her car if it hadn't been for the woman standing in the open doorway of the ice cream parlor. It looked like—but no, of course, it couldn't be. Lori did a double take, and the woman in the doorway shocked her even further by calling out her name.

"Lori, could you spare a few minutes for an interview?" the woman asked.

Lori stepped closer to the woman. "Excuse me for staring," she apologized. "But you look like . . ."

"Arline Vincent?" the woman completed Lori's sentence. "The talk show hostess? I look like Arline because I am Arline. And I'd like to do an interview with you, if you can spare the time."

Lori was stunned. "Why would you want to interview me?" she asked.

"I've done some research on you, Lori," Arline said smoothly. "You're an interesting person whose story can have great audience appeal."

"Me interesting?" Lori repeated. "I don't understand. And I don't understand about this ice cream parlor, either."

Arline laughed. "The ice cream parlor is just a set. It'll be gone by tomorrow morning, I assure you."

"Gone by tomorrow morning? But it looks so real. How did you put a set together with this much detail in such a short time?" Lori asked curiously.

"Believe me, Lori, it was no trick at all," Arline smiled. "The people helping out with this project are a trio of real angels. They really know how to get the job done. Please, won't you step inside where we can wait more comfortably for our second guest to arrive?"

Lori was dumbfounded. Coming face to face with a celebrity like Arline Vincent was one thing, but ice cream parlors from out of nowhere? How was it all possible? And why would anyone be interested in her life? "Second guest, you say?" she asked. "Who?"

"I can't tell you who the second guest is just yet, Lori. It would spoil the element of surprise so vital to a good plot. Please, do come inside."

*   *   *

Brad waited until Loretta closed the door, then shoving both hands in his pockets he slowly walked back to his car mumbling to himself, "I'm sorry, Shannon. I tried. I really tried. But can we not do this again, dear sister?"

Brad opened the Pontiac door and to his shock, he noticed someone in the passenger seat. His reaction was spontaneous. "Who are you?! What are you doing in my car!?"

"Well now, matey," came the reply from the individual inside the car. "Is that any way to be talkin' to yer old friend, the captain?"

"Blake?! Good grief, man. Is it really you?"

"Aye, it be me. In the flesh, says I. Well—perhaps not in the flesh—but it be me, all the same."

"What are you doing here? The last time I saw you, you said . . ."

"The last time ye saw me, things were different, matey. I be livin' on the other side now, with me Angela Marie."

"Are you serious?" Brad asked excitedly. "You actually gave up looking for a descendent of Oscar Welborn and went home where you belong? And after you were so adamant in your refusal to cross over to the other side until you found the legitimate heir to the cargo you were carrying when your ship capsized. I can't believe this, Blake."

"No, matey, I didn't give up me search for Oscar's kin. I found him, says I. He has the map in his hands now, he does. Me word is me bond, and I kept me word—just as I vowed I would."

"You found him? You actually found him? How?"

Blake smiled. "He came to me, Brad Douglas. Just as I told ye he would. Do ye be rememberin' Michael Allen, the gentleman who came to me island the day ye left the place for good?"

"Michael Allen? You mean to tell me Michael turned out to be the descendent you were looking for? How did you find out it was him?"

"An angel told me, says I. Prettiest angel I ever laid eyes on, me Angela Marie bein' excepted, of course."

Brad got in the car and closed the door. "That's great, buddy. I can't tell you how happy I am for you. And not to say I'm not glad to see you or anything, but why are you here? I mean, if you live on the other side now . . . ?"

"I be here on an assignment, matey. Me pretty angel, her name be Samantha, and her husband, Jason, have entrusted me with gettin' yer destiny back on course, lad."

"My destiny . . . ? What are you talking about, Blake?"

"Start up this here motor car and I'll be showin' ye, matey."

"Start my car? What, you're planning to take me somewhere?"

"Aye, matey, that be me plan. It's me assignment. I've given me word, and me word is . . ."

"Okay, okay," Brad said, starting the car. "I get the picture. I've got nothing better to do at the moment anyway. Where to, maestro?"

Blake raised a hand and pointed forward. "Set yer sail on a course for what ye call the Marble Fountain Suites, matey. Ye be knowin' the way."

With a shrug, Brad put the car in gear and pulled out of the lot. "The Marble Fountain Suites, you say? Why would you want me to go to an office complex at this time of night?"

"I think ye be needin' a special dessert, after the dinner ye just packed away. There be a special store at the Suites, says I. Rumor has it they even serve ghost portions in the place I be thinkin' of, matey."

"A dessert store? Are you kidding me, Blake? At the Marble Fountain Suites? The way I remember it, there's never been anything there but business offices. I admit, there have been a lot of changes in the last ten years, but a dessert store at the Marble Fountain Suites? That one's a bit hard to believe, old friend."

"Oh there be a store there, matey. I gives ye me word there be a store, and I gives ye me word the dessert there is out of this here world. But there be somethin' of greater value waitin' there for ye than the taste of mere food, says I."

Brad shot a glance in Blake's direction. "Uh huh. Just as I suspected. You have an ulterior motive in mind, Blake. I've already had my sister's meddling to put up with tonight. The last thing I need right now is one of your hair-brained shenanigans. Come clean, old buddy. What exactly is it you're up to here?"

"What I be up to, matey, is puttin' yer life back on destiny's plotted course. Yer sister, Shannon, had the right idea—only she had the wrong lassie in mind for ye, Brad Douglas."

"Now hold on here, Blake! You're not planning on setting me up with another date tonight, are you? Because if you are . . . !"

Captain Blake squinted his left eye nearly closed. "What I has in mind be for your own good, Brad Douglas. Now be ye ready to argue, or be ye ready to set sail on a sea that Captain Blake guarantees will bring ye to a pleasing port?"

Brad sighed. "All right, Blake. I know you're my friend, and I know you're only looking out for my best interest. Help me get my sails set, and I'll cast off on the sea you're pushing me toward. But so help me, old friend, if this turns out to be another experience like Shannon put me through tonight . . ."

* * *

Lori could not believe her eyes as she stepped inside the ice cream shop. It was certainly no ordinary shop, that much was for sure. There was only one small table with two chairs in the center of the room. What Arline had said about this being only a television set must definitely be the case. But how had it been constructed so quickly, and without her hearing any commotion since she was just across the way working in her own office the whole afternoon? It made no sense at all. Lori looked around for any sign of a television crew, but saw nothing to indicate their presence.

"Sit down, Lori," Arline invited, pointing to one of the chairs at the table. Our other guest will be here shortly. My friend and associate Captain Horatio Symington Blake will see to that."

Lori hesitated before taking a seat. "Captain Horatio who?" she asked.

Arline laughed. "Captain Horatio Symington Blake," she repeated. "The captain is an angel of a guy who I just recently met. If you've seen my show, you must know I'm famous for my angel friends."

"I'm aware of your angel gimmick, yes. But that's all it is, is a gimmick—isn't it?"

"That's the problem with most people, Lori," Arline explained. "They just don't take my angels seriously. Think about it. If I didn't have some pretty powerful help, how do you explain this ice cream shop appearing out of nowhere? You have to admit, it is a pretty strong piece of evidence that my angels are real."

Lori glanced around again at the inside of the elaborate set. "Let me get this straight, Arline. You're telling me this set was put in place by angels? Real ones?"

Arline laughed and nodded yes. "Three of them to be exact. There's Jason Hackett, his wife, Sam, and of course we can't forget the captain. And you know what else? These three angels are here on your behalf. It was their idea for me to conduct this interview, Lori."

Lori was skeptical as she looked around for a hidden camera. "Are we on camera now, Arline?" she asked.

"No," Arline smilingly assured her. "We're not on camera. This interview has nothing whatever to do with my show. This one is strictly for the business of angels. You see, Lori, even though Sam and Jason live in another dimension from ours, they happen to be in charge of certain commitments that take place here in our dimension. One of those commitments has to do with you, and your commitment is in great need of repair. I'm sure you have no idea what I'm talking about right now, and that's to be expected. But I promise, before this evening is over, what I'm saying will make a lot more sense than it does now. Trust me, Lori. Sit down and be comfortable while we wait for our second guest to arrive."

* * *

Brad stared at the "open" sign in the window of what definitely appeared to be an ice cream parlor. But—how could it be an ice cream parlor? This suite was for the accommodation of business offices and nothing more. "This is getting weirder by the second, Blake," he objected. "Are you going to tell me what you're up to, or do I turn around and get myself out of here while the getting's good?"

"By the thunder, Brad Douglas, it be for certain that stubborn streak of yours be thicker than ever. Get yer bones over to that window, says I, and be lookin' at who's sittin' inside. Then, ye'll know better what it is I be up to, matey."

From where Brad stood, he could make out a table in the center of the ice cream parlor where two women were seated. The one with her face toward him looked a little familiar, though he couldn't place where he had seen her. Not positively anyway. It could be he had seen her on some morning television show he had flipped through while searching for the early news, but he just wasn't sure. The second woman had her back turned. "I'm warning you, Blake. If you have thoughts about setting me up with either of those ladies . . ."

Blake pointed to the shop's window. "Just be movin' yerself in closer, matey. Ye need to be gettin' a good look-see at who's inside."

With a disgusted shrug, Brad stepped up to the window just as Lori happen to turn her face far enough for him to see. Brad's eyes opened wide in surprise. His hands went sweaty as his heart pounded with the cadence of a drummer from a hard rock band. "It's Lori," he gasped. "What are you trying to pull here, Blake? I can't face Lori. She's another man's wife. No way can I face her, Blake. No way."

Brad would have turned and fled, but for some unseen power that held his feet glued in place where he stood. "What's happening to me Blake?" he pleaded. "Why can't I move? Please help me, old friend. Don't force me to stay here looking at a scene I'm not ready to face."

"I'll not be helpin' ye run away, Brad Douglas. Yer destiny be waitin' inside this here shop, and by thunder ye be goin' inside to meet that destiny."

To Brad's utter amazement, he found that his feet would move, so long as the direction was forward. Any attempt to turn around was impossible. It was like some invisible giant hand clung to each leg, forcing them to move only one way—toward the shop's entrance. In one helpless, and very fearful moment, he was inside the door in full view of Lori—who was now looking right into his terrified eyes.

* * *

When Lori glanced up to see who had walked into the shop, she found herself looking into a pair of eyes so strangely familiar they actually frightened her. They were eyes containing a distanced look that reflected both tenderness and pain. They captivated her with a magnetism that made looking away nearly impossible. Other than his eyes, the man's face was pretty much hidden behind a full beard. It took a moment or two before Lori even realized there was a second man with the first. He also wore a full beard. And, of all things, he wore what appeared to be a pirate's costume from out of the seventeenth century or so. Could this possibly be the Captain Horatio Symington Blake Arline had spoken of?

* * *

Night after lonely night, for the past ten years, Brad had dreamed of being this close to Lori again. Time and again he had walked the beaches of his tiny island imagining the image of her lovely face in the glitter of the nighttime stars. In his dreams he would hold her, run his fingers through her long silky hair, and kiss her warm, tender lips just as he had done all those years ago when she belonged to him. But this was no dream. There were no glittering nighttime stars. And she no longer belonged to him. She was now the wife of a powerful man who could offer her excitement at life's every turn. Seeing her like this was like admiring a precious diamond inside a thick glass enclosure. The beauty was there to behold, but to touch the precious stone was forbidden. All he could do now was look into her captivating eyes—and wish his legs would allow him to turn and run.

Arline stood to welcome the new arrivals. "Well, Captain Blake," she said. "I see you've managed to escort our friend here in one piece. Bring him on over here so we can get this little show started."

Blake pointed to the chair Arline had vacated at the table. "This way, matey," he said. "If ye'll be so kind as to be takin' yer seat, I'd be much obliged."

* * *

Lori was sure she detected a reluctance on the part of the stranger to join her, but after a quick exchange of glances between him and Captain Blake, he walked to the table and took a seat. Lori studied him more closely. His eyes still enchanted her, but she thought he appeared disgustingly unrefined with his unkempt beard. Even so, everything else about the man seemed polished enough. He dressed neatly and carried himself with dignity. Even his hair was well groomed. Why the beard? But then, what business was it of hers? The man had every right to do as he pleased about his beard, or anything else for that matter.

* * *

The pounding of Brad's heart echoed so loudly in his head he could hardly think. What was he doing sitting at the same table with Lori? How had he allowed his old friend, the captain, to trick him into such a thing? What if Howard were to walk in right about now? He certainly wouldn't be happy finding his wife this close to her ex-husband.

No sooner had he settled into his chair, than he caught a glimpse of someone else emerging from the back room and walking toward the table. A closer look revealed a man carrying a tray with what appeared to be four helpings of ice cream. As the man approached, the woman who had given up her seat to Brad spoke.

"I'd like to have you meet the most famous of all angels ever mentioned on my television show. May I present the prestigious Mr. Jason Hackett, one of my truest friends and the greatest chef I've ever known. The ice cream is one of his concoctions, and let me tell you— you're in for a real treat."

At the mention of the word "angel," Brad turned to Captain Blake, who gave an assuring nod indicating to Brad that Jason truly was from out of this world. A look back to Jason also drew a wink, and Brad knew for sure. But why were they doing this to him? Didn't they know how much he still loved Lori, and how much it hurt to be this near to her, knowing she belonged to another?

"Be honest, Arline," Jason joked in answer to her introduction. "I'm the *only* chef you've ever known. But you're right about me being a good one." He extended the tray in Arline's direction. "Here, serve these up, will you?"

Arline reached for the cup of ice cream nearest her when to everyone's surprise her hand simply slid through the cup—sort of like light slides through a window.

"Oops, sorry," Jason apologized as he quickly turned the tray. "My mistake. That cup belongs to the captain here. The others are for the three of you."

Arline laughed. "Boy does that bring back memories of the first time you and I worked together, Jason," she said. With no further explanation of her remark, she handed one ice cream cup to Lori and one to Brad. The third she took for herself, leaving Blake to retrieve his own special cup.

"Now, if you'll excuse us," Arline said. "We're going to leave the two of you alone to get acquainted while you enjoy your dessert. We'll be in the back room if you need anything."

As Brad looked on helplessly, Arline, Blake, and Jason simply walked away and disappeared into the back room, leaving him alone at the table with Lori. What was he supposed to do now, for crying out loud?

* * *

If Lori was confused before, she was completely in the dark as to why Arline and the others would walk away, leaving her alone with this man. What was she to do? She couldn't just get up and walk out of the place. And then a thought came to mind. *Arline wasn't telling the truth about the hidden camera. She is taping me for a segment of her television show. I'll bet she's doing a take-off on a candid camera clip.* Lori glanced around, trying to decide where the camera might be hidden. Behind the soda fountain a mirror covered one entire wall. *That's it,* she concluded. *It's a two-way mirror, and the camera is behind it. I'll be darned if I'm going to make a fool out of myself for all the world to see on television. I'll just play along with this gag like I knew what it was about from the beginning.*

Looking straight at the mirror, she put on her warmest smile. Then, looking back to the fellow across the table, she boldly introduced herself. "Hi, I'm Lori. And you are—?"

Brad hesitated. "I, uh,—my name is—that is my friend—uh—friends call me Matey."

Lori, of course, had no way of knowing that Brad was using his skill as a voice impressionist to sound like someone other than himself. She did sense his obvious uneasiness, and wondered if he'd been kept as much in the dark about this little stunt as she had.

"Matey?" she repeated. "A nickname, I presume."

"Yeah—yeah. That's what it is, a nickname."

Matey? Lori mused. *What sort of name is that? You don't suppose . . . ? I'll bet this guy's not in the dark. I'll bet he's in on the gag with the others.* "Matey?" she asked suspiciously. "That's a strange one even for a nickname, wouldn't you say?"

"I suppose so. But it's what I go by all the time."

With a smile in the direction of the mirror, Lori said, "Well, Matey, shall we see if this ice cream really is as good as they say?"

Brad nervously pulled the cup closer and spooned out a small taste which he slid onto his tongue. "WOW!" he declared, as anxiety turned to amazement at the flavor of this treat. "This stuff is good." Looking up at Lori, he actually managed a slight smile. "Go ahead. Try it for yourself."

Lori wondered if part of the trick might be luring her into tasting something bitter. Very carefully, she dipped her spoon into the dessert and eased a small bite to her lips. To her surprise, it was good. Very good. She took a full bite and looked up to see the bearded fellow staring at her. He quickly looked away.

"I was wondering," she asked candidly. "Do you have any idea why they've maneuvered the two of us together like this? I was invited here on the pretense that Arline Vincent wanted to interview me."

Brad glanced toward the back of the room hoping for a glimpse of Blake. If ever he wanted that ghost to come to his rescue, it was now. No such luck, there was no sign of any of them. "I really don't know why they've brought us together," he responded. "But I suspect it has something to do with my friend, the captain. It wouldn't be the first time he's set me up with one of his pranks."

Lori made a decision. She would confide in this fellow what she thought this was all about. Even if it turned out that he was a party to the trick, it shouldn't make her look foolish for figuring it out. "You know what I think," she said. "I think Arline Vincent is setting us up with the old hidden camera trick. You do know she has a television show, don't you?"

"No, I didn't know. She does look familiar, I've probably seen her on television without realizing it. But personally I think my friend Captain Blake is at the bottom of this." Brad paused before going on. "I hope you don't think me too blunt, but I can't help wondering what might happen if your husband should happen in while the two of us are alone like this."

Lori caught a quick breath. "My husband?" she shot back. "What makes you think I'm married?"

Brad shoved his spoon into the ice cream and played with it nervously. "I just assumed—that is, I thought your husband . . ."

"Please," Lori pressed as Brad hesitated in his response. "What is it you're trying to say?" Lori's curiosity was growing by the second. Why would this man refer to her husband? Could he possibly know that she had been married once? Was there the slightest chance he might have some information to the whereabouts of Brad Douglas, the man she still loved and dreamed of almost nightly?

Once again their eyes met. The sadness she had seen there earlier was even more intense now, and she wondered why. "I may be wrong," he nervously explained. "But it seems to me I've seen you with the movie tycoon, Howard Placard. I just figured you were probably his wife."

This statement came like a rush of cold water to Lori's face. "Howard Placard?" she choked. "You thought you'd seen me with Howard? When, for heaven sakes. And where?"

Lori looked even deeper into Brad's eyes. "Who are you?" she suddenly demanded. "You're here because of Howard Placard, aren't you? That's what this whole thing is about, isn't it?"

It was at that moment that Arline reentered the room with a strong declaration. "No, Lori, that isn't what this whole thing is about. But your question of who this man really is, is a good one. And it's time you learn the answer to that question. Jason, get in here with your razor. We're ready for our moment of truth."

CHAPTER 11

Brad looked on in disbelief as the ice cream shop, that should never have been there in the first place, was now being transformed into a makeshift barber shop. There was a barber's apron, a stack of towels, a soap mug and brush for the lather, and the biggest straight razor Brad had ever laid eyes on. All that was missing was the hydraulic barber chair, but in its place a bar stool had been set up next to the sink behind the ice cream counter.

"What are you doing?" Brad gulped. "I don't want my beard removed."

Brad knew that removing the beard would simultaneously reveal his masquerade. He would be left to face the unimaginable discomfort of confronting the woman he worshipped and adored, not as a welcomed friend, but rather as an unwanted intruder from out of her past. The pain and humiliation were more than he could bear.

Jason let out a sympathetic sigh. "Don't make me do this the hard way, friend. We're in the middle of pulling off a pretty important enterprise here, and the next step calls for the whiskers to go." Jason paused momentarily, then added, "I'm pretty sure you know why."

Oh, yes, Brad knew why. They wanted him unmasked in front of Lori. This whole thing made no sense. What could it possibly prove? After all, Lori was Howard Placard's wife now, and coming face to face with a bad memory would be just as unpleasant for her as it would be for him. Brad folded his arms and stared defiantly at those beckoning him to the barber chair. "No!" he emphatically stated. "The beard stays in place, and that's that!"

It was Blake who carried the argument to the next level. "I be warnin' ye, matey. Me friend Jason Hackett be not one to trifle with.

Ye be the one on the plank, and Jason be the one with the sword at yer back, says I. Spare the embarrassment to yer dignity, lad. This chap can be forcin' ye to the chair the same as he forced yer feet into this here shop. Give us a favor, old friend. Be sittin' yerself down to yer fate like a man."

Brad glanced at Lori and pictured in his mind her reaction at seeing his bare face. It was hard enough facing her like this, but without the beard? "I can't believe this, Blake. You're supposed to be my friend, and here you are pushing just as hard as the rest to make me drink this cup of humility. You, of all people, should know why I want the beard left alone. Please, old buddy, help me out here."

The captain stood firm, being careful not to call Brad by his name and let the secret out before its time. "Thee and me have been shipmates these many years, matey. I'm askin' that ye trust me now. It be not the cold, shark-infested waters ye be steppin' into by lettin' Jason remove the beard; it be a bright new sunny day on calm seas, says I. Ye know I would never be tellin' a lie to ye. Step to the chair, matey, and face yer destiny with a measure of pride."

Brad exchanged glances between Blake and Jason, paying special attention to the razor in the angel's hand. "What about it, Blake? Can this guy really get me in that chair even if I don't want to go?"

"Aye, matey, he can if ye force him into such a deed. Ye have me word on it, friend. And ye have me word that takin' off the beard be for yer own good."

Brad looked at Lori one last time, then turned his attention to Jason and another matter of concern. "Have you ever given anyone a shave before?" he asked nervously, still staring at the sharp-edged razor.

Jason shrugged. "Well, not actually. But I did take a crash course just this morning from an old army buddy of mine, back during my days in mortality. He was our company barber in Vietnam. The guy was an artist with his razor. I heard him say he could toss an orange in the air and peel it on the way down before it hit the floor. I never saw him do it, of course. But the guy was good. Who knows, he might have been able to do it."

Brad continued staring at the razor. "If the beard has to go, I don't suppose you could talk your Vietnam buddy into coming here to do it, could you? I mean, this is a ten-year growth we're talking about."

"Don't be arguin' with the man, matey. Get in the chair. I be tellin' ye, these second-degree angels can be doin' most anythin' they set their mind to."

Brad eyed Blake through a half squint. "If you're so confident in Jason's ability, let me see you get in the chair. If he takes your beard off without cutting your throat, I'll give it a try. You have to admit, cutting your throat will bring a lot fewer consequences than cutting mine."

"Ye don't know what ye be askin', matey. This here beard of mine has been on me face for more than three hundred years. I started growin' it when I was a mere lad. Ye wouldn't be askin' me to sacrifice a tradition anchored so deep in the sea of me soul—would ye, matey?"

Brad sighed. "No, Blake, I guess I can't ask that. Poor Angela Marie wouldn't know you when you went home to her. And besides, if you're half as ugly as I figure you are behind that beard, I'd be doing the whole universe a disfavor. I'll get in the chair. But if this doesn't work out like you say . . ."

"I be givin' ye me word, matey. And ye knows I never go back on me word."

Jason lay a hot steaming towel over Brad's face, and Brad was forced to silently admit it felt pretty good. If only he could feel half as good inside. It took two more towels before Jason decided the scrubby growth was softened up enough for lathering. Then came the first swipe of the razor. Brad almost felt it would be better if Jason did cut his throat; it might be an easier way out of this than facing Lori. The whole dreadful task was over in less than five minutes, and Jason held up a mirror for Brad to see. With pounding heart, Brad looked at his own bare face for the first time since just before taking his flight home from Acapulco all those years ago. He had aged some, but surprisingly not as much as he might have supposed. His face was pale, but that was nothing a few hours in the sunlight wouldn't cure. Now came the most dreaded moment of all. The moment when Lori would see his face. Slowly, he stood—drew in a deep breath—and turned to face her.

* * *

Howard Placard was just leaving the studio on the way to his waiting limo when his cellular phone rang. Removing the phone from his blazer pocket, he spoke into it. "Yes? Who is it?"

"It's Myro Finderman. My man Hindricks just reported in. He's the guy I've had glued to Brad Douglas the last couple of weeks. It looks like you were right about Douglas being interested in his ex-old lady."

Howard stopped dead in his tracks. "Ex-old lady? Are you referring to Lori?"

"Yeah, man. You said call if the two of them got together. Well, they got together."

"Do you mind being more specific, Finderman? Got together when? Where?"

"I know you're not gonna believe this—I have a hard time swallowing it myself—but Hindricks assures me it's the truth."

Howard was rapidly losing patience. "Cut the stall, Finderman. If you have something to report, then do it. Has Douglas seen Lori or not? If so, when and where?"

"I'm getting there, Howard. Douglas and his ex are together even as we speak. They're in a—and I know you're not gonna like this part—they're in an ice cream parlor at the Marble Fountain Suites."

"An ice cream parlor? There's no ice cream parlor at the Marble Fountain Suites. Have you been drinking, Finderman?"

"Never touch the stuff, pal. I'm giving it to you just as Hindricks gave it to me. Ya want I should put a couple of guys with Hindricks and rough Douglas up a bit?"

Howard was quick to squelch this idea. "No, you fool. No rough stuff around Lori. Go ahead and get your man some help, then grab Douglas just as soon as he's alone. I want him brought to me as soon as possible. You got that, Finderman?"

"Duck soup, pal. I can have him on your doorstep in one piece or in several pieces. What's your poison?"

"I said no rough stuff. Bring him to my home office unharmed. I'll have an easier time dealing with him that way."

Howard shut off his phone and shoved it back in his pocket. The idea of Brad Douglas coming back after all these years infuriated him. Howard prided himself on being one of the most powerful men in these parts, but the one thing that had managed to elude his every effort was the one thing he wanted most—Lori. Though he would never admit it, much of his infatuation with Lori came as the result of her rejecting him. Howard was not one who could accept rejection easily. He vowed never to give up until she changed her mind and came to him with all the passion she once held for Brad Douglas. But now, with Brad Douglas back in the picture, that vow was in jeopardy. An evil smile crossed Howard's lips as he anticipated meeting his old rival face to face after all these years. Handling Brad would be child's play, and forcing him out of the picture again would bring great pleasure. This time Brad would disappear Howard's way. And this time, he'd be gone for good.

* * *

A score of questions came to mind as Lori watched the peculiar exchange leading up to this stranger losing his beard. Why had Arline Vincent brought her here? Were these really angels, as Arline had said? By far, the most intriguing questions of all concerned the man in the barber's chair. Who was he? Why did he seem so familiar to her, even though she couldn't pinpoint why? Why were these people so dead set on her seeing this man's beardless face? With burning curiosity she watched as the cleanly shaven man stood and slowly turned to face her. Then she caught sight of his face, and in one startling instant— she knew.

"Brad!" she gasped, jumping to her feet and laying a hand to her mouth as if speaking his name should somehow be forbidden.

"Hello, Lori," came his quiet response, this time in his own voice.

Lori's eyes locked with his in a magnetic hold that refused to let her look away. "Is it—really—you?" she asked, her voice barely louder than a whisper.

A sad smile crossed Brad's lips. "It's me," he responded. "I didn't intend for you to know, but . . ."

Lori's heart pounded. Her head felt as if it would explode. It was as though she hung suspended somewhere between elation and terror. How many times had she dreamed of the moment she and Brad would meet again? Over and over she had rehearsed her lines for the occasion, and now that it was here—words refused to form. The best she could manage was a feeble "Why? Why are you here?"

Brad's shallow smile remained as he answered. "It was these angels; they brought me here. I swear, Lori, I had no idea what they were up to." Brad paused, and then added, "I know you must think I'm terrible, intruding on you like this."

"No, no—I don't think you're terrible at all." Ever so gradually, the fog began clearing from Lori's mind. One at a time the puzzle pieces started to fit. The ice cream parlor appearing out of nowhere, her chance meeting with Arline Vincent, the "out-of-this-world" ice cream, and the climax in a face-to-face meeting with the only man she had ever loved.

It was true. Arline Vincent's angel gimmick was no gimmick after all. "These people really are angels, aren't they?" she asked meekly.

"I'll be answerin' that if ye'll allow me, lassie," Blake volunteered. "We be angels, says I. We be here to help set yer ship back on course. Brad Douglas' ship as well, I might be addin'. Me friend Jason and his lovely wife, Sam, be the folks in charge of puttin' such wrongs back to the right. Beggin' yer forgiveness if I sound the braggart, but because of me many skills in such matters, I've been chosen to be assistin' them in their efforts. Ye can think of me as yer guardian angel, if ye like."

Brad stared at the captain. "Don't pay any attention to him, Lori. Sometimes this old sea goat just doesn't know when to keep his mouth shut. Believe me, I had no idea what he had in mind bringing me here. The last thing I want is to embarrass you. If you'd like, I can leave now."

"No, please! Don't go. I'd like for you to stay, really. At least until we finish this ice cream."

Brad glanced at his hardly touched cup still on the table. "Yeah," he agreed. "It is pretty good ice cream."

Lori watched as Brad moved his chair back to the table and sat down. "Something's bothering me," she said, as he took another bite of Jason's treat. "Why did you ask if I was married to Howard? You didn't really think that was possible, did you?"

Brad rubbed his fingers ever so lightly over his cleanly shaven face. "I did see you kissing him, Lori. And I saw the pictures."

"And you found the cell phone in the Pontiac and figured out that I was taking your calls from somewhere other than home. All that's true, Brad, I don't deny it. I made a foolish mistake letting Howard come onto me like he did. I was young and unsure of myself at the time. But I swear—you're the only man I ever loved. All these years

I've wondered about you. But never in my wildest dreams did I think you believed I'd actually married Howard."

"Aye, lassie, take me word for it. Brad Douglas be speakin' the truth. I'm the one to be knowin', since I was there by his side all these many years. Brad be thinkin' ye belonged to Howard right enough. And I be speakin' the truth when I tell ye the man be eatin' his heart out over this thought."

"Confound you, Blake! Will you stay out of this! Lori deserves better than to listen to your running off at the mouth."

"You're wrong," Lori objected. "I do want to listen to what the captain has to say, Brad. I had no idea you believed I would marry Howard. That's why you never tried to contact me all these years, isn't it?"

"Yes, I did think you were Howard's wife. And yes, that is why I never tried to contact you. I wanted you to be happy, and I figured—"

"You wanted me to be happy? With another man? Is that what you're saying, Brad? Because if it is . . ."

Captain Blake removed his hat and tossed it on the table between the two of them. "I be thinkin' it's time to lift anchor and be castin' off on the next part of the plan, says I."

Brad threw up both hands. "Next part of the plan? What are you talking about now, Blake? Haven't you done enough already?"

"Be nice to the captain," Arline spoke up. "He's telling the truth, you know. Your destiny is Lori, and her destiny is you. A lot of work and planning has gone into preparing the little adventure you're about to embark on under the captain's lead. Make the most of it, Brad. And you too, Lori. Your destinies depend on it."

Lori was confused. "What adventure are we about to embark on? I don't understand."

"Of course ye not be understandin', lassie," Blake explained. "But take me word for it, ye be in good hands. The two of ye be about to hoist sail on a cruise back through time to when all this mutiny first took root, says I. And the two of ye will do well to be listenin' to what I say. Ye be not allowed to return from yer journey 'til ye be settin' yer destiny on its true bearing, and be sealin' that bearing with a kiss of promise."

"Blake!" Lori heard Brad loudly protest. "What are you . . . ?" His question was never finished as it was interrupted by as strange a phenomena as Lori could ever imagine in her wildest fantasy. The room suddenly felt as it were spinning beneath her feet. Faster and faster it spun until everything in sight molded into one massive blur of brilliant light. It was like one of those carnival rides that spin away the senses to the blaring sound of fast and obnoxiously loud music, only this time the music was missing. Then, just as quickly as it had begun, it was over. As Lori regained her presence of mind, she immediately recognized they were no longer in the ice cream parlor. They were instead standing on a sidewalk leading to the door of a very familiar house.

"What happened?" Brad muttered, holding onto his still spinning head. "Where are we and how did we get here?"

Lori tried to shake off her own dizziness. "You're asking me, Brad? They're your angels, remember? But would you look at this? We're right in front of your house."

"No way is this my house. It looks like my house but . . . "

"I see what you mean," Lori quickly observed. "Something is definitely different about the house. The tangerine tree for one thing. It's small again, like it was when—"

"When the two of us lived here together," Brad interrupted.

"And look at all the cars at the neighbor's houses," Lori added. "They're all ten-year-old vintage, at least. The captain said something about taking us back through time—you don't suppose he's actually managed to do it, do you?"

"I don't know," Brad shrugged. "I've never seen him do anything like this before, but he's changed now. He crossed over the line to the other side. No telling what that ghost is capable of doing these days."

Lori looked confused. "How is it you know so much about Captain Blake?" she asked. "Was he telling the truth when he said he's been with you the last ten years?"

This brought a laugh from Brad. "He was telling the truth, all right. Tried his best to scare me off his island the first few months the girls and I were there, he did. But when he found I wasn't one to be pushed aside by a ghost, the two of us actually became good friends."

Lori wondered what island Brad was referring to, but she let it go for the time being and turned her attention back to the house. "Just look at this, Brad," she said excitedly. "It's all the same, down to the tiniest detail. It's just like it was ten years ago. Do we dare take a peek inside?"

Brad looked at her questioningly "Peek inside? Why?"

"Aren't you the least bit curious? If we've somehow been moved back in time, wouldn't it be neat seeing inside the old place again? I have a zillion memories in this house." She paused before adding, "Most of them are good ones. I still drive by it every once in a while. You know, just for old time's sake."

"You do?" Brad asked, a bit surprised at the thought.

"Yes, I do. Does that strike you as strange?"

"No! Well—that is—yeah, sort of. You have to understand, I've spent these years thinking of you as sharing the exciting world of Howard Placard. It's a little strange realizing you might have missed— well you know—what we once had."

You thought I lived in an exciting world? she reasoned. *Ha! You don't know the half of it, Brad Douglas. You have no idea how much I've missed what we once shared, and how I've dreamed of someday waking to find it had all returned.* "I really would like to see inside, Brad. What do you say?"

Brad looked at the closed door. "Maybe it would be neat to see inside," he conceded. "What the heck, let's give it a try."

Together, they walked to the door, where Brad tried the handle. "It's locked," he said.

Lori smiled. "I guess that means our younger versions aren't home, huh? How much do you want to bet there's a key hidden in that flower pot next to your feet?"

"That's right. You did keep a key hidden, didn't you? That's because you were always losing your keys." Brad glanced down at the flower pot and laughed. "I can't believe how many key rings you lost back then, Lori. I spent so much time at Al's hardware store having keys made that the guy knew me on a first-name basis." Brad looked at Lori. "Do you still have that problem?" he asked.

Lori returned his laugh. "No, I've learned to take better care of my keys since I started having to have them remade myself. You can't believe how self-sufficient I've become. So—are you going to check for a key, or shall I?"

Brad paused a moment just looking at her. "Do you know what we just did?" he asked. "We just laughed together."

"I guess we did, didn't we?"

"Did it feel as good to you as it did to me?"

Lori blushed. "It did feel good," she admitted. "We used to laugh a lot."

Brad felt inside the flower pot. Sure enough, the key was there. Smiling he held it up for Lori to see, then used it to unlock the door and they stepped inside.

Lori shivered. "This gives me goose bumps," she said. "It's like I'm dreaming, only I know I'm awake. Those angel friends of yours are something else, Brad."

Together, they made their way down the hall and into the family room. "Look!" Lori said, pointing to the table in front of the sofa. "There are your slippers on the table, right where you always left them for me to pick up. I never could break you of that habit."

"I'm better about that sort of thing now," Brad shrugged. "I guess being on my own has taught me some things, too. Like you and your keys."

Lori's smile widened. Just hearing Brad's voice again made her feel so warm all over. Being in this old house with him again—well—that added a certain tingling to the warmth that penetrated to the very heart of her senses. She'd gladly pick up his slippers off the coffee table now, even if it meant doing it every day for the rest of her life. It's funny how some things can be complained about one minute, and in the next minute, become something to be desired.

"Check this out," Brad said, pointing to the table where his slippers lay. "It looks like the angels have left us each a cup of hot chocolate. Remember how we used to sit on the sofa in the evenings drinking hot chocolate and talking about the day's events?"

"I do remember," Lori beamed. "That's something I hadn't thought about in years."

"I think about it all the time. No one could make hot chocolate like you, Lori."

"Well this hot chocolate isn't mine, Brad. These cups are fresh. Like you said, the angels must have left them for us."

Brad picked up a cup and took a taste. "Oh wow," he exclaimed. "If this isn't your chocolate, it's the best imitation I've ever tasted. Come on, let's sit on the sofa and enjoy it. Like you say, for old time's sake."

Lori tasted the chocolate. Brad was right, it was good. She couldn't believe this was happening: here she was sitting on the same sofa as

Brad, drinking hot chocolate just like in happier days. Only one thing made this setting less than perfect—the distance between them. They used to sit side by side. Now she was on one end of the sofa and Brad on the other. Suddenly, she noticed something she had missed before. On the open bar, between the family room and kitchen, sat a dozen red roses. She instantly realized they were the roses from Brad, when he returned from Acapulco. A cold chill passed through her as she shot a quick glance in Brad's direction to see if he had noticed the flowers. Apparently he hadn't. Her attention shifted back to the roses. They looked so fresh and alive. She wondered what Brad would think if he knew she still had the roses at home on her mantel, where they had been kept all these years after having them preserved in wax.

"This chocolate sure has a way of stirring up old memories," Brad said. "Times were good back then, Lori. Better than they've ever been since, I might add."

"Back then," Lori laughed. "Back when I was just a kid, you mean?"

"Back when we were both kids," Brad corrected. "It's funny how something so traumatic as a broken marriage can pile on the years." He sighed. "At least that was the case for me."

"Me too, Brad. As the old saying goes—if I'd only known then what I know now."

Brad swallowed a drink of chocolate and changed the subject. "So, are you still into interior decorating? It was always your first love, as I remember."

Lori laughed bitterly. "My first love?" she mocked. "You don't know this, of course, but it was my love for interior decorating that led me down the path to the biggest mistake of my life. But to answer your question, yes. I have my own business now. My office is just across the outside hall from the ice cream parlor where the angels had us meet."

"You're doing well, I hope. You'll always be a great lady in my book, Lori. And I wish you all the happiness in the world."

Lori looked into Brad's eyes again. *You wish me happiness?* she reflected. *That's very sweet of you, Brad. But the only way I can ever really be happy again is back in your arms. After what I did to you, I know that can never be.* "I'm doing well enough in my business," she replied. "I'm not getting rich, but I'm not starving, either. How about you? Are you still directing pictures?"

"Oh, no. I haven't directed a picture since—you know—the one in Acapulco. I manage to get by performing my old routine, like I did before we were married. I play the piano, tell a few jokes, and throw in a voice impression here and there."

Lori turned serious. "It's Howard, isn't it? You can't get work directing because he has you blacklisted, isn't that right?"

Brad shrugged. "It's no big deal."

You really have reason to be proud of yourself, girl, Lori thought. *Not only did you drive Brad away with your foolish antics, you've ruined his career, as well.* "I'm so sorry, Brad. I can't help but feel responsible."

Brad tried to laugh. "Hey, don't go beating yourself up, Lori. What's done is done, and as for Howard—that man isn't worth working for. I'm much better off out of his world."

"So, if you don't mind my asking—where have you been staying these last years?"

"No, I don't mind you asking at all. Actually I've had it pretty soft. I sort of homesteaded a small island in the Caribbean, which I shared with Shannon and Tanielle. I'm sure you read my letter, the one I left when—"

"I read the letter," Lori broke in, raising her hand to wipe the corner of one eye.

"Yeah, well, we spent all those years hiding out on the island until James Baxter found us. He tried to kidnap Shannon and ended up getting himself killed in the process." Brad shook his head in wonder. "I guess it was the angels who set that one up, too."

"An island in the Caribbean?" Lori echoed. "I should have known; that sounds just like you. How did James Baxter find you?"

"Shannon made a mistake," Brad explained. "She wrote, and had published, several novels while we were on the island. She picked a pen name that Baxter recognized. Once he had that much figured out, he used his money and power to uncover the rest. Anyway, with Baxter out of the way, it was time for the girls and me to come home so I asked Tom to set the girls up with a flight back here. He even helped them move into an apartment in the same complex where he lives."

Lori knew that Tom Reddings had been Shannon's first love, long before she married James Baxter. "Are Shannon and Tom seeing each other, by chance?" she asked.

"Oh, yes. They're seeing each other all right. I expect to be eating wedding cake sometime in the near future."

"That's great!" Lori exclaimed. "And what of Tanielle? She must be nearly grown up by now."

"Tanielle's sixteen and a real heart stopper. Shannon's going to have her work cut out keeping all those guys in line."

"I'm so happy for them, Brad. I'd love to see them again sometime."

"Hey, no problem. Just say the word, and I'll set it up. Maybe we could all go out for dinner someplace."

"I'd like that," Lori agreed. Suddenly, the handle broke loose from her cup, spilling the now lukewarm liquid all over her white blouse. "Oh!" she shrieked, leaping to her feet and looking for something to wipe up the mess.

Brad made a dash for the kitchen, looking for a towel. He found one, right where it should be, and headed back to Lori. "Did you get burned?" he asked in concern.

"No, I'm okay. But this is embarrassing. How could I have been so clumsy? I can't even get home to change, thanks to your angels."

"Wait a minute," Brad said. "Maybe you are home, Lori. I mean, the dish towel was there, right where we always kept it. Maybe . . ."

Lori was quick to pick up Brad's meaning. "You don't suppose . . . ?"

"Your clothes. The ones you wore ten years ago, at least. Maybe you'll find them hanging in the bedroom closet. It's worth a try, isn't it?"

Lori's eyes shifted to the door leading to their old bedroom. Apprehension tugged at her mind as she contemplated what she might find behind the door. But Brad was right; it was worth a try. "Would you mind checking it out for me, Brad? Opening a door leading into yesterday is just a little frightening for me."

Brad smiled and walked to the door. "You're darn right I'll check it out," he bragged with a spring in his voice that hadn't been there in a very long time. "It's sort of fun being your hero again, even if it is for something as small as checking behind a door."

Lori watched nervously as Brad opened the door. Though she didn't admit it to him, it felt good to her, too. Him being her hero again.

"It looks exactly like our room used to look, Lori," he said. "Just like the rest of the house."

Lori made her way to the door and peeked inside. Brad was right. "At least I'm the same size I used to be," she said, trying to loosen the tension some. "If any of my old clothes are here, I should be able to get into them. Even if they are a little out of style."

She stepped through the door and pulled it closed behind her. It was then she noticed the red dress lying across the bed. "That looks like . . . ," she started to whisper.

"The red dress," a feminine voice finished her sentence. Lori looked up to see an attractive blonde standing next to the bed. "The one Brad bought for you that you only wore once, to see him off at the airport on his way to Acapulco," the woman explained.

"Who are you?" came Lori's bewildered question at seeing the stranger in her old room. "Another angel, I presume?"

The angel held up her hand. "Hey, I'm not just another angel—I'm the angel in charge of this operation. You can call me Sam. And I know what you're thinking. Did I knock the cup of chocolate out of your hand?" the angel named Sam asked with a smile. "I did. And I'm the one who laid this red dress out for you, too. You and I have our work cut out if we're going to break down that ten-year-old wall of male stubbornness Brad's hiding behind."

Lori shook her head. "This is the strangest evening of my life. What is it you and the others are up to?"

"What are we up to? Good heavens, girl, I'd have thought you would have that figured out by now. We're here to set destiny straight. You know, like in getting you and Brad back together where you belong. And don't tell me you're not still in love with the guy, because I know better. I wasn't born yesterday."

Something about this beautiful angel left Lori with a feeling of trust and easiness. "I admit it. I am in love with him. But I assume you know what I did to him."

"Oh yes, I know all about your little antics with Howard Placard. Unfortunately, that happened long before I was in charge of your destiny. And you'd have to know my predecessor to appreciate how he let your mistake get so far out of hand. Gus is a great guy and all, but when it comes to matters of the heart—well—let's just say he's a typical man."

Lori looked first at the red dress, then at her stained blouse. "Did you really have to go to all this trouble?" she asked. "This happens to be my favorite white blouse. If you wanted me in that red dress, you could have tried asking."

Samantha grinned and shrugged. "Sorry about that, but I'll have the blouse cleaned for you and have it good as new."

"You can get this chocolate stain out of a white blouse?"

"Don't worry about it, okay? Just give me the blouse and I'll bring it back whiter than you've ever seen it. We have some darn good cleaning shops on my side of forever."

* * *

As Lori stepped through the door into the bedroom, Brad was left to himself to try and sort out all that was happening. His heart was torn with the things he had learned. Unbelievable as it seemed, Lori had never married Howard Placard. Brad couldn't deny the sense of relief and satisfaction this revelation brought, but memories of pain and broken trust refused to leave him. He still loved her. Seeing her again like this only deepened those feelings. But the tormenting question still loomed in his mind. Could he ever trust her, or any other woman, with his heart again? Then, too, there was the question of how she felt about him after all this time. True, she was friendly enough, and she seemed to enjoy seeing him again. But after ten years of separation, he had no idea of her true feelings for him today. A brusque, familiar voice interrupted his moment of contemplation.

"By thunder, matey, I be disappointed in ye. After all me trouble to get ye back together with this lassie, and ye haven't so much as hoisted anchor yet. What are ye waitin' for lad? Sweep the lassie off her feet and get on with it."

Brad looked up to see Captain Blake before him. "Oh, it's you again, is it? What do you mean you're setting me up with Lori? Let it go, Blake. I've seen pictures of Cupid and believe me he looks nothing like a salty old sea captain."

"Put away yer dagger. I be here to help ye, matey."

"Help me? How, by pushing Lori and me back together after all these years? Oh, I'm not saying I haven't enjoyed seeing her again. But sharing a few old memories is about the best the two of us can ever do, Blake. What we had back then is long dead. Probably even deader than you, if the truth be known."

"There ye go with that stubborn streak showin' through again,

matey. Think back to the promise ye made to this lassie when the two
of ye first set sail on yer forever voyage, says I. Ye knows what I think
about a man goin' back on his word."

Blake's comment struck with painful accuracy. Brad and Lori had
set a course intended to traverse the fields of forever. Was it his fault
the marriage came crashing down short of its intended goal? What
more could he have done? Hadn't he proved to be everything a faithful husband should be?

"You're wrong, Blake," Brad shot back sharply. "I didn't go back on
my word. And don't get the idea I'm pointing all the blame at Lori, either.
We were just kids back then. Kids make mistakes. I was the only man Lori
had ever dated, so how could she really know I was the right one? I don't
blame her for what happened. When Howard came along he represented
an excitement she had never known with me. She started to wonder if
she'd made a mistake by marrying me—and you know the rest."

"Ye be wrong, matey. If ye weren't such a stubborn man, ye might
be givin' the lassie the benefit of the doubt. Howard did his best to
lead her away with his flatterin' tongue, but she was wise enough to be
seein' through the man's lies before he snared her in his net. If ye had
been man enough to give her the chance back then, the two of ye
could have put ashore in time to be avoidin' the worst of the storm.
Aye, and all that's left now is to be tuggin' yer ships into dry dock
where the damage can be undone, says I."

"Say what you will, Blake, it's too late for dry dock. The storm is
over, the ship is sunk, and there's no way it can ever be salvaged again.
Haven't I gone through enough pain? Call off this little game of yours
and let the two of us go home. All you're doing is wasting your time
as well as ours."

"Nay, matey, I'll not be hoistin' the white flag. But I will be leavin' ye to yerself for the time being, says I. Yer about to see some things
that may change yer mind about not givin' the lassie another chance.
Do the old captain a favor, Brad Douglas. For once in yer life, think
with yer heart and not with yer head. Ye never were much good at that
sort of thinkin'." Having said this, Blake simply vanished from sight.

"Blast you, Blake," Brad called after him. "I hate this new weapon
of yours. The way you were before, I could at least finish an argument
without your going up in a puff of smoke."

* * *

Lori stared at the image of herself in the full-length mirror on her closet door. "I'd forgotten how beautiful this dress was," she admitted. "But it is a little out of date now, you know, Sam."

"Doesn't matter. For the evening I have planned, the only one who'll see you in it is Brad. Everyone else you come across will be holographs."

"Holographs?" Lori asked. "What are you saying, Sam?"

"What I'm saying is you and Brad are about to go on a specially prepared tour through a few pages of your past. This old house is only the first stop along the way."

Lori looked away from the mirror and straight into Samantha's eyes. "None of this is real, is it?" she remarked. "I'm really fast asleep, and dreaming—just like I've dreamed of finding Brad again for all these years."

Samantha quickly set Lori straight. "This is no dream, Lori. It's all real. And you can rest assured you have the best Cupid in the universe on your side. Trust me, I know what I'm doing."

Lori turned to stare at the door leading back to the room where Brad waited. "All right, Sam, I'll trust you. But I'm not sure Brad can ever trust me again. And the worst part is, I can't blame him. I hurt him pretty badly, you know."

When Samantha didn't answer, Lori looked around to discover she was gone.

CHAPTER 12

For ten long, lonely years Lori had dreamed of the time Brad would step back into her life, sweeping away all the hurt and pain caused by her senseless mistake with Howard Placard. This time it was no dream. Brad was really here—just on the other side of that bedroom door. Lori drew a deep breath and stared at the door. Was there a chance she could win back Brad's love and trust? The angel named Sam had said there was. With head held high, Lori opened the bedroom door and stepped through it.

Brad's eyes opened wide when he saw her. "Lori . . . ," he spoke her name as though in a trance, seemingly not even realizing he had said it. "You look—beautiful. That dress—isn't it . . . ?"

"It's the dress you bought me just before you left for Acapulco, Brad. I wore it when I went to the airport to see you off, remember?"

"Of course I remember. How could I ever forget? I've pictured you the way you looked that day for the past ten years. Whenever I would close my eyes, you were there, wearing that dress."

Lori smiled. "I still have the dress, you know. I keep it sealed in a plastic bag in my closet. I never wore it again, but I couldn't bear the thought of parting with it. It was the last gift you ever gave me—other than the roses you left me that last night. And, silly as it may sound, I still have them, too. I had them preserved."

Brad's eyes softened and the hint of a smile crossed his lips. "You kept the dress? And the roses? I don't know what to say. I never supposed . . ."

"That I missed you as much as you say you missed me? Well I did. You have no idea how many times I've relived that dreadful night. There are a thousand things I'd do differently if I could start my life over from the day I first wore this dress. But that can never be, can it, Brad?"

"No, it can't," Brad affirmed. "In life, we get one shot at a target and that's it. Once, when I was a small boy, I had a dog. I called him Jumper because he loved to jump up and give me dog kisses all over my face. He wasn't anything special, just a mutt, but oh how I loved that dog. Late one afternoon I was playing catch with Jumper. I didn't see the car when I tossed the ball into the street. I screamed his name, but it was too late. Jumper didn't have a chance. He was only doing what any good dog would do—going after the ball his master had thrown."

Brad paused for a breath. "I relived that instant in time over and over again, but it never changed a thing. Jumper was gone, and that's all there was to it. My mother tried giving me another dog, but I refused it. If I couldn't have Jumper, I didn't want any dog."

Lori stared at Brad and would have said something if she hadn't been interrupted by the return of the phenomena that had swept them from the ice cream parlor to this house. Once again, the room went into a blurring spin. Just as before, the experience climaxed with the scene around them changing to a different place and time. This change left them standing on the banks of a gurgling little brook, one oh so familiar in Lori's memory. It was nighttime and the reflection of a full moon danced off the surface of the rushing water with millions of tiny sparkles. "Do you know where we are, Brad?" Lori asked excitedly.

"Yeah," he beamed. "I know. This is Beaver Creek. This is the very spot where I—"

"Where you asked me to marry you," Lori cut in. "And it was on a night exactly like this one."

"You're right, it was. I remember, Lori."

"I'm surprised you do," Lori said, with a faint laugh. "It wasn't much of a proposal, you know."

Brad took exception. "What do you mean? My proposal wasn't all that bad. You did say yes if memory serves me right."

"Not all that bad? Are you kidding me, Brad? If you knew you were asking me here to propose, did you really have to bring your fly-rod along?"

"I only fished a few minutes, Lori. Just long enough to catch that rainbow that had been eluding me for weeks."

"You fished a few minutes, did you? Ha! More like an hour. And after you caught the darn thing, all you did was throw him back in! I could have pushed you in after him, Brad. I mean, look at this place. It oozes romance, and all you could think of was fishing."

"All right, so I'm not the most romantic guy in the world. I was in love with you, and this was the best way I could think of to ask you to marry me. I admit, I should have left the fishing pole at home. But I was young back then. Didn't I deserve to make a mistake or two?"

The question hit Lori with bitter impact. Brad's mistake was small alongside the one she later made. "You're right, Brad," she concurred. "You were young and so was I. We both made mistakes. But I'll tell you this much, if any man ever asks me to marry him again I'm going to expect something more elaborate than what I got from you. And that's a fact."

"Give me a little credit, Lori. I did bring along my transistor radio for some background music when I finally did get around to popping the question. That should count for something."

Lori's eyes moistened as she remembered. "That's right. You did bring along your radio. And do you remember what song was playing when you proposed?"

Brad squirmed nervously. "Uh—no. I guess I don't remember that for sure." He looked at Lori. "Do you?"

"Oh yes, I remember. Elvis was singing 'I Can't Help Falling in Love with You.' To this day I get goose bumps when I hear him sing it."

"Goose bumps? You just said my proposal was a disaster. Why would anything about it bring goose bumps?"

"Because I loved you, that's why. Bad as your proposal was, it was something I had been hoping for, for a very long time."

Brad reached down and picked up a rock, which he tossed into the stream. "Yeah," he said. "It was something I had tried to get up enough courage to do for a long time, too." He laughed. "Do you remember how excited I got when you said 'yes'?"

"Do I remember? How could I forget. My ears rang for days after the way you yelled. But the thing I remember most is the way you kissed me. If ever I doubted your love, that kiss erased it all."

"Yeah," Brad answered quietly. "I remember that kiss, too."

Lori's heart pounded as he looked at her, and she thought she saw something in his eyes. They were standing only inches apart, and from somewhere off in the distance she could swear she heard Elvis' voice singing those immortal words. She leaned forward, just as Brad leaned toward her. Their lips brushed ever so slightly. She longed for him to pull her into his arms, but instead he backed quickly away.

"I—I'm sorry," he said. "I had no right . . ."

Lori's heart sank. Once again she wished time could somehow rewind back to when this bittersweet replay was real. Wouldn't it be wonderful if second chances were there for the taking? Chances where mistakes—like the ones that lay ahead from this point—could be eradicated from the pages of her life.

Something inside told her this particular scene was about to run its course. She quickly looked around for one last drink of the nostalgic beauty and glowing memories contained here. Within seconds her suspicions turned to reality when the setting faded into darkness much like the lights dimming to blackness at the final curtain of a captivating play. In little more than a heartbeat, a new scene came to light. This time they were in a hotel room. A room she couldn't remember seeing before.

"Where do you suppose the angels have dropped us off this time, Brad?" she asked, looking around. "I'm at a loss on this one."

"We're in Acapulco," Brad explained. "This is the room where I lived for more than three months while directing what was to be my last film. Of all the places the angels could show us, why would they choose this one?"

A sudden surge of guilt shot through Lori as she examined the small room. There was a bed, an overstuffed brown sofa, a chest of drawers, a small table with a single chair, and a small adjoining bathroom. On the table she spotted a picture of herself next to the phone. Her heart ached as she thought of the times he had called from this drab, lonely room, thinking she was just as lonely on the other end of the line. Time and again her end of the line had been received from somewhere other than the lonely walls of home as he had supposed. Some of Brad's calls she had taken in fine restaurants, and others while she was walking along on the soft white sands of a romantic beach at Carmel by the Sea with Howard at her side. All thanks to Howard's cellular phone.

Never had her feelings of self-blame been more piercing than here, in this hotel room. Brad's question rang with stinging wonder in her own mind. Why had the angels brought them here? It was more than she could stand. Burying her face deep in both hands, she fought to block out the pointing fingers that appeared from every corner of this room. Ten years of tormenting shame seared her heart with unquenchable guilt—and she wept bitterly.

Brad lay a hand on her shoulder. "What is it, Lori?" he asked, sympathetically.

Without even thinking, Lori buried her tear-streaked face deep against his powerful chest. She felt his arms slide around her, pulling her tightly against him—and she cried even more.

"It's all right, Lori," Brad whispered. "This isn't real. It's only a trick the angels are playing in our minds."

Lori slid her arms around Brad and forced herself to speak. "I—never knew how lonely this was for you, Brad. Not until now. Seeing this room is more than I can bear. Oh, Brad. I'm so sorry. So very sorry."

"Hey, it's all right, Lori. This all happened a long time ago. Let it go. It's over now."

"Please," Lori begged. "Ask the angels to take all this away. I just can't bear another second in this awful place."

"It's sorry I be indeed, lassie," came Blake's unmistakable voice. "Me friend, the beautiful angel Sam, assures me your seein' this room be a necessary part of her plan."

Lori turned her head just far enough to peek past Brad's chest with one eye. There stood Captain Blake, wearing the most understanding smile she had ever seen. "Captain Blake?" she choked out. "Can you take this scene away please? I just can't stand looking at it any longer."

"Aye, lassie, I can be doin' as ye ask. Once the cannon fire falls to silence, it be time to move on to the next battle, says I. If ye'll be so kind as to be closin' yer eyes now."

Lori had no inclination to argue. She quickly did as the captain asked and closed her one eye that had been open. A cool breeze brushed by, leaving in its wake the familiar smell and sounds of an oceanfront beach. Venturing to open her eye once more, she realized Blake was gone, and so was the hotel room. This time they were standing on the moonlit shores of a white sanded beach she instantly recognized as Carmel by the Sea.

"Oh great," she moaned. "Talk about out of the frying pan into the fire. Thanks a lot, Captain Blake. Of all the places you could have taken us, why did it have to be here?"

Brad released Lori and backed away a step. "It's all right, Lori. Stop punishing yourself. What's past is past. Even if the angels are forcing us to look back on it, it's still the past. Don't let it bother you, okay?"

Lori wiped an eye with her hand. It only managed to streak her makeup worse than ever. She was glad when Brad offered his handkerchief, which she gladly used to dry away the remainder of her tears. "I can't help it, Brad. I'm so ashamed. You know I wasn't always at home when you called me from Acapulco."

"I know, Lori. I found the cell phone, and I saw the pictures. Some of them must have been taken right here, on this beach."

Lori felt herself shudder. "Yes," she admitted. "I spent two weeks here with Howard, just before you came home. He was producing a film on location, and he used it as an excuse to lure me here. I don't know what possessed me to do it. It's just that Howard—I don't know—he paid attention to me, pampered me. I became infatuated with him, Brad. I don't mean to make excuses, and I'm certainly not proud of myself, but that's the way it happened."

Brad released a long sigh. "I don't suppose Howard was unromantic enough to bring along his fishing pole on your dates, was he?"

"They weren't dates!" Lori shot back emphatically. "At least, I didn't think of the time we spent together as dates. It was just sort of business—mixed with a little pleasure. I give you my word, I was never unfaithful to you, Brad. At least not in an intimate way, if that's what you thought. Is that what you thought?"

"I tried not to think about that part," Brad whispered. "But I admit, hearing you say it never happened does make me feel better. Who knows, if I'd only given you the chance to explain back then . . ."

This time it was Lori's turn to be reasonable. "Like you said, Brad. The past is dead."

Brad tried to laugh. "Yeah, I did say that, didn't I? There I go, giving out advice I can't even follow myself."

"It's hard advice to follow, since the mistakes of the past have had such an impact on our lives, I'd say," Lori philosophized.

Brad shrugged. "Yeah, and while we're about the 'what if's'—what if I'd learned to be a little more romantic myself? Maybe then you wouldn't have been so tempted when Howard turned on the charm."

"There's one thing I never did with Howard," Lori said with a seductive smile. "I never walked this beach with him in the glow of the full moon."

"Like right now, you mean?" Brad asked.

"Uh huh."

"What the heck, we might as well enjoy this holograph or whatever it is. What do you say, Lori? Shall we take a little stroll?"

"Yes!" she responded without hesitation. "I'd love to."

Lori smiled as she felt his hand slide into hers, and together they walked. She drew in a deep breath of cool salty air and gazed up at the image of a sea gull silhouetted in flight against the big round moon. Off to the right, a gentle wave broke, sending a flood of foamy water rolling to within inches of their feet before being swallowed up by the thirsty sand. "One thing I can definitely say, Brad," she stated quietly. "The man I'm walking with now is much more handsome than the one I walked this beach with those ten years ago."

"Yeah? You really think so?"

"I do. And you know what else? The guy I'm with now is ten times the man the other fellow was. No, make that a hundred times. I failed to recognize that once, but that's a mistake I'd never make again."

Smiling, Brad retreated into thought for a moment, then asked a question. "Do you still see him, Lori? Howard, I mean."

The question left Lori with an empty feeling in the pit of the stomach. It was a question Brad certainly had the right to ask, but one she didn't feel all that comfortable in answering. "I suppose that all depends on what you mean by seeing him," Lori responded. "I speak to him every now and then, if that's what you're getting at. And we've had lunch together occasionally—but only when he's happened by unannounced. I don't go out of my way to see him, and I certainly don't date him, if that's what you're asking."

Lori tightened her hold on Brad's hand and looked upward at the thousands of stars surrounding the moon's luminous glow. "I'm not sure if you can understand this or not, Brad. But I feel like I'm guilty of not only wronging you by my past actions, I feel I've wronged Howard, too."

Brad came to a stop. "You what?!" he gulped. "I'm sorry, Lori, but I fail to see your point. How could you possibly think you've wronged that man?"

Lori never took her eyes off the stars as she explained. "My point is, I should have acted the part of a happily married woman, never giving him reason to believe I could be anything else. That's not what I did. By responding to his flattery, I left myself wide open. To Howard, it was a sure sign he was winning my affection. When I finally came to my senses and insisted there could never be anything between us, he refused to accept it. He still refuses to accept it, no matter how hard I try to discourage him. But just in case you have doubts, let me set the record straight. I made the mistake of giving in to his pressure once, but that will never happen again. I'm a lot wiser now, and that's a fact."

* * *

Even though Lori's acknowledgment offered a degree of comfort to Brad's troubled mind, his acceptance of what she was saying fell short of total trust. Brad knew Howard all too well to believe the man was capable of accepting Lori's rejection. Howard would never give up, and Brad wasn't sure Lori could resist him forever. With his fabulous wealth, an exciting lifestyle, and unlimited romance, Howard's arsenal was filled with weapons he hadn't even unsheathed yet. Brad had to admit that Lori sincerely meant to stick to her word. After all, she had resisted Howard's advances for more than ten years—but ten years is far short of forever.

Another thing Brad had to admit, being this close to Lori again was nothing short of wonderful—but he knew their evening could amount to nothing more than reliving a few warm memories. Unfortunately, the warm memories weren't the only ones being relived. Some memories came with a painful bite, like the memory of Lori in Howard's arms— her lips pressed to his in a forbidden kiss. Tempting as the thought might be, Brad knew he could never trust his heart to Lori again. Once this night was over, he would go his way and she would go hers.

Brad's attention was suddenly drawn to a shooting star at the edge of the horizon. The star grew increasingly brighter as it streaked across the night sky, until it soon outshone the moon. Still it grew brighter, lighting everything in sight with the brilliance of a noonday sun. The brightness became so intense, Brad was forced to cover his eyes to block out its rays. Moments later, it was over. The star was gone, and the night was back to normal. Or was it? Something was definitely different. He was still holding Lori's hand, and they were still standing on a beach. Only this beach wasn't near the ocean. They were standing near a lake, one he couldn't remember seeing before. "It appears we've moved again," he observed. "Do you have any idea where we are this time, Lori?"

* * *

Lori had more than just an idea where they had ended up in this change; she knew exactly. How could the angels be so cruel as to bring them here? "Yes," she hesitantly admitted. "I do know where we are. We're on a private island once owned by Howard."

Brad looked surprised. "This is Howard Placard's privately owned island?"

"Not any more," Lori went on to explain. "Howard sold the island several years ago, to a man named Jedikiah Marshall. We're evidently seeing the island the way it was ten years ago. Jedikiah has since built a fabulous resort on it."

"This makes no sense at all," Brad mulled aloud. "Howard always bragged that his island was his favorite place of retreat. Only his closest friends were ever allowed to see it." Brad paused in thought and Lori cringed in anticipation of his next question. "How do you know this is Howard's island, Lori? Were you one of the select few he brought here?"

What was she to do? Denying she had been alone on the island with Howard was futile since the angels were apparently dead set on bringing it to light. And—there had been too much lying already. The lying is what sealed her fate and cost her marriage to Brad in the first place. Releasing his hand and looking him straight in the face, she began the hardest confession of all. "Much as I hate to own up to it, Brad, I was on this island with Howard the evening you came home from Acapulco."

The hurt in Brad's eyes evidenced what was taking place in his mind. Lori wished for a way to soften what had to be said, but the only ally she had left was the truth. "I had no idea Howard was bringing me here that night, Brad. I swear, if I'd known, I would never have consented to come with him."

Turning his back to Lori, Brad stood looking out across the lake for nearly a minute. When he spoke next, it was to pose an unexpected question. "You say Howard sold the island? Why would he do that, Lori? This place meant more to the man than anything else he owned."

"He sold it because it was here I rejected him, Brad. You know as well as I do, Howard can't accept rejection of any kind. After that night, he could never stand coming to this island again, and so he eventually sold it."

Still Brad would not look back at Lori. "You say you rejected him. Can I assume he asked you to leave me and marry him?"

"That was his intention, yes. That's what brought me to the realization of the magnitude of what I had allowed myself to become involved in. I asked Howard to take me home, with the intention of telling you everything. As we both know, I never got that chance."

"She be tellin' the truth, matey. It was yer stubborn streak that got in the way and set yer course on the rocky sea ye've been sailin' ever since, says I."

Lori glanced around to see Captain Blake standing just behind her. She wondered how long he had been there, but didn't venture to ask.

At Brad's silence, the captain repeated himself. "Aye, Brad Douglas, the lady be tellin' the truth and I be fixin' to prove it to ye."

Brad turned to look at Blake, but for once in his life he didn't respond to the ghost's prodding. This time he only listened quietly to Blake's disclosure. "So far, in this flashback of yer past lives, ye and the lassie have seen only places. This time, says I, ye'll be seein' a bit more. Yer about to see for yerself, Brad Douglas, exactly what took place between the lassie and Howard Placard on the night in question."

Lori couldn't believe what the captain said. "You mean, we're going to watch what actually went on between Howard and me that night?" she gasped.

"Aye, lassie. That be me meanin'. Me matey here refused to let ye tell him the truth, so now he'll be seein' it for himself. And don't be worryin' yer little heart none about his reaction. It all be part of the lovely angel Sam's plan to be settin' yer destinies on the proper course. Ye know where the house be, says I. I be leavin' it up to ye to be takin' Brad there now."

Removing his hat, Blake made a deep bow to Lori, then vanished just as before. Lori looked back to Brad, and their eyes met. "This isn't going to be easy for me," she softly admitted.

"Nor for me," Brad added. "But it seems the angels aren't about to let us out of watching this part."

Lori swallowed hard and tried to quell the anxiety from her fevered mind. Extending her hand to him, she said, "Come on. I'll lead you to the house."

Brad hesitated. "I hope these angels know what they're doing," he said anxiously.

"Me too," Lori added worriedly. "Me too."

Brad took hold of her hand, and together they made their way toward the house, and a moment of truth neither knew if they were ready to face.

CHAPTER 13

Even though Lori had seen Howard's island only once, the exact location of his exquisite home was etched deeply in her mind, as was every other detail about that fateful evening so long ago. Finding the house now presented no problem at all; forcing herself to go there with Brad was another matter. Still, what choice did she have? She couldn't fight the angels. And if there was the slightest chance that allowing Brad to see for himself what actually took place that evening might help as the angels claimed, well . . . Swallowing her pride, she quelled her fears, took Brad by the hand, and led him straight to the front door.

The house was exactly as she remembered it. Just as Captain Blake had predicted, the holographic figures of Howard and herself were right on cue. What a strange sensation it was, watching herself and Howard performing a perfect replay of what had actually taken place those ten years ago.

As the two figures approached the door and prepared to enter the house, Lori glanced at Brad and saw that the color had drained from his face, leaving him pale and drawn. He spoke and his voice reflected the pain he was feeling inside at seeing, firsthand, his wife on the arm of this powerful man, Howard Placard. "That gown you were wearing," he observed in a shaken whisper. "It's the same one you wore when I saw you and Howard kissing at our front door."

Lori wished she could shrink herself down in size and hide from Brad's view under some nearby rock. "I didn't solicit that kiss," she feebly attempted to explain. "Howard forced it on me unexpectedly." She breathed a slow, lingering sigh. "But, yes, the gown is the same."

Brad made no comment on her explanation of the kiss, but remained on the subject of the gown. "It looks like satin," he remarked painfully. "Was it a gift from Howard?"

"No!" Lori quickly corrected. "The gown wasn't a gift from Howard. I bought it myself."

Bewilderment filled Brad's eyes as he stared at the younger Lori's image. "You bought the gown yourself?" he asked. "May I assume you bought it just for this evening's occasion?"

"I did," she hesitantly admitted.

Brad rubbed a hand across his brow. "That gown must have cost more than you normally paid for ten dresses, Lori. I never knew you to be so extravagant. You must really have wanted to impress Howard."

Lori closed her eyes and shook her head. "I tried to explain to you earlier, Brad. I thought Howard had something altogether different planned for this evening. I was led to believe we would be at an event that included the others at the studio. You know, some sort of celebration for the progress we had made on his film in Carmel by the Sea. I admit, I wanted to look nice, but not just for Howard, as you probably suppose from what you're seeing here. I wanted to fit in with the others I expected to be at the occasion. Which brings us to another matter I've never told you about. The gown cost a great deal of money, but it didn't pinch my budget like you may think. I was able to afford the gown because I had a job you knew nothing about."

Brad looked more confused than ever. "A job I didn't know about? You mean you weren't teaching at Sanderson's College while I was away?"

"No, Brad. I wasn't teaching at Sanderson's College. The truth is, Howard set me up with a dream job as a set designer for some of his productions," Lori admitted.

Brad stared at Lori. "A set designer? I—I don't understand. How did that happen, Lori?"

Lori sighed before going on. "I was an experienced interior decorator, you know that, Brad. And you know I had aspired to being a set designer at times when I visited the studio to watch you direct. I read everything I could get my hands on about the subject of set designing long before you left for your filming in Acapulco. Though I didn't know it at the time, Howard knew about my skills in interior decorating, and about my meddling in set designing. Since the two are closely related, Howard used my skills as a means of getting me close to him. He offered me the job as set designer, and I was just too overwhelmed to turn him down. I took the job, and that's what started my spiral toward the night you came home and found us together."

"So you were a set designer? I assume you mean at the film studio?" Brad clarified.

Lori nodded. "Yes. I worked at the studio. Most of the time, anyway. I did help out on the one film at a remote location."

Brad drew a breath. "At Carmel, you mean?"

"Yes."

"When did Howard set you up in this job? Did you know about the job when you saw me off to Acapulco?" Brad asked slowly.

"No, I didn't know then. Howard offered me the job the next day after you left. He showed up at the airport right after you left; he said he wanted to see you off. Then he invited me to lunch and starting talking about a job for me. Like I said, it was all part of his plan to lure me into getting to know him better. He used the job to get close to me, and ashamed as I am to admit it—his plan worked."

"That's the reason you were at Carmel with Howard. You were helping with a film he was producing. He used your job as an excuse to get you there with him, am I right?"

Lori was glad for a chance to explain. "That's the way it happened, Brad. Howard convinced me I would be going along because he needed me to help design the sets."

Brad's face showed a flicker of relief. "So you didn't just go there because you wanted to be near him, like I've always supposed."

Lori hesitated before answering. True, at the time it had been her job that lured her to Carmel. But it would be wrong to say she didn't take advantage of the situation to enjoy being lavished by Howard's extravagant attention. There could be no more lies to Brad. Still—was it necessary to tell everything she knew? "It was my job that brought me to Carmel," she said, and let it go at that. "And that's how I afforded the gown. Not only was my new job exciting, the pay was incredible."

Brad forced a laugh. "You can't imagine all the ways I've conjured up how you and Howard might have gotten together, but I never would have guessed this. Not that I don't agree with him; you would be perfect for the job."

"I'm not proud of myself for hiding it from you, Brad, but that's the way it happened. I desperately wanted the job, and I didn't want you worrying because it meant I had to deal so closely with Howard. I was sure, at the time, I could keep everything on a professional basis with the man." Lori paused, and then added, "Guess I was wrong, huh?"

Brad overlooked her remark. "I have to admit, you did look beautiful in the gown. But not half as beautiful as you look in the red dress you're wearing now. The one I bought for you."

Lori had one more thing to say. "Just to set the record straight, I never wore the gown again. In fact, I burned it the morning after you left. I never returned to my job at the studio, either. Not that Howard didn't pressure me to come back—I just couldn't do it. Not after what the job—and the lies that went with it—had cost me."

"You burned the gown and you never went back to your job at the studio? Are you saying what I think you're saying Lori? Are you suggesting that if I had stayed and talked things out, we might have gotten back together?"

Lori smiled sadly. "'If' is a big word, Brad, and as you've already observed—it never changes a thing. We might as well pay some attention to this ten-year-old rerun," she suggested. "I'm sure the angels don't want you to miss a word that was said."

The two of them stepped forward and managed to slip inside the house before the door was closed. Lori still marveled at the elegance of it all. Nothing was missing. The music, the candles, the beautifully set table, the view of the moonlit lake through picturesque windows— it was all there. Only this time, it wasn't hidden from Brad's eyes. Together, they watched the events of the long-past evening play out once more, right down to the most intricate detail.

* * *

Howard removed Lori's coat and lay it over the back of the sofa. "I really don't feel comfortable with this," Lori said nervously as Howard led her to the prepared table.

"Nonsense," he smilingly objected. "What's to feel uncomfortable about? Sit down, Lori. You're about to taste a shrimp cocktail prepared so exquisitely, it'll drive your taste buds wild. After that, it's swordfish, sautéed to perfection by the finest chef this side of Paris."

As Lori sat down, Howard took her empty wine glass and dipped it in the ice bucket, swirling it a few times before dumping the ice back in the bucket. Next he uncorked the wine bottle and filled her glass, but she refused to take it from him.

"You know I never touch wine, Howard. Why even offer it to me?"

"Lori, I'm offering you much more than a glass of the finest wine the grape can produce. I'm offering you a whole new life. Take this glass. Try one sip. When you do, I guarantee your palate will never say 'no' again. And, the wine will enhance your taste for the food that follows. Relax, Lori. Let me teach you how to enjoy life's richest offerings."

Lori stood abruptly, knocking over her chair in the process. "No, Howard," she bluntly declared. "I won't taste your wine. And suddenly I'm not very hungry either. I'd like you to take me home."

"Please," Howard sighed. "Not just yet. We'll forget dinner for now if you like; maybe we can come back to it a little later on. I'd like you to go for a walk with me around the island. There are some things I want to say to you."

"I'd really rather go home now, Howard," Lori insisted.

Howard held up his hand, saying, "All I ask is that you hear me out, Lori. Just walk with me while I explain some things to you. Then, if you still want to go home—we can go."

Lori glanced through the glass windows at the lovely evening. "I'm wearing high heels, Howard. Walking in the sand would be a little difficult."

"There's no need to walk in the sand. I have a concrete sidewalk that spans the whole island. You're dressed perfectly for a walk next to my lake, Lori."

"All right," Lori conceded. "We'll walk, and I'll listen to whatever it is you have to tell me. But that's it. I want to go home."

* * *

Brad lay a hand to his head. "I'm sorry, Lori," he excused. "This isn't easy for me. For ten years I imagined you and Howard together in every possible situation—but seeing you like this takes it a step beyond imagination. I feel a little ill at the moment."

Lori was feeling a little ill herself. Although she was thankful that the angels had picked this scene for Brad to witness instead of Carmel, she still couldn't help but wince as the pangs of guilt penetrated to the depths of her soul. "I'm sorry, Brad," she earnestly declared. "If I could erase it all, I would. If I could relive it all, I'd handle it differently. But we both know I can't do either."

Brad shook his head slowly, as if it hurt him to move. "I'm really having a hard time understanding this, Lori," he said. "When we were married, I thought we were pretty open with each other. No secrets and that sort of thing. Why didn't you tell me about your new job? I would have been elated for you, you should have known that. And if you thought your dealings with Howard were strictly business, why did you hide this from me?"

Lori sighed. "I don't know why I didn't trust you with everything, Brad. I've asked myself that same question a thousand times since. When Howard offered me the job, I wanted it so desperately I couldn't bear the thought of saying 'no.' But it meant working closely with him, and I wasn't sure how to approach you with that one. I just kept thinking I'd find a way to tell you later. Only when later came, it was too late. I lost everything—the job, my marriage, my self-respect. Everything. And as if that wasn't enough, I ended up ruining your life while I was at it." Lori shook her head and laughed derisively. "That's a track record to write home about, wouldn't you say?"

"It's not all your fault, Lori," Brad objected. "Now that I think about it, I can see why you didn't confide in me at first. Maybe if I'd given you half a chance near the end, things could have worked out differently."

"Maybe so," Lori speculated as she and Brad followed the two holograph figures out of the house on their way to the lake's edge. "Maybe so, but we'll never know for sure, will we?"

She and Brad both turned their attention back to the ten-year-old scene being played out before them.

* * *

For several minutes Howard and Lori walked along the edge of the lake with neither of them speaking. At last, Howard stopped and leaned against the white iron rail that paralleled the walkway on the lake side. Lori folded her arms and stood a little ways off.

"You remember the day at the airport?" Howard began. "The day we met by chance while seeing Brad off to Acapulco?"

"I remember," Lori acknowledged coldly.

"It wasn't by chance that we met, Lori. It was by design. I planned it that way."

When Lori, obviously shocked by this declaration, didn't bother to answer, Howard continued, "I planned it all. Even to the point of hiring Brad to direct the movie in Acapulco. I wanted him out of the picture for a while, and that seemed like the perfect way."

Lori dropped her hands to her side and stared at Howard. "Let me get this straight," she said sharply. "You hired Brad to do the film in Acapulco because of me?"

Howard turned to face her. "The truth is, I'm in love with you, Lori. I've been in love with you from the first time I laid eyes on you at my father's ranch. You were with a group of high school girls who came to the ranch for a field trip into the mountains on horseback. That's when I first saw you, Lori, and I couldn't keep my eyes off you. You were the most beautiful woman I had ever seen. You didn't know, of course, but I saddled my own horse and followed you into the mountains that day. I watched you all day, staying just far enough away that you wouldn't notice."

Lori was horrified. "This is insane, Howard. You can't possibly be in love with me."

"I am in love with you, Lori," Howard insisted. "I would have stepped forward to introduce myself that day at my father's ranch, except my parents already had my future wife picked out for me. They were set on me marrying a girl named Betty Wilson, because she was socially acceptable in their minds. You'll never know how much I wish I could live my life over from that point. If only I had been brave enough to go with my instincts right then, I would have given Brad Douglas a real fight for your hand, Lori. But I didn't. It wasn't until years later that I managed to bolster my courage enough to oppose my parents. I never did marry Betty Wilson, but by the time I made that choice you were already married to Brad. I do love you, Lori. I love you enough to do whatever it takes to win you away from Brad. I thought if you saw all the exciting things I have to offer, you might be tempted to leave him for me. I know you've enjoyed these last months. You can't deny that, Lori."

"I—I'm not denying that I've enjoyed the time we've spent together," Lori stammered. "And I admit, I may have inadvertently done some things to encourage you. But . . ."

Before Lori could stop him, Howard stepped forward and kissed her. Instantly, she pulled away. "Stop that, Howard! You have no right. I'm a married woman."

"Yes, you are a married woman, Lori. But tell me you love Brad now that you've had a taste of how life can be with a man like me. Go ahead, tell me you love him. You can't, can you?"

"Yes!" she shouted in Howard's face. "I do love Brad Douglas. I don't know how I'm going to face him again, but I do love him. I'm sorry if I led you to believe there could ever be something between us, Howard, but I'm telling you now—there can't be. Now I'm begging you, please take me home."

* * *

Tears streamed heavily down Lori's face as she watched and listened to this painful moment from out of her past. "Please, Captain Blake," she quietly sobbed. "Take this scene away like you did the one at the hotel. I can't bear any more of this."

Though the good captain didn't appear this time, he obliged her wishes nevertheless. No sooner had she uttered the words than the figures from the holograph faded and were gone.

"Is this really true?" Brad asked, once it was just the two of them again. "Howard wanted me out of the way long enough to destroy our marriage?"

Lori swallowed away the lump in her throat. "Yes," she whispered. "Breaking up our marriage was his intention from the beginning. And I was naive enough to play right into his hand. But I swear to you, Brad, what you just witnessed was the turning point. When he lured me here to this island, it was my wake-up call. Unfortunately, it came too little and too late."

"Then, when I saw you and Howard kissing at our front door—it was all his doing?" Brad asked.

Lori nodded, her cheeks wet with tears. "He caught me completely off guard with that kiss, Brad. Just like he did here on the island."

Brad lifted his hand to the back of Lori's head and gently stroked her hair. "If I'd only known," he whispered. "If I'd only known."

Lori managed a slight laugh. "There's that word 'if' again."

"Yeah," he agreed softly. "What's done is done, I guess. How do the words to that song go? *'We don't have tomorrow, but we had yesterday.'*"

Lori wiped her eyes with Brad's handkerchief. "What I told Howard was true, Brad. I was in love with you. And I'm not ashamed to admit—I still am."

"Aye, lassie, that ye be. And me matey here is still in love with ye."

"Oh, I see you're back," Brad said to Blake. "Are you having fun, popping in and out like a sewing machine needle?"

"Whether I be havin' fun or not all depends on ye, says I. For ten long years all I heard from yer lips was how ye yearned to be kissin' this lassie. I be givin' ye the chance, and all ye can do is wave yer jaw like a mainsail in the breeze."

Brad blushed. "Blake, when will you ever learn to control that wagging tongue of yours. You never did know when to keep quiet. Come to think of it, it was your mouth that got you in trouble with Oscar Welborn. If you hadn't given him your word to deliver that precious load of gold, you could have saved yourself three hundred years of grief."

"Aye, matey. But I did give me word. And ye gave yer word to this lassie. Somethin' about keepin' her around forever, if I be rememberin' right."

Speechless at last, Brad turned to look at Lori. Though not a word was spoken between them in that brief instant, Lori knew he was struggling with the truthfulness of Blake's words. Out of the corner of her eye she noticed Blake wink, and she knew he was about to put the next part of the plan into action.

"Hold onto yer britches, matey," he said. "We have one last stop to make afore I considers takin' ye home again. And remember me words before we started this journey through yer past days. You're to be sealin' yer destiny with a kiss of promise before ye can be goin' home, says I."

Captain Blake smiled, and a flash of blinding light filled the night with the brilliance of a hundred noonday suns. For several seconds, Lori couldn't see a thing. As her vision slowly returned, she discovered Howard's island was gone. *Why can't that rustic old angel stick to one way of changing these scenes?* she asked herself. *They say variety is the spice of life and evidently Blake is adding lots of spice to these changes.*

Lori looked around and saw that they were standing in front of another house, one that was definitely more modest than Howard's island mansion. She didn't recognize the house at all. "Where are we now, Brad?" she asked. "I hope you know, because I certainly don't."

Brad drew in a deep breath. "We're at the place I called home for ten long years, Lori. We're standing in the center of a tiny island not far from the shores of Saint Thomas in the Caribbean Sea."

"This is the island where you lived these last ten years?" Lori asked unbelievingly. "It's certainly not what I pictured when you mentioned an island in the Caribbean. Where are all the girls in bikinis and tourist shops? This is hardly more than a jungle."

"Actually it's a rain forest. And there are no girls in bikinis or tourist shops. What you see is what you get."

"You lived here with Shannon and Tanielle? What did you do for entertainment, count leaves on coconut trees?"

"It's not as bad as it looks, Lori. I owned a good boat, and Saint Thomas Island is only a short distance from here. They have all the tourist shops anyone could want."

"Uh huh, and I suppose they have the girls in bikinis, too?"

Brad laughed. "They have them, but I never went shopping in that department."

"Come on, Brad," Lori pressed. "Surely you didn't go ten years without dating once in a while? Admit it, there's someone special on Saint Thomas, isn't there?"

"Hey, what can I say? I was just never interested in dating," Brad defended himself. "I'm not saying I didn't get lonely, but through it all I could only think of one lady. And so far as I knew, she was married to someone else." Brad paused to look seriously at Lori. "Are you saying you did date others?" he ventured.

Lori shook her head. "No," she said. "The only fellow I was interested in fell off the edge of the world and was never heard from again."

Lori stepped up next to Brad and ran her hand through his thick red hair. "Not until tonight, that is," she added.

Brad reached up and placed his hand on hers. For a very long time, they stood silently looking into each other's eyes. At last, Lori broke the spell with a question. "You built that place, didn't you?" she asked.

Brad nodded yes. "Every nail and board in it," he affirmed. "What prompted you to suspect it was my creation?"

"Look at the place, Brad. You don't have to be an Einstein to see how much it resembles another house. One you built several years ago for your young bride."

"Oh," Brad acknowledged, rolling his eyes. "You mean the house you used to call drab?"

"Oh, yeah," Lori squirmed. "I guess I did refer to the old place as drab, didn't I?"

"Not more than a thousand or so times," Brad snickered, tongue in cheek. "Not that it hurt my feelings, or anything. Actually I like my creations referred to as drab."

"Well, Brad. If it's any consolation, I wouldn't call the place drab anymore," Lori said. "I've learned that painted-on glamour doesn't mean nearly as much as I used to suppose it did." She lowered her eyes and stared at her feet for several seconds, then looking back at Brad, she smiled. "I'm glad you didn't date any of those girls in bikinis. Isn't that silly of me?"

"No, it's not silly. You can't believe how glad I am to know you weren't with Howard all those years. And I'm just as glad you didn't date any of those romantic guys I'm sure were lined up at your door. What do you think, Lori? Do you suppose you might consider having dinner with me one of these evenings?"

Lori's face lit up with excitement. "Yes!" she said, unable to hide her excitement. "I'd love to have dinner with you, Brad Douglas."

"I'm not saying anything will come of our having dinner," Brad quickly explained. "I just thought . . ."

"We'll have dinner and see what happens next," Lori agreed, then changed the subject. "You might not believe this, Brad. But I worried about you while you were gone. I had no idea where you might be or what you might be doing. I didn't even know for sure if you were still alive."

"Well, as you can see, I am alive and doing all right. Other than the loneliness, this island made a pretty good home."

"Could I see inside the house?" Lori suggested.

"I guess it would be okay. The real house isn't in very good shape anymore, but I assume this flashback model is pretty much intact. Inside and all."

"What happened to the house?" Lori asked as they approached the front door.

"It was torn up pretty bad by a horrendous hurricane. We barely made it out alive."

"A hurricane?" Lori asked. "The one that barely missed Florida a couple of months back?"

"That's the one," Brad said as he tried the door and found it open. Poking his head inside he looked around. "Yep, everything seems to be exactly as it was when we lived here."

The two of them stepped inside where for the next several minutes Brad presented Lori with a master tour of the place. "Oh look!" Lori exclaimed as they stepped into Brad's den. "You had a piano. You do still play, don't you?"

"Sure I still play. Both piano and guitar. That's how I made a living while we lived here. I performed for the folks on Saint Thomas and Saint John islands. I played, did voice impressions, told a few jokes, you know the old routine."

"Play something for me now, Brad. I love hearing you play."

Brad shrugged and sat down at the keyboard. "Anything in particular?" he asked.

"You pick something, Brad."

His fingers touched the keys, and the notes began to flow smooth and easy. Tears soon filled Lori's eyes as she recognized Elvis' song, "I Can't Help Falling in Love with You." Lori could never listen to this song without getting sentimental. It always brought back a vivid impression of the day Brad proposed to her. With Brad himself playing it, there was no stopping the flood of emotion. Suddenly, she was filled with one thought alone. Ten years of lonely nights, unfulfilled dreams, burning desire, and a constant longing to be near the man she loved motivated her to gather up her courage and slide onto the bench next to him. The music stopped as Brad turned to face her. With a pounding heart she leaned toward him until her lips nearly touched his, and the world stood still. Closing her eyes, she silently prayed for a miracle. The miracle came as she felt the warmth of his lips brush gently against hers. The dam of emotions ruptured as she threw her arms around his neck pulling him into a kiss that ended a decade of emptiness and waiting—and she thought her heart would explode.

She kissed him a second time, and for good measure she kissed him a third. Then laying her tear-soaked cheek next to his, she whispered, "Do you know how long I've dreamed of this moment?"

"Not one second longer than me," he whispered back. "Please don't let me wake to find this is just another dream, like I've done a thousand times before."

Brad ran his fingers through her long, blond, silky hair, as he had done so many times in ten years of dreams. "Maybe you should have a look at the rest of my island," he whispered. "Before you make a statement like that one, I mean."

"I want to see the rest of your island, Brad, but that can wait. Right now I want to kiss you again." She did, and darned if he put up the slightest struggle.

As Brad led her along the well worn path to the seashore, Lori marveled at the beauty and denseness of the rain forest. A brilliant glow from the still present full moon provided all the light they needed.

"Oh, this is gorgeous!" Lori declared at first sight of the beach. Towering palms lay silhouetted against a backdrop of the moon above calm, black Caribbean waters. Quiet, gentle waves lapped dreamily over the sandy shore providing a setting worthy of the artist's skillful brush. Hand in hand they walked down to the water's edge.

"I can't begin to count the number of nights I stood on this beach and thought of you, Lori," Brad softly observed. "I never dreamed I'd live to see the night when you were here with me."

"It's more beautiful than anyplace I've ever seen, Brad. I'm so glad you at least had this place. Maybe we can come back here sometime. You know, for a vacation."

Brad pulled her around to face him again. "Are you saying you'd like to have me back in your life?"

"That all depends," she smiled. "Are you asking me to be a part of your life again?"

Brad sighed. "My head tells me no," he admitted. "But my heart is turning a deaf ear to my head. Be honest with me, Lori. Could you really be happy with a rusty old character like me, when someone like Howard is yours just for uttering one simple 'yes'?"

"Howard who?" Lori asked, laying a hand to Brad's face. "The only thing rusty about you, Mr. Douglas, is your bright red hair. And that I love just the way it is."

For a long time Brad stood just looking at Lori. Then, taking her hands in his, he said, "Captain Blake said we had to seal our destinies with a kiss of promise before we could go back to our own time, Lori. What do you suppose he meant by that?"

Lori looked deep into his dark blue eyes. "I'm not sure what he meant for your part of the promise," she ventured. "But for my part— I think he meant giving my promise never to let another Howard come between us."

"Could you do that, Lori?"

"In a heartbeat," she said, over the sob that escaped her lips after hearing his question.

"Then I guess that leaves the ball in my court, huh?"

"I guess."

"All right," he gulped. "I give you my promise, pretty lady, to forgive and forget everything that's ever come between us. I love you, Lori. I've always loved you, and I always will."

Tears glistened in Lori's eyes as she looked into this man's face and believed his words. "I give you back my heart, Brad Douglas. It's yours and yours alone. For today—and forever. This is my promise to you."

Brad took her in his arms and they kissed. As they did, the flowers smelled a little sweeter, the breeze felt a little fresher, the music of the night sounded a little fuller, the very island itself seemed to be smiling, and the world instantly became a more beautiful place. As the kiss ended, lightning flashed and thunder rolled. In the night sky a shooting star burst forth in a glory more brilliant than the moon. Somewhere off in the distance a bird started singing. And a smiling old sea captain stood suddenly beside them.

"Aye, matey, and it's proud I am of ye. Now I be askin', be ye ready to go home?"

Lori looked first at Blake, then at Brad. "We be ready, matey," she grinned. "And ye have me thanks for makin' this night the most wonderful of me life."

"That goes for me, too," Brad added with a thumbs-up to Blake. "Take us home, old friend."

The trip back to their own dimension was less dramatic than some of the other transfers through time and location, but it was not without its element of surprise. The first surprise came when Lori realized they hadn't returned to the ice cream parlor at all. They ended up, instead, near the fountain in the outer corridor of the office complex. In fact, the ice cream parlor was no longer there. In its place was the group of offices that should have been there all along. Gone, too, was any sign of Arline Vincent or the other angels.

The second surprise came when Lori realized she was no longer in the red dress, but was again wearing the white blouse and pants suit—and the blouse had never looked brighter. Not one hint of a chocolate stain remained. It took several seconds to put her thoughts straight, and one look at Brad told her he was having the same dilemma.

"Talk about weird," Brad observed. "Did any of this really happen, or am I losing what little mind I have left?"

"It happened," Lori assured him. "And look, the sun is just breaking in the east. It must have taken our whole night."

"You're right, Lori, it is morning. I don't know about you, but I'd say what we did beats watching the *Late Night Show* anytime."

"Umm, me too," Lori said, snuggling next to Brad and kissing him on the cheek. "I never cared that much for Jay Leno anyway. Wanna come to my place for some breakfast?"

"Breakfast sounds great. Uh—where do you live, by the way?"

"I have a condo not far from here. You can follow me there. That is, if you have a car."

Brad laughed. "I have a car, Lori. And if you think about it, I'm sure you can picture exactly what it looks like."

"The Pontiac?" she laughed. "You got that old thing running again?"

"Hey, didn't I tell you that it was a dependable car when we bought it?"

"Oh, yes, that you did. And I told you it was an ugly car, didn't I? If the thing is still running, I guess we were both right, weren't we?"

"If you say so," Brad chuckled. "So how about you, Lori? Did you ever get that sports car you always wanted?"

"Sort of," she responded. "I'm driving a six-year-old Mazda Miata. Of course, I could be driving a Porsche 911 if I were willing to accept it from Howard. He's offered me one at least a dozen times over the years." Lori laughed. "You're the guy I'm in love with, Brad Douglas. And you're a hundred times the man Howard is, but I have to admit he does have better taste in cars than you."

"Humph. Even if I did want a Porsche 911, I could never afford one. You might as well know that up front if you want me back in your life, Lori Parker."

Lori's smile faded. "Lori Parker?" she asked. "Why did you use that name, Brad?"

Brad shrugged. "It is your maiden name, Lori. I just assumed you took it back when you divorced me. I mean, for ten years I thought you were Lori Placard, but . . ."

After a moment or so to think about it, Lori's smile returned. "You're pretty happy with the idea I'm not Lori Placard, aren't you?" she asked.

"You got that right, lady. Come on, I'll walk you to your six-year-old Mazda Miata, if you'll show me where it is."

CHAPTER 14

How long had it been since Lori's last excuse to fix a real breakfast? She had to admit it was great fun, right down to stopping off at the grocery store to pick up the makings. The box of corn flakes and day-old doughnuts she had on hand just didn't seem appropriate somehow. Especially since the excuse for all of this was the return of Brad Douglas to her breakfast table. And if anyone had ever told her she would enjoy washing dishes—well—what could she say? But with Brad on drying duty, she found herself laughing through the whole chore.

With breakfast out of the way, they simply sat and talked. They talked and they laughed. Each had plenty to talk about—after all, there was a decade's worth of catching up to be done. It was nearly eleven when Brad finally suggested he should leave. Even then, Lori wasn't ready to let him go. Not when she was this engrossed in reweaving their lives back into the tapestry of togetherness that should never have come unraveled in the first place.

"You are going to call me, aren't you, Brad?" she persisted as he stepped out her door. "You promised me dinner, you know."

"I'll call," he smiling assured her. "Wild horses couldn't stop me."

She reached out and stroked his lapel. "You'd better, big guy. If you don't, I know where you live, remember? I might even still have a key to the place somewhere."

Brad smiled. "You kept a key to the old place? I like that. It means you never gave up hope on me completely." Taking her in his arms, he kissed her.

What a difference a kiss can make, she marveled to herself. *It was a forbidden kiss that drove Brad out of my life all those years ago. And now, in the warm splendor of a belonging kiss—he's come home to me.*

Melting in his arms, she listened as he whispered softly in her ear, "Just in case I should be of a mind to re-propose to you sometime," he asked, "how elaborate do I have to get?"

She felt goose bumps erupt on her arms at Brad's question. "Pretty elaborate," she whispered back. "And if you're holding a fishing pole at the time, I'll bend it around your neck."

Lori watched the old brown Pontiac until it disappeared at the end of the block, then with a vibrant "Thank you, angels!" she stepped back inside with the idea of getting some sleep and dreaming some wonderful dreams. Not necessarily in that order.

* * *

Brad pulled away from Lori's condo with one thought in mind—and that was Lori. So deep was his concentration, he completely failed to notice the black Cadillac parked two doors down even when it pulled onto the road a short distance behind him. It wasn't until he turned into the driveway of his own house with the Caddy right behind him that he became aware of something strange. By the time he was out of his car, two suspicious-looking men were hurriedly approaching. "Is there something I can do for you gentlemen," he asked uncertainly.

"Yeah," one of the men came back, obviously doing his best to sound gruffly authoritative. "You can get in the Caddy, pal. You have an appointment with a very important man, and we wouldn't want to keep him waiting, would we?"

As Brad looked on in confusion, the man stepped forward and shoved a short-barreled automatic pistol into his ribs. Brad glanced down at the pistol, which brought back vivid memories of James Baxter's attempt at kidnapping Shannon off their island a couple of months back. His first thought was that these men were somehow connected with Baxter. Was it possible that even in death, Baxter's hatred was still reaching out to strangle Shannon? The thought infuriated him to action.

With a lightning-fast backhand, Brad dislodged the gun, sending it flying to the grass several feet away. Before the culprit could gather his wits, Brad had him twisted into a one-armed choke hold. "Stay back!" he yelled at the second man. "Or I may have to rearrange this guy's neck so he's looking where he's been instead of where he's going."

The second fellow appeared stupefied, as if he didn't know what to do next. "I—I've got a gun, too," he stammered, but made no attempt to show a weapon. "Let my brother go, or I'll—I'll . . ."

"Shut up, you idiot!" the constrained man gasped out. "This guy means business. He could break my neck."

"That's right, I could," Brad threatened, applying a little extra pressure. "Who are you guys, and what do you want? Does James Baxter have anything to do with you being here?"

"Take it easy on the neck, pal. We don't know any James Baxter. We're just a couple of guys trying to earn a buck. I'm Lefty Hindricks and this is my brother, Ralph. We do odd jobs for a private eye by the name of Myro Finderman."

"A private detective?" Brad asked. "What would a private detective want with me? You're lying through your teeth! You're here because of James Baxter, admit it!"

"No, pal, I'm not lying, I swear. We're here because some big shot movie producer wants to see you. All we were supposed to do is get you to his office, and that's the truth. Who knows, maybe the guy wants you for the star in his next film."

Brad took a closer look at the pistol lying a few feet away on the ground. To his near disbelief, he realized it was nothing more than a cap gun. "A movie producer?" he asked, his mind shifting from James Baxter to other possibilities of why these men were here. "His name wouldn't be Howard Placard, by any chance, would it?"

"Yeah, that's the guy," Lefty quickly agreed. "Howard Placard."

Brad released Lefty, who quickly joined his brother, where he stood rubbing the feeling back into his throat. "You got a mean streak in you, you know that, pal?" he remarked.

"I've got a mean streak?" Brad scoffed. "Let's take a look at who accosted who here, shall we? Let me get this straight. You were sent here to take me to see Howard Placard?"

"So help me, pal, that's the way it is. If you'll just be kind enough to come along with us, we'll take you to him. You'll be none the worse for the wear, and my brother and me will still be on Myro Finderman's payroll. What's it gonna hurt, eh?"

Brad thought about the proposal. "Exactly where is it you want to take me?" he asked. "Howard Placard has offices all over the city."

"We're supposed to bring you to his home office," Lefty went on to say. "He's expecting you there in the next few minutes."

So the infamous Mr. Placard wants to see me, does he? Brad questioned himself. *The guy's certainly stooped to an all-time low, sending henchmen with toy guns to escort me to his office.* "I don't suppose either of you have any idea why Mr. Placard wants to see me?" he asked.

"I ain't got a clue," Lefty admitted. "All I know is we're supposed to bring you in, and if we fail . . ."

"Well, guys. This may be your lucky day. I'd sort of like to know what Howard Placard has on his mind myself. And since I know how hard it is getting past all the security he surrounds himself with, I may just let you escort me to him."

"Can I have my cap gun back?" Ralph questioned. "You promised nothing would happen to it when I loaned it to you, Lefty."

"Shut up, Ralph!" Lefty barked. "Forget the cap gun. This guy's giving us the chance to come out of this in one piece. After the way you botched it, I'd think you'd be appreciative."

"I botched it? You're the one who suggested flashing a gun. And I need it back. It belongs to my kid."

Brad shook his head. Reaching down, he picked up the cap gun and handed it to Ralph. "Where did Myro Finderman find a couple of guys like you to do his dirty jobs?" he asked. "If there were another one of you, I'd suggest you meet with Howard Placard yourselves. Who knows? He just might be looking for a new Three Stooges act."

"Thanks, man," Ralph said, taking the cap gun. "Myro is my wife's uncle. He hires us for family sake, you know."

"Shut up, Ralph," Lefty said, with a moderately hard slap to his chest. "Myro hires us because we're capable hands, that's all."

"How 'bout if I follow you in my own car?" Brad suggested. "That way, I'll at least have a ride home."

"No, pal," Lefty objected. "We're supposed to bring you in. It wouldn't look good with you driving up in your own car, get it?"

* * *

Samantha glanced up from her desk just in time to see Captain Blake step into the office wearing a smile that easily peeked through his heavy black beard. "Ah, Captain," she said. "How did it go down there? From the look on your face, I'd say Brad and Lori must have enjoyed their little adventure."

"Aye, lassie. Everythin' went the way ye said it would. The wind is full in Brad Douglas' sails, says I. He'll be sailin' on a course straight back to his sweet Lori or me name's not Symington Blake. How did I do on me first voyage, lassie? Would ye be signin' me on for another hitch when the tide rises to the occasion?"

Samantha stood and returned Blake's smile. "You did great, Captain. And yes, I would sign you on for another hitch, as you put it. But you're not quite through with this one yet. Things aren't as rosy on the old home front as you seem to suppose they are."

Blake looked at her skeptically. "By the stars, lassie, me mind cannot grasp what more need be done."

"That's because you're standing watch at the wheel, Captain. You need to climb the mast and get a bird's eye look at the whole of the battle scene."

Captain Blake squinted his left eye. "Ye be puttin' it in words I understands, lassie. Lead me to the mast where I can take a better look for meself."

"I'll be glad to, Captain. First of all, let me jog your memory a notch. When you said good-bye to Brad on the day he left the island for good, do you remember giving him a gift?"

"Aye, lassie, I be rememberin'."

"That gift," Samantha explained, "just happens to be a very big part of the rest of our plan. You see, thanks to our old friend Howard Placard, there's a fly in the ointment, so to speak. Jason's taken the liberty of borrowing your gift from where Brad had it stored, and he has placed it in the capable hands of Bruce Vincent, along with an explanation of what we want him to do with it. Bruce has connections in all sorts of places, thanks to his years as a psychologist to the rich and famous."

Samantha paused and smiled at Blake. "By the way, there's a question I need to ask you, Captain. How are you and Bruce Vincent getting along in your workings on the case? Any problems between the two of you?"

"Nay, lassie, there be no problems. I be quite fond of the lad. We be hittin' it off like longtime shipmates. Be your question one I should concern meself with?"

"No, Captain. No need for you to concern yourself. But Jason had better be concerned. When he gets back here I have a little chore for him to perform. He owes me for a wager, and I intend to claim that payment in writing. I want no less than one hundred words."

"Aye, and it's hopin' I never owes ye payment for a wager meself, says I. Ye seems to be a mean one in that department, lassie."

"Only when it comes to my cute little ghost of a husband, Captain. Now, if you'll be so kind as to pull up a chair, I'll fill you in on the rest of the plan."

* * *

Ralph and Lefty had no trouble getting inside Howard's home, as he had left instructions allowing them to enter. Once inside, they escorted Brad to Howard's home office. The door was open, and they stepped inside, one on each side of Brad. "We got him here, Mr. Placard," Lefty said. "Just like ya wanted us to."

Howard was seated at his massive desk. Brad caught his breath at first sight of the man he hadn't seen since the night Howard had kissed Lori. Strangely, the man hadn't aged at all. He still looked the part of a wealthy producer from his $500 custom-designed shoes to his personalized haircut costing more than most men pay for a three-piece suit. "Hello, Howard," Brad said coolly. "You wanted to see me?"

"Brad," Howard answered with a slight nod. "Yes, I do want to see you, old friend." Howard gave a flick of his wrist toward the door. "You two may leave now," he said to Lefty and Ralph. They stepped from the room without hesitation.

Howard looked back at Brad, who was still standing near the door where he came in. He got right to the point. "I understand you've spent some time on an island in the Caribbean, Brad. So let me ask you, what brings you back here now?"

Brad laughed dryly. "You've done your homework, I see. But actually I think I'm the one entitled to some answers. To start with, why am I here in your office? If you plan on asking me to direct a movie,

I'll have to decline. I have more pressing matters to spend my time on these days."

Howard smiled ever so slightly. "I think we both know I won't be asking you to direct any movies, Brad Douglas. Let's get straight to the point. I understand you've been spending some time with Lori. Is that right?"

"Well, Howard, not that it's any of your business, but I have seen Lori. That shouldn't come as a surprise to any clear-thinking individual. She is the woman I was married to until a slimy snake slithered out of the tall grass to take her away from me. Now that she understands just how slimy that snake is—who knows what might transpire between the two of us?"

Howard crumpled up a paper he had been looking over and threw it hard into the waste basket next to his desk. "You call me childish names," he said pointing a huge finger at Brad. "Truth be known, I'm more of a shining knight on a fine steed than a snake in the grass. Lori deserves more than someone of your caliber has to offer. This may come as a surprise to you, but I happen to be in love with her. I intend to have her as my own one day."

"Aren't you forgetting something, Howard? Lori doesn't want you or your lifestyle. I think she's made that pretty clear to anyone willing to listen to what she's been saying."

Howard's hand rolled into a tight fist which he held up in Brad's direction. "That's where you're wrong, Brad Douglas. I'm not sure what she's told you in an effort to spare your feelings, but she's made it plain to me that she doesn't want you around ever again. I'm the one she came to for help in divorcing you."

Brad broke out laughing. "You think of yourself as a shining knight," he snorted. "Well, someone should tell you just how rusty your armor is, Howard. All the lies you can conjure up won't change the fact that I'm the one Lori loves. There'll be a new wedding real soon, and by the way—you're not invited."

"I'M THE ONE LORI LOVES!!!" Howard shouted, standing abruptly and shaking his fist violently. "Has she even told you of the time the two of us spent together? We've traveled all over the world these last years. And yes, we do stay in the same room at night, in case you're wondering."

Brad shook his head. "What's happened to you, Howard?" he said. "I never thought I'd see the day you'd reach such a low. It wasn't enough you tried to steal my wife; now you've become a liar. What does a man have left, if his word no longer has any value?"

Howard raised his head and stared down the point of his nose at Brad. "Step over here next to this window," he said, doing his best to prove he was the one in control of this conversation. "I'd like to show you something."

Brad hesitated a moment, then accommodated by joining Howard next to the window.

"Take a look out there," Howard said, pointing through the wall-length window. "Tell me what you see, Brad."

"I see a beach," Brad said with a shrug. "So what? I've seen hundreds of beaches in my lifetime. I just spent ten years looking at one nicer than this."

"A beach nicer than this one?" Howard snickered. "Ha! I doubt that. This is the finest beach for hundreds of miles around. And I own every inch of it. I own an entire empire, Brad. And part of that empire, as you should be keenly aware, is my controlling interest in our local motion picture studios. By the way, I happen to know you went there looking for work recently. Too bad there was nothing available for a man of your past talents."

Brad threw up both hands in a gesture of disgust. "All right, Howard. I concede to your wealth. So what? I'll get by without directing any of your films and you'll be the one losing in that deal, believe me."

"This has nothing to do with your directing, Brad. This has to do strictly with Lori."

"Give it a rest, Howard. Your empire will never see Lori's shadow on the wall. She's all mine."

Anger flared in Howard's eyes. "Why would you say something like that, Brad, when you know perfectly well you don't love her?"

"I don't love her? What an asinine thing to say, Howard. Even you couldn't be that blind."

"And I suppose you think she doesn't love me," Howard pressed.

"You got that right, Howard," Brad said with a harsh laugh. "I can't believe you still think Lori could love you after all that she's done to convince you otherwise."

Howard's face twisted into a sly grin. "We both know how you led me to believe you wanted an excuse to get her out of your life all those years ago. And how you encouraged me to show an interest in her in the hope she would take the initiative and ask you for a divorce."

Brad couldn't believe what he was hearing. "I think you've lost your mind, Howard. You're raving like a maniac."

"You do know I could have you thrown out of my office for saying that, don't you, Brad?"

"Of course I know that, Howard. But you're the one who brought me here in the first place."

What Howard said next left Brad thinking he had really gone off the deep end. "You're here after my money, aren't you, Brad. Go ahead, admit it. You want money from me."

Brad shook his head. "You want me to say I want money from you, is that it? Would you mind telling me what it is you suppose I want your money for?"

"You want money so you can run off and hide again, just like you did before."

Brad stared at Howard, and struggled to make sense of this conversation. "I see," he said, releasing a slow breath. "I want to drop off the edge of the world just like I did before. I never want to see Lori again because I don't love her. And I want money from you to pay for my getaway. I think you should be seeking some counseling, buster. You've lost it."

Howard let out a burst of loud laughter. "Thank you, my friend. You have no idea the gift you've just handed me. And just to put the record straight, you are nothing but a fool. Lori lied to you once, and she's still lying to you. She belongs to me now, just as she has since I took her away from you ten years ago. And there's nothing you can do about it. Yes, I use my money and power to get what I want. It works, Brad. It'll work just as well with you as with anyone or anything else I set out to control. I know your weakness, and I have no reservations using that weakness against you. I'll come to the point. Ten years ago you vanished into the night as though the world had swallowed you up. That's what you're about to do again, Brad. Only this time, you're never to show your face around this place again."

"Oh, I see," Brad snorted. "This fantasy you have that you can somehow turn Lori's head your way is in jeopardy with me around. You want me out of the picture again. Well you can forget it, Howard.

You took my life from me once, I'm not giving you that pleasure a second time."

"I think you'll change your mind when you hear what I have to say. I've already mentioned knowing your weakness. You see, Brad, because I own controlling interest in the motion picture studio, I hold several hundred lives in the palm of my hand. I'm talking about people you've known and worked with from your earliest days in the business. Now I ask you, what would happen to all those people if something should persuade me to close down the studio. I'll tell you what would happen, the lot of them would end up on the street, that's what. And just in case you think they could get work elsewhere, think about yourself, Brad. Once on Howard Placard's black list, working in the motion picture industry no longer comes easy."

Brad was stunned by this unexpected turn of events. "No, Howard. Even you wouldn't stoop that low."

"I would and I will. You have my word on it, Brad. I'll be watching you like a hawk. If you blow your nose, I'll know about it before you toss away the Kleenex. Now listen to what I'm telling you—if you so much as blink in Lori's direction, or even try to call her, I'll close down the studio so fast you won't have time to think. Is that understood, Mr. Douglas?"

Brad's mind whirled in confusion. How could this be happening? After watching a decade of nightmares end in one wonderful evening, now he faced a new dilemma even worse than the first. How was this possible? Wasn't it true that the very angels were on his side? Was it possible that even angels were subject to Howard Placard's control?

Never had Brad felt so helpless—so totally empty. What was he to do? How could he be responsible for costing all those people their jobs? But on the other hand, how could he walk away from Lori again?

Howard let out a cruel laugh. "I see by your silence you get my drift, old friend. And just to show you I'm not without a heart, I'll give you a little something to help with your next vanishing act. Say—a couple hundred grand? How does that sound? You can live pretty high on the pork with that kind of money, provided you pick the right spot to disappear."

"I don't want your money, Howard," Brad spit back. "And don't call me 'friend.' You gave up that title in my book a long time ago."

"Suit yourself about the money, I never make an offer more than once. But mark my words, any attempt on your part to contact Lori—any attempt at all—and the studio is history."

Brad gathered his courage for one last attack, feeble though it appeared. "I don't know how I'm going to do it, but I'm going to beat you this time, Howard. To quote an old friend, 'Ye has me word on it, and I never goes back on me word'."

Howard laughed all the harder. "If I were you I'd tell that friend to take some speech therapy, and as for you—I'd get a grip on reality. You can't beat me, Brad. I'm a powerful man and I always get what I go after. Right now, I'm going after Lori, and there's nothing you can do to stop me. Now unless you have anything more to say, I'll have my people take you home."

"Forget it, Howard. I'll walk."

"Suit yourself, Brad. I couldn't care less if you want to play the martyr. Just be sure you stay away from Lori. Understood?"

Brad didn't bother with an answer. Stepping out of Howard's home office, he made his way to the front door. By the time he made it, three security guards were there to greet him. One of them blocked the door. "You want to move aside?" Brad grumbled. "I'm in no mood for games at the moment."

"It's all right," Howard called from behind him. "Let the man out."

The security guard stepped aside, and Brad hurried through the door into the late morning sunshine. Scores of thoughts passed through his mind as he walked away from Howard Placard's lavish home. Had he made a mistake in not accepting Howard's offer to at least drive him back home? It was at least five miles to the nearest pay phone where Brad could call a taxi. Funny how walking on an open sidewalk seemed so much more unpleasant than traipsing through the rain forest of his island home for the past ten-plus years. Of course the heat of the open sun was not the only thing bothering Brad right now. Confusion still ran rampant through the halls of his mind at Howard's threat to sell the motion picture studio. Talk about a no-win situation—either he would submit and turn his back on Lori or hundreds of his friends would be out of their jobs in the industry.

Brad turned a corner and started down a long stretch of road paralleling the beach when he noticed a red Mustang convertible with the top down coming toward him from the far end of the block. As the car drew near, it slowed and pulled up alongside where he was walking.

"You're Brad Douglas, I assume," the driver said as he brought the Mustang to a stop.

"That's right," Brad responded warily, as he eyed this stranger closely.

The fellow leaned across and opened the passenger door. "You look like you could use a ride, Brad. And besides, we need to talk. Get in."

* * *

As the sun went down that evening, Brad had to admit, this had been a day of many twists and turns. Would Captain Blake allow Howard to win out once all the chips had fallen? Brad couldn't believe his old friend would let this happen. He had to wonder, Was this afternoon's meeting with the man in the red Mustang one of chance, or could it be this meeting was part of a plan put together by Captain Blake and his angel friends. Only time would bring a final answer to this question.

One thing for sure, Brad knew he had to write the letter. There was no other choice—not if the studio was to be protected from the immediate threat of closure. Setting up his laptop, Brad bit the bullet and typed in some of the hardest words he had ever been forced to author.

> *Howard, You probably know I won't stand by and see you close the studio. With this in mind, I feel I have no choice, but to concede to your terms. You can keep the money. I want no part of that. However, if dropping off the face of the earth will keep the studio open, I suppose I have little choice but to comply. I have some friends in Johannesburg, South Africa. I'm sure they can help me get a start there. You provide the airfare to Johannesburg, and give me your word not to close the studio, and I'll catch the plane. The ball is in your court, Howard. Let me know of your next play. Brad Douglas*

Three days later the tickets were in Brad's hands. By this time Brad knew for sure that Captain Blake's hand had been in the meeting. For better or for worse, the die was cast.

CHAPTER 15

Lori was a little surprised, and more than a little disappointed when several days passed without Brad's call. Getting through her daily activities took all the energy she could muster when her every thought was drawn like a giant magnet to the anticipation of HIS call. At least it was Friday, and at least she didn't have any clients scheduled for the weekend. It was pretty easy to get away from the office for an early afternoon lunch. She drove herself to the North Side Mall where she had called in reservations for one at the Texas Star Steakhouse. She was shown to her table and handed a menu that she looked over with little enthusiasm. Eating alone was not her idea of excitement. Oh well, she would just have to be patient. Surely Brad would call soon, making good on his promise for dinner. She decided on the New York cut and lay the menu aside just in time to see Howard Placard approaching her table.

Oh, no, she cringed inside. *What does he want? What rotten luck! I wish for Brad and I get Howard. Where's the justice, anyway?*

"Good afternoon, Lori," Howard said in a cheery voice that irritated Lori to the quick. "I see you're eating alone. May I join you?"

Lori explored her options. She could simply stand and walk out without saying a word. But then Howard would probably just follow her. She might tell him to get lost, that she wanted to eat alone, but that could cause an unpleasant scene, which she certainly was in no mood for. No, the only thing to do was swallow her frustration and invite him to sit down. Too bad she didn't have one of those angels here to zap her to a different scene like they had done in the holographic replay the other night.

"Hello, Howard," she responded coldly. "Pull up a chair. You can share my menu, I've already decided what I'm having."

Howard sat down just as the waitress approached the table. "May I get either of you something to drink?" she asked politely.

"Water, please," Lori answered. "And I'm ready to order, too, if that's okay. I'll have the New York Steak, medium well with baked potato, and hold the sour cream. For my salad, the light Italian dressing sounds good."

The waitress wrote the order, then turned to Howard. "And you, sir?"

Howard didn't bother with the menu. "Make mine the same, except I'll go with the bleu cheese dressing."

As the waitress walked away, Lori opened the conversation with a pointed question. "Okay, Howard, how did you know I was here? Wait—let me guess. You're still having me watched, right?"

Howard's chest expanded with a deep breath. "I'm sorry, Lori, but I feel I must keep a close check on you right now. When I learned that Brad had returned, I called Myro Finderman's detective agency and asked to have you guarded. It's for your own good, Lori. There's no telling what that man might do. I just don't trust him."

Lori scowled. "You know how I feel about your having me watched. I've asked you over and over to let it rest, Howard. Now you're at it again."

"With Brad on the loose, I'm left with little choice, Lori. I know he's made contact with you. How many times have I warned you about ever seeing him again?"

"Who I see and who I don't see is none of your business. And as for Brad ever hurting me—that is preposterous. I'm telling you once and for all, call off your watchdogs, and stay out of my life."

Howard refused to drop the point. "Lori, Lori, Lori, how can you be so naive? Even if Brad never hurts you physically—and I'm not giving up the idea he might—you know perfectly well he'll walk out on you again just as before. The man is irrational. I can't stand seeing you hurt by one of his disappearing acts again."

Lori paused in thought. "You've pulled another one of your shenanigans, haven't you? That's why Brad hasn't called; you're meddling in my affairs again." Sudden anger filled Lori's eyes. "Tell me the truth, Howard. You've seen Brad yourself, haven't you?"

Howard picked up a knife and began drumming it lightly against the table. "I admit, I did see Brad," he said, without looking Lori in the face. "Brad came to my home office asking for money."

Lori narrowed her eyes. "Brad asked you for money? That's pretty hard to believe, Howard," she said.

"It's not hard when you know the whole truth of the matter, Lori. There are things about Brad I've never told you. I've always kept them to myself in order to spare your feelings. Now that he's back, I've decided it's time to bring these things to light."

"What are you getting at, Howard?" Lori said impatiently. "What things have you supposedly kept from me?"

Howard still would not look Lori in the eye. Instead, he stared at the knife in his hand. "Ten years ago, when I sent Brad to Acapulco so you and I could have some time to get acquainted—I always told you that was solely my idea. Actually, Lori, that wasn't quite true. You see, Brad knew about my feelings for you. I often told him how I envied him for having you waiting there when he came home every night. One day, out of the blue, he came to me with a striking confession. He told me he didn't love you anymore."

"That's a lie, Howard, and you know it!" Lori countered angrily.

"No, Lori, it's not a lie," Howard insisted. "Brad explained how you were the only one he had ever dated, and that marrying you had turned out to be a mistake. He's the one who suggested I show some interest in you. He wanted out of your marriage, but he didn't have the courage to ask for a divorce. At first I opposed him, but I have to admit, Lori, I was in love with you the whole time. So, I was finally persuaded to go along with the idea. I'm sorry now I did. If I'd stayed out of it, Brad probably would have gone ahead with the divorce and then I could have courted you properly."

Lori stared in disbelief at the man across the table from her. "What is with you, Howard?" she accused him. "You're lying, and we both know it. How can you stoop this low?"

"I'm not lying, Lori, and I have the proof. Let's finish lunch, and then if you'll take a little ride with me I'll show you."

Lori stood and shouldered her purse. "Suddenly I'm not hungry, Howard. I've listened to all your lies I can handle. Enjoy your steak, and the bill's on you."

* * *

As Lori walked away, Howard quickly removed a one-hundred-dollar bill from his wallet and dropped it to the table with the intention of following after her. When he stood, he suddenly found himself looking in the face of an old acquaintance who managed to position himself directly in Howard's intended path.

"Hello, Howard," Bruce Vincent said, extending his hand as he spoke. "How long has it been since we last saw each other?"

"Uh, hello, Bruce." Howard leaned to the right trying to catch a glimpse of Lori, but Bruce leaned in the same direction blocking his view.

"So how's business in the movie industry?" Bruce asked, maintaining his trumped-up stall maneuver.

Howard was growing impatient. "The movie industry is fine, Bruce," he answered sharply with a quick handshake. "But if you'll excuse me, right now I have some pressing business to attend to."

"What's the hurry, Howard? You have your henchmen watching Lori. You can catch up with her later on."

Howard froze in his steps and stared at Bruce. "What do you know about Lori?" he asked, his demeanor turning from impatient to demanding.

"I know a lot more than you might think, Howard. I know about how you broke her and Brad apart once, and I know you're planning on a repeat performance. I'm here to give you a warning, Howard. Back off, while you still have the chance. Because if you don't, you'll have me to contend with. And if you think those henchmen of yours are thorough, you should get a load of my supporters. They're a bunch of real angels."

Howard exploded in contempt. "I'll have you to contend with?" he scoffed. "You're getting a little big for your britches with remarks like that, Bruce. I have no idea what your game is here, but my advice to you is stay out of my way. I'll steam roll you into the ground so deep, a well digger won't be able to find you. Now get out of my way!"

Bruce still refused to let Howard pass. "I know exactly what you're up to, Howard," he said firmly. "My supporters have been glued to you like trained hounds on a fox. I know every move you've made for the past month, Howard. And I do mean EVERY move. Now listen up, this is my final warning. Back away from Brad and Lori, or you have my word—there will be consequences. And you can take my word for it, you won't like the consequences."

Howard attempted to push Bruce aside, but since Bruce was the larger of the two men, Howard got nowhere in his effort. "I'll have your head on a platter for this!" Howard loudly threatened. "No one makes a fool of Howard Placard and gets away with it."

Bruce smiled. "Can I take it you're rejecting my warning then?" he asked.

"Your warning? HA!" Howard countered. "Your warning means about as much to me as a canary warning a cat. As for you, I'd say you had better watch your back. And while you're at it, you can tell your wife she can kiss her television career good-bye. As of today, her show is history."

"Have it your way, Howard," Bruce said, stepping to one side. "But just remember, I warned you."

* * *

After leaving Howard at the restaurant, Lori headed immediately for her car and drove away as fast as possible. She was sure Howard was lying about most of what he had told her, but she did believe he had something to do with why Brad hadn't called. Determined to get at the bottom of the matter, she headed the car south toward the old house. That would be the best place to begin looking for Brad and find Brad she must. Her whole life depended on it.

* * *

By the time Howard managed to work his way around Bruce, it was too late. Lori was nowhere in sight. Removing the cellular phone from his jacket, he dialed Myro Finderman.

"Myro, here," came the fast response. "To whom do I have the pleasure of speaking?"

"This is Howard. I lost Lori at the Texas Star Steakhouse. Do your boys have her covered?"

"Oh, yeah, pal. My boys got her covered. Do you want I should check with them for her whereabouts?"

"That's exactly what I want, Finderman. Get back with me on this one ASAP. And what about Brad? Did you get the videos of him boarding the plane and give them to my crew at the studio like I instructed?"

"Had 'em there by noon, boss. Just like you wanted."

Howard laughed into the phone. "You did good, Finderman, and if these videos turn out half as good as I'm hoping, there'll be a little something extra in your check to show my appreciation. Now find out where Lori's gone, and get back to me when you do. Timing is very delicate right now, and I don't want any slip-ups."

Howard hit the "End" button on his phone to terminate this conversation, then immediately dialed in a second number. This time he reached the security desk at the filming studio. "Walt, this is Howard," he said. "By any chance, is Steve still in the cutting room working on the project I gave him?"

"Yes, Mr. Placard. As a matter of fact, he is. About an hour ago, he called and asked me to have someone from the cafeteria take him in a sandwich. He told me he was nearing completion on your project. Would you like me to transfer your call there?"

"That's why I'm calling. I want to make sure everything is moving along according to schedule."

"Hold on, sir. I'll transfer you."

There was silence for the space of a few seconds, then another male voice came on the line. "Howard? Steve here. How's it going, man?"

"That's what I was about to ask you. Is the video about finished?"

"Just putting the finishing touches on it now, Howard."

"Ah, good. How'd it turn out? Will it pass for the genuine article?"

"Oh it'll do that, all right, Howard. It's a masterpiece, if I do say so myself. And I have the audio tape you wanted, too. I talked Herb Sullivan into cutting it for me. Herb is the best there is at impersonating another's voice. In a way it's funny, turning one of Brad's tricks around so he's the goat this time. That guy's a pretty darn good impressionist himself."

Howard was elated. "Good, good, good. Now I want you to get these items to my yacht, along with the equipment necessary to play them both. How soon can you have them there?"

"Half an hour. Forty minutes at the longest. Is there anything else you'll be needing me for after that? I have a hot date lined up for tonight, and I'd really hate to let the lady down, if you know what I mean."

"Just get the stuff to my yacht, Steve, and you can have the whole weekend to yourself."

Howard hit the "End" button again and slid the cell phone back into his pocket. A cruel smile crossed his lips as the thought came to mind that he, too, was anticipating a hot date for the weekend. Lori just didn't know it yet. Walking to his Cadillac, he sat inside and waited for Myro Finderman's return call telling him where he could find Lori.

* * *

Lori pulled to a stop in front of the old house. It looked different in the light of reality than it had looked in the holographic replay. She hurried to the door and rang the bell. There was no answer. Without hesitation, she looked in the flower pot for the spare key. To her great relief, it was there. Stepping inside the house brought cold chills along with deep nostalgia. Calling out Brad's name, she made a search of the entire house. A check of the garage found the old Pontiac missing. Her heart pounded as she searched her mind for any clue where she might find him. Then it hit her. The answering machine. There might be some clue to his whereabouts on the machine. Quickly she made her way to the phone and pressed the play-back button. To her complete and utter shock, she heard Arline Vincent's voice.

Bruce, I know you and Brad are supposed to be at the movie studio, but on the off chance you get this message, give me a call. I just had a visit from Sam, and she brought a red folder by that will knock your socks off. The papers in the folder concern some of Howard's financial dealings. Call me if you hear this, okay? Love ya!

"The movie studio?" Lori asked herself. "Why would Brad go with Bruce Vincent to the movie studio? No matter, girl. You had better get to that studio as fast as possible." She had no way of knowing how old the message was, but maybe someone at the studio could at least give her a lead, even if Brad wasn't there now.

Lori turned and headed out of the house. To her disbelief, she stepped from the door to find Howard waiting on the front porch.

"What are you doing here?" she shouted at him. "What right do you have following me all over this city?"

"We have to talk, Lori," Howard insisted. "I have some information about Brad that will prove what I was telling you back at the restaurant is true."

"Get out of my way, Howard," Lori said as she brushed past him on the way to her car. She twisted the key and heard the starter grind, but the car refused to start. A quick glance out her window revealed the problem. There stood Howard, holding an ignition wire he had presumably taken from her engine while she was in the house.

"Why are you doing this, Howard?" she pleaded. "You and I have nothing to talk about. Put that wire back where it belongs so I can start my car."

"Get in the Cadillac," Howard insisted. "Showing you my proof is extremely important to me, and I refuse to take 'no' for an answer."

Lori got out of her car and slammed the door. Without a word, she started back toward the house, intending to call a taxi. Howard caught her roughly by the arm. "Listen to me, Lori!" he shouted. "You asked if I knew where Brad is. The answer is yes, I do know where he is, and I'll be glad to show you if you'll give me the chance."

"Stop it, Howard! You're hurting my arm. If you know where Brad is, then tell me here and now."

"I'm sorry I have to do it this way, but I insist on you seeing my proof. I give you my word, I will tell you where he is if you'll only come with me now."

Lori couldn't remember Howard ever being more adamant than now. He was frightening her, and her arm throbbed from his grip. "What is going on with you, Howard?" she pleaded. "I've never seen you like this. Why won't you just tell me where Brad is and face the fact the two of us are getting back together again. Nothing you can show me will change that one tiny bit."

"You're wrong, Lori. What I have to show you will come as a cold shock, but I guarantee it will change your mind about some things. And I give you my word, if you don't come with me now and let me show you these things, you'll never see Brad again as long as you live!"

Lori stared at Howard. "Is that a threat?" she gasped. "Because if it is . . ."

"It's not a threat, Lori. It's merely a statement of fact. Now, please, get in the Cadillac and let me enlighten your mind to some things you've never understood."

For a long time Lori stood looking at Howard. What was he up to? A rush of thoughts passed through her mind. Why hadn't Brad called her? What did Howard know about Brad that he wasn't telling? Was Brad in some kind of danger? Would Howard go so far in his obsessed efforts as to kidnap Brad? Much as she hated to admit it, there was only one way to find out. If she wanted Howard to open up with what he knew, then she would have to give in to doing it his way. "Where is it you want me to go with you?" she asked coldly.

"That's my girl," Howard smiled. "Get in the Cadillac and I'll show you where we're going. I'd rather not tell you just yet. It would spoil the surprise."

Lori still hesitated. "I've seen some of the things you've had in mind for me in the past, Howard. I'm in no mood for any of it now. Just show me what you know about Brad and get it over with."

"Get in the car," Howard pressed. "You have my word. Nothing bad is going to happen to you."

Not knowing what else to do, Lori walked to Howard's Cadillac and got in. She sat staring straight ahead as he closed the door and rounded the car to his own side. Seconds later, Howard had the car in motion. "Well, would you get a load of this," Lori observed coolly. "Howard Placard driving his own limo. What happened, another chauffeur walk off and leave you?"

Howard shot her an accusing glance. "I don't need a chauffeur for what I have in mind right now," he quickly affirmed. "I'm perfectly capable of driving my own vehicle when I chose to."

The drive took a little over half an hour, and Lori soon realized they were headed in the direction of his private beach. Several times Howard tried to lure her into conversation, but she remained stone silent the entire trip.

At last Howard pulled off the highway and drove a short distance along a rock-covered road to the docking pier where he kept his yacht moored. Lori had heard about Howard's yacht, but had never seen it for herself. When she caught sight of it, it was just as luxurious as she supposed it would be. "Are you expecting me to get on that yacht with you?" she asked as he parked the car and proceeded to step out.

Howard closed his door and leaned in the open window. "What I have to show you needs to be seen in privacy," he explained. "Surely after all this time you have no fears about being alone with me on my yacht?"

Lori opened her own door and stepped from the car where she stood staring at the fabulous yacht. "Why not just tell me here and now what it is you want me to see, Howard? Why ask me to go alone with you on the yacht when you know perfectly well I'd rather not? In fact, you know what this reminds me of, Howard," Lori continued. "It reminds me of the night you brought me home after luring me alone to your island. I tried to talk you out of walking me to the door, but no—you insisted. That's when you kissed me in front of Brad, and sent my life tumbling into chaos for the next ten-plus years. How do I know you're not setting me up for another experience like that one? How can I be sure that's not your motive for getting me on your yacht?"

Suddenly, as if from out of nowhere, a man appeared standing next to Howard. No, a second look revealed it wasn't a man at all, it was . . .

"To be puttin' yer mind at ease, lassie, this blackguard can neither see nor hear me, says I. So just hold yer tongue and listen to what I be sayin' to ye."

The sight of Captain Blake was such a relief to Lori, her heart leapt inside her. A bright smile crossed her face, and she nodded her understanding of what the captain was saying. Seeing her smile, Howard misunderstood it to mean she was warming up to his wishes.

"The yacht does look pretty inviting, doesn't it, Lori?" he grinned. "You have my word, Brad is nowhere around. In fact, he's probably half way to Johannesburg, South Africa, by now. At least that's where he told me he intended to disappear to this time."

"Play along with him, lassie," Blake instructed. "It be part of our plan. Aye, and ye have me word no harm will come to ye. Not so long as Captain Blake is on hand. Especially once I gets me sea legs under me on this here fancy cutter."

Lori felt as if a ton had been lifted from her shoulders. "All right, Howard. I'll come aboard with you. And I'll look at whatever it is you want to show me. Lead the way."

* * *

Now we're cooking, Howard reasoned to himself. *It was the sight of my yacht that won her over. Never underestimate the power of wealth. In the end, it wins out every time.*

Howard extended his arm, and was pleasantly surprised when she slipped her own arm through his. After escorting her onto the pier and up the ramp to the boat, he paused on deck long enough to press a switch that automatically raised the ramp.

"Why are you raising the ramp, Howard? Are you planning on taking the yacht out to sea?" Lori asked.

"I said we needed privacy, Lori. Surely you're not worried about a boat ride with me, are you?"

Though Howard didn't know it, Lori's answer came only after checking to see that Captain Blake was still near and still smiling. "No, Howard. I'm not worried. Not at all."

Howard was elated. Maybe Brad's sudden return had been a blessing in disguise. For the ten years he was gone, Howard hadn't made one inch of headway at winning Lori's heart. Now, with the little masterpiece of art he had waiting to present to her, maybe things could finally work out between them.

* * *

Lori stood next to Howard as he maneuvered the yacht out of the channel onto the open sea beyond. The view was spectacular. Several sea gulls hung majestically on the smooth breeze, adding their own special touch to the already beautiful early evening sky. Lori drew in a deep breath of the tangy sea air and wished she were here with Brad, instead of Howard. About twenty minutes out, Howard cut the engine and let the boat drift to a stop.

"This will do nicely," he smiled at Lori. "Let's step to the front of the yacht where I have everything ready to give you the show I promised."

Howard led the way with Lori close behind. Near the bow of the boat, he had prepared a table with a VCR and tape recorder on it. Howard pulled out a chair for Lori, who stood looking at the setup. "You're planning to show me one of your movies?" she asked.

"I do plan on showing you a movie of a sort," Howard agreed. "However, this movie stars our own Brad Douglas. And I really don't think you have any idea what you're about to see and hear from the man. Sit down, Lori. I'm sure this will come as a shock to you."

Lori sat down and watched as Howard picked up a video tape from the table and inserted it in the VCR. "The first part of this video was shot in my home office," he explained. "You see, for security reasons, I keep several surveillance cameras running constantly. A few days ago, Brad came to my home and insisted on seeing me. When my security people informed me of his presence, I had them bring him in. I'd like to show you some excerpts from the tapes on my surveillance cameras."

Howard hit the "Play" button. The screen lit up and Lori focused in. She had never seen Howard's office, but from its elaborate appearance, it fit what she would have imagined perfectly. "That's me at my office window," Howard explained. "I'm about to invite Brad to have a look outside."

Lori watched intently as the video began to play.

* * *

"*Take a look out there,*" *Howard said, pointing through the wall-length window.* "*Tell me what you see, Brad.*"

"*I see a beach, so what? I've seen hundreds of beaches in my lifetime. I just spent ten years looking at one nicer than this.*"

"*A beach nicer than this one?*" *Howard snickered.* "*Ha! I doubt that. This is the finest beach for hundreds of miles around. And I own every inch of it.*"

"*All right, Howard, I concede to your wealth. So what?*"

"*You're right, Brad. This conversation has nothing to do with my wealth, does it? This has to do with Lori, and with the fact you don't love her in the slightest.*"

"*You got that right, Howard.*"

* * *

Lori caught her breath at Brad's statement. Was he actually agreeing with Howard's contention that Brad no longer loved her? There had to be some mistake. She must have heard wrong. She listened more closely as the video tape continued.

* * *

Howard continued, "We both know how you led me to believe you wanted an excuse to get her out of your life all those years ago. And how you encouraged me to show an interest in her in the hope she would take the initiative and ask you for a divorce."

"Of course I know that, Howard. I want to drop off the edge of the world just like I did before. I never want to see Lori again because I don't love her. And I want money from you to pay for my getaway."

* * *

"No!" Lori cried. "Something has to be wrong. Brad wouldn't say those things."

Howard shrugged. "Sorry, Lori, but Brad did say those things. You see, he's been putting on an act for you for a very long time now. I have no idea why he came back after being gone all those years, but it certainly wasn't to be a part of your life again, no matter what he may have told you. Just keep watching the video and you'll learn what Brad did with the money he talked me out of. The next part of the video was shot by the men from the private detective agency I have working for me. They followed Brad to the airport only this morning and caught him on tape catching a plane to Johannesburg, South Africa, just like I mentioned earlier."

Lori could hardly believe her eyes as she witnessed Brad disappearing into a 757, luggage in hand. "There has to be a mistake," she whispered.

"There's no mistake, Lori," Howard assured her. "I'm sure you don't want to watch the next ten minutes of tape showing that Brad never left the plane before departure, but it's there if you need further proof. And that's not all I have either. I'd like you to listen to this audio tape Brad made and left with me at the end of our meeting."

Howard pressed the "Play" button on the audio tape player. As Lori listened with stunned attention, she heard Brad's voice speaking directly to her.

Hi, Lori. I'm sorry to have to say good-bye to you this way, but after giving our future a great deal of consideration, I've come to the conclusion it's best for me to go away again. This time for good. I know we had a great marriage once, but people change. I changed. I'm not sure why I came back this time, but whatever the reason I've found I feel nothing of the old love I had for you. Forgive me. I've asked Howard for enough money to give me a new start in a remote part of the world, and he graciously obliged. The guy really loves you, Lori. He can give you the life you deserve if you'll only let him. Well, I have some packing to do before catching a plane to nowhere. See you around someday, kid.

Lori sat speechless for nearly a minute after the tape ended. Slowly, she rose and walked to the bow of the ship where she stood with her long blond hair flowing delicately to the rhythm of the brisk sea breeze brushing past her face. There, she contemplated the possibility of a future with the only man she had ever loved. The tears that might have moistened her eyes were quickly dried by the wind. Howard stood just behind her. Good old Howard. How many times she wished she had never met this man, or even so much as heard his name? But, she did meet him. That chapter of her life was well behind her now—just as were so many of her dreams. She felt Howard's hand on her shoulder as he carefully pulled her around to face him.

"It's over for you and him, Lori," Howard said, with a pleading in his eyes that sent cold chills through her. "Can't you see that now? Give me the chance to make you happy as I know I can."

Before Lori knew what was happening, Howard took her left hand in his and slid a diamond band on her finger. "You know how I feel about you," he continued. "Take this ring, say 'yes,' and make me the happiest man in the world."

Lori stared at the ring. Apprehension filled every corner of her mind as the fullness of Howard's intentions became vividly clear. Here, in the shadow of all that had happened these last few days, he was asking her to marry him. He was offering her yachts, a beach home, fine cars, life in the fast lane—he was even willing to accept the fact that she didn't love him.

Instinctively, Lori's right hand moved to the gold chain around her neck. The chain Brad had given her so long ago. The chain that held a secret known only to Lori, and to none else.

"All you have to do is say the word, Lori. My yacht is stocked with supplies. I have enough gas to sail anywhere you desire. I've taken the liberty to fill one closet with clothes bought especially for you, Lori. Another closet holds my own clothes. Just tell me where you want to go, and we're on our way. We can be married at the first port we come to. Say the word, Lori. Hawaii? The Phillippines? Tahiti? Any place you name is yours for the asking. What about it, Lori? Do we have a deal?"

Just then, Captain Blake came back into Lori's view. With all she had just seen, she had momentarily forgotten about the captain. "Don't be disturbed by what ye've just seen, says I," Blake comforted her. "It all be lies, lassie. Don't be forgettin' this culprit be one who produces these picture shows ye be so familiar with. He has what is called a *cuttin' room* at his disposal as well as folks who can be imitating Brad's very own voice. I don't suppose you'll be havin' much trouble figurin' out how he made Brad appear to be sayin' these blackened lies, will ye, lassie?"

Lori broke into a smile as the captain spoke. He was right, of course. The video was a fake, and so was the audio tape. Looking deep into Howard's eyes, she gave him her answer. "Yes, Howard. I will marry you. I love you so much it hurts."

A giant smile covered Howard's face. "Oh, darling, that's wonderful. You'll never regret your decision, I promise."

Then, as Howard looked on in dismay, Lori pulled off the ring and shoved it into his shirt pocket. "There, that should prove I can lie as well as you when I set my mind to it, Howard. Although I've never gone so far as to manufacture a trumped-up video and audio tapes to perpetuate one of my lies."

Howard felt the ring in his pocket and glared at Lori. "How can you not believe what you saw and heard?" he asked abruptly. "It was Brad's own face you saw, and his voice."

"Give it up, Howard. I can't believe a producer with your reputation would try to pawn off a botched video like that one as real. Now do me a favor, will you? Get this boat back to shore so I can call a taxi to take me home."

"No!" Howard shouted. "I refuse to take you home. This yacht is equipped to sustain us as long as necessary for you to change your mind; and by all the power I hold, I refuse to take you home until you do."

"What are you saying, Howard? You're talking about kidnapping here. You can't get away with holding me on this yacht against my will."

"When you're as rich as I am, you can get away with anything. All it takes is a good lawyer, and believe me—I have the best. I'm not taking you ashore. Not until you agree to marry me."

CHAPTER 16

Samantha slipped up behind Jason and slid her arms around his waist. "So how goes the watch?" she asked, after giving him a kiss on the cheek.

"Umm, hi, Sam," he said, laying a hand on hers. "Everything's going about like we expected. Howard refused to back off after Bruce presented him with a warning, so Plan Two is moving right along."

Jason had been keeping an out-of-sight watch on the activity between Lori and Howard ever since their meeting in the restaurant. He was careful not even to let Captain Blake know of his presence for fear of undermining Blake's confidence. No sense in letting the fellow think he wasn't trusted. Still, Jason wanted to stay on top of everything to be sure Lori was all right and that the overall plan kept moving along in the right direction. Jason knew that Blake had Brad and Lori's best interest at heart, but he also knew that Blake lacked the experience to handle any of those unexpected problems that show up every now and then. Jason had to smile as he wondered at the close tabs Gus must have kept on him back when he was a greenhorn angel courting Samantha.

"I'm proud of you, babe," Samantha said softly in his ear. "You've been one step ahead of old Howard all the way on this case. Personally, my cute little ghost, I think you're getting a handle on this Special Conditions Coordinator thing. Who knows, I might even trust you to help me out when it comes time for my brother, Michael, and Jenice Anderson to go after the captain's sunken gold where it lies on the floor of the Atlantic."

Jason grinned. "Wow, now that is showing confidence in me, Sam. By the way, how are Michael and Jenice doing? I hope she's not having second thoughts about marrying him. Old habits are hard to break, you know."

"No way!" Samantha asserted. "Those two are together for the count. And guess what Jenice is up to with Michael? Betcha can't guess."

"Okay, I give up. What is she up to?"

Samantha laughed. "She's trying to make a reporter out of him. And you know what? He's not doing all that bad with it. I have to admit, I misjudged that lady. She's been nothing but good for Michael since I maneuvered him into putting the ring on her finger."

"Yeah, well I'm glad for both of them. But about this Special Conditions Coordinator thing, I'm not exactly sure I'm getting a handle on it. It took all I had getting Lori to that restaurant where Howard could make his move. She had her mind set on Chinese takeout at home."

Samantha smiled. "So how'd you handle it, tiger?"

"I just conjured up a whiff of one of my own personal barbecued steaks. That put her mind on beef in a hurry. Then I worked in a commercial for the Texas Star Steakhouse on the radio station she was listening to."

"Not bad, Jason. Not bad at all. But don't think you're the Lone Ranger, cutie. I had a couple of problems, myself," Samantha laughingly acknowledged. "First, I had to round up Howard's old chauffeur, Don Harrison, and get him involved in the action. And as if getting him involved wasn't hard enough, he was determined to handle things the old-fashioned way and strongly resisted my idea for Howard's future. I finally got through to him, though. I tied him up in a traffic jam that left him unable to do anything else but listen to my subliminal suggestions. Am I clever or what?"

Jason took Samantha in his arms. "You're having great fun with this, aren't you, Mrs. Hackett?" he asked with a kiss to her lips.

Samantha tapped her finger on the tip of Jason's nose. "Yes, Mr. Hackett, I am. In fact, I'm having the time of my life on both sides of forever."

Jason became serious. "Speaking of which, have you ever been sorry you crossed the line to marry me instead of staying on the mortal side to marry Bruce?"

Samantha was appalled. "Jason Hackett! You know better than to ask a question like that. Of course I've never been sorry. I'll tell you one thing, though. After my experience with Bruce, I know how Lori feels having a rich admirer trying to lure her away from her true love with the promise of fun, games, and unlimited luxury. And believe me, it does have a way of turning a girl's head."

"Uh huh," Jason responded. "And I know how Brad feels having to wait ten years to be in the arms of the woman he loves. Only in my case, it was twenty years. So how come you're so interested in old Howard's future, anyway? The way I see it, the old-fashioned solution is exactly what the guy deserves."

Samantha smiled. "I may have to find a way of tying you up in a traffic jam, my cute little ghost. If you'd been paying attention to me, you'd know I have other plans for Howard. I spent some time checking him out in my computer, and I learned some interesting things about the man, Jason. I know why he's so taken with Lori. And I know his name is about to show up in our upcoming caseloads."

"What are you saying, Sam? That Howard has some contract you and I are responsible for?"

"That's exactly what I'm saying, my cute little chef. And all I'm doing with my plans for him is giving us a head start once his case ends up in our in-basket."

"Howard Placard?" Jason choked. "You and I are going to be responsible for Howard's contract? I don't know, Sam. Personally, I'd say Howard is as close to being a lost cause as a person can get."

"That's what you thought about Bruce, too, remember? I surprised you in his case, didn't I?"

Jason had to think a moment. "Yeah," he finally conceded. "But Bruce wasn't as bad as Howard. I still say this guy's a throwaway of the worst sort."

Samantha shook off Jason's remark. "I don't think so. And neither do the higher authorities, or they wouldn't be placing him on our list of clients. You saw a change in Bruce, and I predict you'll see a change in Howard when the time comes. All he really lacks is a little humility."

"A little humility? Ha! Try a ton of humility to start with. And what about his lack of integrity? This guy wouldn't recognize the truth if he fell in a lake of it."

"Okay," Samantha shrugged. "So he needs lessons in both humility and integrity. You have to admit, what I have in mind for him will be a good start."

"Uh oh," Jason said with a slap to his head. "I feel a Cupid coming on, Sam. Who do you have in mind for Howard?"

"It's not what I have in mind that matters. It's what the higher authorities want that counts. Do you want to argue with them, Jason?"

Jason shook his head. "Okay, Sam, we'll do it your way. You've evidently done your homework on the man. But frankly, I have a hard time thinking he's worth the effort. Personally I'd say even if Howard is a future client, we'll lose this battle. To quote Captain Blake, 'Them be me words, and I be standin' by me words till the ship be scuttled.'"

"Oh?" Samantha asked indignantly. "Be that a challenge, asks I?"

"It's not a challenge, Sam," Jason said reasonably. "It's just my opinion."

"Okay, you're entitled to your opinion, even if it is wrong. And by the way, I've looked over your proposed apology about Captain Blake and Bruce that I expect you to read when we have Gus and Maggie's families over for dinner. I've marked up a few proposed changes in it. You didn't grovel enough to suit me," she teased.

Jason shook his head in mild disgust. "I should have known better than to make a wager like that with you, Sam. Unless I miss my guess, you'll have me on my knees when I read the thing."

Samantha perked up. "I hadn't thought about it, but that does sound like a good idea. Thanks for suggesting it, sweetie."

"Yeah, yeah," Jason grumbled. "Back to the business at hand, what's the deal with Brad? I saw Howard's video of Brad boarding a plane to Africa. I didn't see him come back off. How did you and Arline manage to get him off the plane before it took off?"

"Simple, my dear Watson," Samantha chuckled. "If you'd seen the whole video, you would have seen a uniformed pilot step off the plane."

Jason snapped his fingers. "And that uniformed pilot was . . ."

"Brad Douglas," Samantha answered coolly. "Who else? You don't think Howard and his cronies would be smart enough to catch something that complicated, do you?"

"Evidently not, Sam. They all think they have proof Brad is gone permanently. I guess Howard's in for a little surprise."

"I'd say so, my cute little ghost. What do you say we grab ourselves a ringside seat and get comfortable for the upcoming show. It'll be fun watching Howard handle a few surprises."

* * *

"What about it, Lori," Howard pressed. "Do you care to tell me what destination I should navigate for, or shall I pick one?"

Captain Blake spoke up with a suggestion. "Tell the blackguard ye be wishin' to visit me island in the Caribbean, lassie. That should anchor his tongue for a spell, says I."

Lori took the hint. "If you insist on forcing me to stay on your boat, then I suggest we go through the Panama Canal and do a tour of the Virgin Islands. I want to see the island where Brad lived for the past ten years."

Howard glared at her. "The island where Brad lived? How provincial. I'm looking for a place filled with excitement and romance, one where I can teach you the finer qualities of life. I'm sorry, but some tasteless speck of lava in the Virgin Island chain with nothing but rain forest and wild animals will never do. I'll make the decision myself. We sail to Tahiti."

With Captain Blake as her motivator, Lori took courage. After all, if she had the angels on her side, what chance did Howard have at accomplishing his insidious plan? "What's the matter, Howard?" she chided. "Afraid Brad might show up on his old island again? You pride yourself on being a powerful man. I think you're afraid to face Brad because you know he's going to beat you this time."

"Nonsense!" Howard snorted. "Saying Brad could beat me is ludicrous. I have the power to bury the man in a heartbeat, and you know it, Lori."

Lori broke out laughing. "Words. That's the best you can come up with. Just words. You think you have me trapped on this yacht, but you're wrong. Brad will come after me, Howard. You don't know it, but he has someone more powerful on his side than you've ever matched wits with. He'll come, and when he does—you are in for the defeat of your life."

"You think Brad will somehow show up with a means to interfere with my plan?" Howard laughed. "That's the most preposterous idea I've ever heard. In the first place, you don't need rescuing. I'm not holding you hostage, I'm only using this means to help you make the decision to open the door to a whole new future. In the second place,

Brad wouldn't dare show his face in my presence again. I've taken precautions to insure that little fact."

"Wrong, Howard. Wrong on both counts. No matter how you try to justify what you're up to, you are holding me hostage. And pretending to believe Brad is out of the picture is only lying to yourself. Brad will come. I'm sure you've found some way to try to scare him off, but he will come."

"Nonsense! Pure nonsense!" Howard insisted.

"Nonsense is it? Let me explain something to you, Howard. You claim to love me, but the fact is you have no idea how to love a woman. It's Brad who really loves me. And you mark my words, he will find a way to make you pay for what you're trying to do."

Howard broke into vicious laughter. "Brad can't come," he contended. "The man is thousands of miles from here by now, and he knows better than to ever return. We sail to Tahiti and there we stay until you come to your senses and accept my offer to give you the world."

"I don't think so, matey," Blake declared. "It be time for ye to face yer keelhaulin'. Take heart, lassie. The tide be ready to turn, says I. If ye'll be so kind as to be castin' an eye toward the east, ye'll soon realize the meanin' of me words."

Lori glanced up to see what the captain was referring to. The only object in the eastern sky, other than a few sea gulls floating lazily on the early evening wind, was a helicopter at barely visible range. A helicopter? Could it possibly be . . . ?

In a matter of seconds it became obvious the helicopter was defiantly coming in the direction of Howard's yacht. "What are you staring at?" Howard asked, noticing Lori's interest in the approaching craft. "It's only a helicopter. Helicopters and light planes are common this close to shore."

The size of the smile on Lori's face was matched by an equally all-encompassing frown on Howard's as the helicopter grew nearer and nearer, until at last it pulled to a height of less than fifty feet above the yacht where it hovered noisily. As Lori looked on, she witnessed a breathtaking feat as a man on a rope platform appeared from inside the helicopter and began a slow descent toward the front deck of the yacht. Not just any man, though. This guy was an all-out Elvis impersonator right down to the guitar strapped across his back.

"What is this?!" Howard grumbled. "I didn't order an Elvis impersonator. These fools have obviously mistaken my yacht for someone else's." Howard waved his arms frantically at the craft. "No! No! You have the wrong yacht! Leave us, at once!"

The helicopter pilot, who was visible through the window of the craft, only smiled and passed on a salute. When Elvis was a foot or so off the yacht, he released the hoisting line and stepped onto the deck. At that point, someone inside the helicopter began tossing out long-stemmed red rosebuds by the handfuls. Soon, it was raining roses. They fell in droves, laying a thick red blanket on the forward deck. Some even spilled over the sides, leaving the surrounding waters alive with the delicate flowers.

As the spectacle of roses ended, the helicopter moved swiftly upward and turned back in the direction of shore. Still, the show was not over yet. Fireworks propelled from the craft suddenly decorated the evening with one brilliant burst after another. The sky came alive with giant flashes of blue, orange, and red. Some burst into rapidly expanding circles, while others were more like colorful waterfalls; still others shot upward in a spiraling motion drawing their flaming corkscrew patterns against the purple of the early evening sky. As the noise from the helicopter faded and the last of the fireworks display drifted upward as blue smoke, Elvis removed the guitar from his back and began strumming a familiar tune. After a few notes of introduction, he began to sing:

Wise men say—only fools rush in . . .

Lori's eyes went damp and goose bumps arose as she recognized the song. This guy not only looked the part; he had Elvis' voice down like no other she had ever heard.

But I can't help falling in love with you.
Shall I stay—would it be a sin?
If I can't help falling in love with you.

Lori quickly glanced at Howard, who was totally astonished by all this display. Looking back to Elvis, she was surprised to see him moving leisurely in her direction.

Like a river flows, surely to the sea.
Darling so it goes—
Some things—are meant to be.

By this time, Elvis was directly in front of her. Dropping the guitar to his side, he reached down and picked up a rose. Breaking off most of the stem, he pressed the flower gently into her hair. Then taking her hand in both of his, he sang on:

Take my hand—take my whole life, too.
For I can't help—falling in love with you.

Lori's heart jumped within her as she listened to the final words. And then—she knew. Reaching out with her one free hand, she removed the long black wig and stared into the most beautiful pair of blue eyes in the whole world. Tears flowed freely now as Brad slid to one knee. "Is this elaborate enough?" he asked. "There's not a fishing pole within miles of here. Will you marry me—again?"

Lori was crying openly now. But they were happy tears. "I told you he'd come, didn't I, Howard?" she said just before pulling Brad to his feet and planting a big kiss on his lips.

"Can I take that as a 'yes'?" Brad asked as she paused to look in his eyes and stroke his hair. Her only answer came as a second smothering kiss.

"What are you doing?! You said you were going to South Africa," Howard shouted venomously. "What are you trying to pull?"

"All I said is that I would catch the plane," Brad said grimly. "I got on the plane, then I got off—before it left."

"Perhaps I'm the one who should address that question," came an unexpected voice from behind Howard. Spinning around, Howard found himself face to face with Bruce Vincent. "How did YOU get aboard my ship?" the movie producer demanded.

"Elementary, Howard. You were so engrossed in watching the helicopter show, you never noticed the news boat approaching from behind."

Glancing past Bruce, Howard was dumbfounded to see a second boat with the markings of Channel Five News on the side. The boat was only part of what he saw. There also appeared to be an entire news team boarding his yacht. Of all things, the cameras were already rolling. And holding a wireless microphone to her smiling lips was none other than Arline Vincent herself.

"Hello, Howard," Arline said. "Welcome to the taping of Monday morning's show." She held out the mike toward him. "Is there anything you'd like to say to my audience before we get started with this part of the documentation?"

Howard rudely pushed Arline aside. "Shut those cameras down and get off my yacht!" he demanded.

Bruce took one step closer to Howard. "I'd appreciate it, Howard," he said coolly, "if you were a little less physical with my wife. She's only doing her job. If you feel like shoving someone around, make it me, friend. Do you hear what I'm telling you?"

Howard's face was nearly purple with rage. "Hang what you're telling me, you fool! I'm the one calling the shots around here. You listen to what I'm telling you, Bruce Vincent. Shut those cameras down now! I'll see to it that not one person among you ever works in this industry again if you don't get off my boat instantly."

Bruce smiled. "Just like you planned on closing down the studio?" he asked. "Oh yes, I know about your meeting with Brad. I happened to be in the neighborhood as he was leaving your place, Howard. The two of us had a very nice chat about several things, including the studio. And by the way, we've come to the conclusion not to shut it down. We may even expand its operation in the near future."

"You're insane, Bruce," Howard spluttered. "I'm the only one who can make the decision to keep the studio open or to close it. And by blazes—I will close it. I'll close it so tight a cricket couldn't manage his way inside."

"You threatened to close the studio?" Lori gasped. "So that's what your game was, Howard. I think you're despicable. Is there anything you won't do to insure that Brad and I never get back together?"

Howard's voice softened somewhat as he addressed her. "No, Lori. There's no length I won't go to, to make you mine. Don't you see? I'm only looking out for your own good." His voice ended on a pleading note.

"No, Howard, I don't see that at all," Lori responded. "All I see is a selfish, power-hungry man trying to force his intentions on me at any cost—including depriving me of the only man I've ever loved. You lose, Howard. And let me say this, Brad packs a pretty powerful kiss for someone who's supposed to be thousands of miles away in Africa."

"Stop it, Lori," Howard begged. "You don't know what you're saying. You have no idea what you're giving up by rejecting what I'm offering. If you won't think of yourself, then think of those people at the filming studio. If you'll agree to forget Brad and come with me now, I'll spare the studio. What about it, Lori? Will you come with me?"

For ten long years, Lori had tried to be civil to Howard, but his devious actions since Brad's return had caused her to completely lose patience with him. "You know what the two things I dislike most about you are, Howard?" she said coldly. "Your face. And if I don't see either one of them ever again, it will be too soon."

Arline, who had been catching all this conversation on her mike, moved in close to Howard again. "So, Mr. Placard. Just so our audience will have no trouble understanding your intentions, you say you'll close down the local filming studio, putting hundreds out of work unless Lori denounces the man she loves to become your personal property. Is that about it?"

"Get that mike out of my face, and turn off those cameras! The fate of the studio is no one's business but mine. And if you think your show will air Monday morning, you're sadly mistaken, young woman. Your show is off the air as of this instant."

"I don't think so, Howard," Bruce cut in. "You have nothing to say about Arline's show, nor do you have any say in the fate of the studio. Just for your information, you no longer hold controlling interest in the studio. In fact, you don't hold any interest in it at all. You see, Brad and I liked your idea of selling the studio so well, we decided to beat you to it. So, we called a meeting of all the stockholders and presented them with two proposals, yours and ours. Guess what, Howard. They didn't like your proposal one bit. So they went with ours. We had the perfect buyer, so they voted unanimously to sell. Oh, and if you're wondering why you weren't invited to the meeting, I guess we just forgot to call you. Too bad, huh?"

Bruce opened a briefcase he had been holding and removed a three-page document, which he handed to Howard. "I'm sure you won't believe me, Howard," he said. "So I'll let you read it for yourself. By the way, you'll find a check in the package for your share of the sale. I know you can use the money."

Howard looked like he was ready to explode. He grabbed the document from Bruce and looked it over start to finish. "This is preposterous," he grumbled. "It says here Brad Douglas is the one who purchased the studio. Where would the likes of Brad Douglas come up with money to buy a corner hotdog stand, let alone a filming studio? This is a fake, Bruce, and we both know it."

"Excuse me just one second, will you, Lori?" Brad asked, releasing her arm and moving in front of Howard. Speaking directly to Howard, he said, "Remember that night so long ago when I caught you kissing Lori? Yes, of course you remember, Howard. And do you remember the way I thanked you?"

Howard's eyes grew wide as he watched Brad's hand roll into a fist. "No!" Lori shouted, quickly stepping between Brad and Howard. "You hit him once, Brad, and I won't have you hitting him again."

Brad looked at Lori, and with a sigh relaxed his fist. Howard suddenly reached out, grabbing Lori by the left arm and pulling her around to face him. "Please, Lori. I'm asking you one last time!" he shouted.

"Let go of my arm," Lori said in a slow deliberate voice.

Howard gripped her all the tighter. "You've got to listen to me, Lori! This is all wrong!" Lori's hand shot forward at lightning speed, striking Howard a stinging blow to the side of his face. Instantly, she pulled her arm free.

Brad couldn't believe his eyes. "Lori!" he cried out. "You hit him!"

"Yes, I did, didn't I?" she grinned. "He deserved it. And what the heck, why should you have all the fun?"

"Nice job, Lori," Bruce complimented her. "And by the way, Howard, you're wrong about this document being a fake. It's every bit as real as that red mark on your face. Brad does own the studio. You no longer have any say in what happens to the place."

Howard rubbed his face and stared first at Bruce, then at Brad. "How can he own the studio? Where could he get the kind of money necessary for such a transaction?"

"Allow me to introduce a friend of mine to you, Howard. He's an angel of a guy when you get to know him." Bruce pointed to what appeared to be empty space just in front of where Howard was standing. "I'd like to have you meet Captain Horatio Symington Blake," Bruce smiled. "I'll let the good captain explain where Brad's money came from."

"Have you lost your mind, Bruce?" Howard growled. "There's no one standing where you're pointing."

"Ah, but there is," Bruce contended. "It's just that until now you're the only one who couldn't see him. But the time has come to rectify that little discrepancy."

Howard gasped, and took a quick step backward as the figure of Captain Blake became instantly visible to his eyes. "What—how . . .?" Howard stammered. "This is impossible."

"Aye, ye blackguard, how indeed, asks I," Captain Blake spoke up. "It was me gift of gold to Brad Douglas when he was leavin' me island for the last time. That be how he got the money to make yer shiverin' bones hang at the tip of his sword. It's walk the plank and into the deep with ye, says I."

Brad flashed a smile in his old friend's direction, then took up the torch himself. "Actually it was your own doing that provided me the money to purchase the studio, Howard. If you'd never interfered with my marriage, I never would have fled to an island in the Caribbean. If I'd never been on that island, I'd never have met the good captain here, and I'd never have acquired those rare gold coins I brought back with me. They were worth a hefty fortune, it seems. You can't believe the deal Bruce was able to set me up with, especially since the coins were in mint condition."

"Gold coins?" Howard gasped, as he looked again at the document in his hand.

Howard wasn't the only one surprised by this new turn of events. Lori was also caught off guard. "Captain Blake gave you some gold coins?" she asked. "And you sold them for enough to buy the studio?"

"That's just the way it happened, Lori, except that with Bruce's help I was able to sell them for much more than it took to buy the studio. For your information, pretty lady, I'm the one now who can afford to give you some of the finer things in life. Marry me again, and you can live in the most fabulous home you can dream up, and you can forget the old Pontiac while you're at it. I've already ordered you a brand new Porsche 911, and I'm having it custom painted candy-apple red. It'll be here in less than two weeks, and it's all yours."

Lori's mouth dropped in surprise. "You bought a Porsche for me? And you're offering me an expensive house to live in? I'm surprised at you, Brad Douglas. Howard is the sort of man who thinks he has to buy my love; I thought you were above his sort of thinking. I don't want expensive houses from you, and I don't want your candy-apple red Porsche 911, either. I'll be perfectly happy living in the house you built for me when we were first married, and you can cancel the car deal tomorrow morning."

"What?" Brad was stunned. "But you've always wanted a Porsche 911. I just don't understand you, Lori."

"I don't want it because it reminds me of something Howard would do. I love you for who you are, Brad. Not what you can afford. The car goes back."

Howard kicked at a few of the rosebuds near his feet, then crumpled the document Bruce had given him and threw it on the deck of the yacht, as if that would somehow help make the problem go away. "Don't count your winnings just yet, Mr. Douglas," he growled. "Sometimes it's necessary to lose a battle in order to win a war. You may have the studio, but I have countless other irons in the fire. You won't be laughing so loud when I bring your newfound world of petty wealth crushing down around your head, now will you?"

Bruce extracted a red folder from his briefcase and held it up for Howard to see. "Maybe you should take a look at this before you seal Brad's casket closed, Howard. Do you recognize this folder?"

The color drained from Howard's face. "Where did you get that?" he snapped, attempting to grab the folder from Bruce who easily kept it out of Howard's reach.

"Ah, I see we've struck a nerve this time," Bruce grinned. "I'll bet you would like to get your hands on this file, wouldn't you, my man?"

Great drops of perspiration appeared on Howard's forehead as he continued to stare at the folder. "This is impossible," he reasoned aloud. "My security system is impregnable. I keep my classified files in a place so secure even a tank battalion couldn't get in. That folder is a fake, Bruce."

"Oh, no, Howard, it's no fake. And yes, you did have them secure from most intruders. Problem is, you didn't reckon on my friends Sam and Jason Hackett. Sam and Jason have a way of doing the impossible so slick it makes David Copperfield's antics look like a schoolboy trying to palm nickels. To them, getting past your security system was child's play." Bruce opened the folder for Howard to see and slowly fanned through the pages. "Satisfied now that the document is authentic?" he asked.

"Get those cameras in close," Arline called out to her crew. "I don't want to miss any of this. Not when it's the icing on the cake."

At this point, Howard's attention was so keenly drawn to the red folder, he didn't even bother objecting to the cameras. "Name your price, Bruce," he pleaded. "I'll give you anything. Just let me have those files."

"What is it about these files that makes you want them so badly, Howard?" Bruce asked innocently. "Could it be the little fact that they contain records showing how you've been cheating on your income tax for the past decade and a half?"

"Stop playing games, Bruce," Howard ordered. "Every man has his price. Tell me yours, and we can come to some sort of understanding here. You want this yacht? How about if I throw in my beach home? It's all yours, Bruce. Just let me have those papers."

Bruce smiled. "In the first place, Howard, I don't need your money. It just so happens I can afford all the yachts and beach homes I might happen to want. And in the second place, I'm not greedy enough to let you have these files at any price. There's someone I'd like to have you meet, Howard. Or should I say someone I'd like to have you become re-acquainted with?"

As Bruce spoke, a man who had been standing out of sight near the back of the yacht stepped forward to join the group in front of the cameras. "You do remember Don Harrison here, don't you, Howard?" Bruce asked, placing a hand on Don's shoulder. "It's been a few years, but I doubt you've forgotten the man."

"Of course I remember Don Harrison," Howard answered nervously. "Don was my chauffeur once. That is until he walked out on me the night I . . ."

"The night you took me home after you tricked me into being alone with you on your private island," Lori exclaimed. "I thought I recognized you, Don."

"That's right," Don said with a polite nod to Lori before addressing Howard directly. "I've been out of the chauffeur business since the night you forced your advances on this lady and interfered with her marriage. I swore on the spot if I ever had the chance to show my contempt for what you did, I'd stop at nothing to get the job done. Well, guess what, Howard? The red folder Bruce is holding gave me that chance. You see, I'm an investigator for the IRS now. Sort of leaves a warm spot in your heart, doesn't it, old friend?"

Howard pulled out a handkerchief and wiped his brow. "You work for the IRS? You've examined the files in that folder, I assume."

"Oh yes, Howard. I've spent hours pouring over your files. Offhand, I'd say you're treading deep water about now."

Howard squirmed. "Listen, Don," he bargained desperately, "I'll give you the same deal I offered Bruce. I'll set you up so you never have to work another day in your life. What are you going to get out of bringing me down? A worthless pat on the back from your supervisor? A moment's fun of thinking you somehow got even with me? It's all so empty, Don. Think about what I'm offering you. The means and freedom to enjoy life to its fullest."

Don smiled. "That's your answer to everything, isn't it, Howard? Throw money at the problem. I'll tell you what I'm going to get out of pressing your case—I'm going to keep my integrity, that's what. What good would all you're offering me be if I couldn't look myself in the mirror long enough to shave in the morning? And just so you'll know how serious I am, I'd like to remind you, your attempted bribe came in front of Arline's television audience. I'd say I have all the witnesses I'll ever need to put you away for a good long time."

Howard quickly surveyed the taping crew that he'd forgotten about in his determination to get the red file back. "No!" he choked out. "I wasn't bribing you—I was only . . ."

"Sorry, Howard," Don shrugged. "You're grown so accustomed to using your money to get what you want, you've lost all sense of right and wrong. There are some things even your fancy lawyers can't justify. Trying to bribe an IRS agent is one of them."

"Please," Howard begged. "Shut off those cameras. I'll give all of you anything you want, just shut off those cameras."

"You want us to stop the cameras?" Arline asked, putting the mike in front of Howard's face once again. "Think about what you're asking, Howard. This should be your greatest production ever. I mean, how many of your other productions have you actually starred in? It'll give you something to think about all those long nights in prison when you have so little else to do."

Don pulled a two-way radio from his belt clip. Pressing the transmit lever, he spoke into the device. "Okay, you guys can come in now. We're ready for you."

"What are you doing?" Howard asked anxiously. "Who did you call?"

Don slid the radio back on his belt. "There's a police boat about a mile away, Howard. They were only awaiting my signal. They're on their way to get you, old friend. You're under arrest for some rather serious tax evasion. And while we're waiting for them to get here, let me ask you this, what do you think of the idea of spending the next ten years in a federal prison?"

"Ten years?" he gasped. "No, please, Don. Give me the chance to come up with the money I owe. I'll pay it all back, I assure you."

"Oh you'll pay it all back all right, Howard," Don affirmed. "Every dime of it. But we're not waiting while you come up with some scheme to get the job done. We'll simply confiscate your assets and turn them into the necessary cash. I think we'll start with this yacht since it's handy. And that check you shoved in your pocket from your part of the studio sale is next. Sort of gets to you, doesn't it?"

Howard fell limp into one of the chairs near the table containing the VCR he had used to show his altered video a few minutes earlier. Had it only been a few minutes? It seemed like another lifetime ago.

Don spoke up again. "My first inclination was to send you to prison, Howard. But fortunately for you, this could be your lucky day. While I was stuck in freeway traffic earlier today, I came up with an alternate plan. Because of you, Brad Douglas was forced to spend ten years of his life on a lonely island in the Caribbean Sea. The thought came to me that it would only be fitting if you had a taste of what life was like for Brad on that island."

Howard swallowed hard and stared at Don. "What are you suggesting?" he gulped.

"I'm suggesting an agreement between the two of us, Howard. I'll agree not to press for a prison term, if you'll agree to spend the next five years on Brad's island. I'm offering you a way to pay your debt in half the time, and spare yourself the disgrace of prison life while you're at it."

"But—how would I survive? I'd need food and shelter."

Brad broke into laughter. "Are you serious, Don?" he asked. "You're offering Howard a five-year stay on my island in lieu of ten years in prison?"

"I'm dead serious," Don assured him. "And Bruce assures me his angel friends can work out the details. What do you think? Does the idea have any merit?"

"I love it," Brad responded. "My tools are still there someplace along with a ton of unused building supplies. With a little elbow grease, Howard should be able to put my old place back into livable condition. Of course knowing Howard, it'll probably take him a month to figure out which end of the hammer drives the nail."

Lori looked long and hard at this man slumping motionless in his deck chair. What she saw was definitely a different Howard than the one she had come to know over the past decade. Gone was his air of all-encompassing confidence; gone was his demeanor of supreme control; gone was the mantel of power he so blatantly held up for all the world to see. Here was a man wearing the garments of bitter defeat. She almost felt sorry for him.

Howard reached into his inside coat pocket to retrieve a handkerchief to wipe the perspiration from his brow. As he did, something else slid from his pocket and fell to the deck in front of his feet. Glancing down, he realized it was the medallion. The one belonging to Lori that he had carried for the past ten years, ever since the day he engineered his first meeting with Lori after Brad had caught his flight to Acapulco, Mexico.

Howard wasn't the only one to notice the medallion. Lori spotted it immediately. Without hesitation, she bent down and picked it up. "Where did you get this?!" she asked. "I haven't seen this medallion for the past ten years. I assumed I lost it somewhere. How did you come by it, Howard?"

Howard wiped his brow. "It must have come off in my pocket the day I met you at the airport. You know, when we went to lunch at the Hunter's Cottage. At first I kept forgetting to give it back to you. After a time, I just kept it because it reminded me of the happy times we spent together back then."

"Happy times?" Lori asked. "Humph, by your standards, maybe. Not by mine." Lori looked again at the medallion. "Maybe it's fitting that I found this now," she mused aloud. "I lost it the day you first started interfering in my life. Now I find it on the day you're finally out of my life." She dropped the medallion into her purse and stared at Howard.

"This can't be happening," he muttered meekly. "What went wrong?"

"You messed with the wrong guy," Lori stated coldly. "You got away with driving him out of my life once, but this time he had the help of some very angelic friends. And by the way, just in case you misunderstood me before all our last-minute guests arrived—no, I won't marry you, Howard. And YOU can take that to the bank!"

Lori glanced up to see the black and white police boat just pulling alongside the yacht. Two police officers came aboard and after reading Howard his rights, put him in handcuffs and led him away.

"I'll take that red folder now, if you don't mind, Bruce," Don said.

"Yes, of course," Bruce responded, handing Don the folder. "Thanks for all your help, Don. And I was wondering, might I ask you one more favor before you leave?"

"Name it, Bruce. If it's in my power, I'll give you anything you ask. After all, you gave me the chance to put Howard away and that's something I've wanted to do for a very long time."

Bruce cleared his throat. "You mentioned the IRS confiscating this yacht. I was wondering, since Brad and Lori could use some time alone . . ."

"If I'd consider leaving the yacht in your hands for safe keeping for a while?"

"Something like that," Bruce nodded.

"You got it, friend. Keep the yacht as long as you like, Brad. I know where it is, and I figure Howard owes you that much."

Don slid the red folder into his briefcase and walked away to join the others on the police boat.

"I'd say our business with Howard is about finished, darling," Bruce said to Arline. "I'm sure your editing department has all the tape necessary to put together a great Monday morning show."

The last rays of the evening sun were just vanishing from the horizon when Brad and Lori found themselves alone on the yacht; or so they thought. As the news boat disappeared into the night who should suddenly show up, but Samantha?

"I said you were in the hands of the most capable Cupid in the universe, didn't I, Lori?" she asked with a big smile. "Well, was I lying?"

Lori slid her arm through Brad's and pulled him to her. "No, Sam. You weren't lying. And I'm not lying when I say I'll never let this guy go again. I've learned my lesson—you can count on it."

Brad kissed Lori on the cheek. "I can't believe all this is really happening. You'd better believe you have my thanks, Sam."

"Tell Jason we said thanks, too, will you, Sam?" Lori asked.

Samantha laughed. "Tell him yourself, Lori. He's right behind you."

"What?" Lori said, turning to see. "Well, I'll be . . ."

Jason was behind them all right. He was there putting the finishing touches on a table set for two. No sooner had Lori seen what he was up to, than the aroma of his meal reached her nostrils. It smelled heavenly, especially since Lori had been cheated out of her dinner earlier when Howard showed up at the Texas Star Steakhouse. "Wow, Jason," she remarked. "Is that by chance for Brad and me?"

"Yep," Jason said, tipping his chef's hat toward them. "I figure you two deserve the best for the start of your second honeymoon, and naturally the best could come from no one but me."

Samantha walked over to Jason and took him by the arm. "We'll be leaving now, guys," she said. "Tonight is yours. The last thing you need is a couple of angels overstaying their welcome."

"Will we see you again?" Brad asked.

"Oh yeah," Samantha was quick to answer. "But probably not for a good many years to come, until the two of you finish your term in this dimension. You don't need us anymore, Brad. Destiny is back on course, and I'm sure it will stay right there. And besides, we have a dinner of our own to attend." Samantha looked into Jason's eyes, and smiled. "My cute little ghost here is just dying to offer up an apology he owes me. Our guests are waiting for us even as we speak."

As Brad and Lori looked on, Jason and Samantha faded from their view. It was only then that they realized Captain Blake had taken his leave, as well. Now, they were quite alone. "Shall we?" Brad said, motioning to the table Jason had prepared.

"You're darn right we shall," Lori said, starting toward the table. "This lady is starved."

CHAPTER 17

It was after midnight now. Brad pulled Lori to him and they kissed in the moonlight as the gentle feel of an ocean breeze quickened their senses. "Do you know how wonderful this is, being alone with you like this, Lori?" he whispered. "If only . . ."

Lori stroked his hair and returned his kiss. "If only what?" she asked softly.

"If only I didn't have to take you home," he sighed.

Lori giggled. "Why would you have to take me home?" she questioned.

Brad shrugged. "Because, Lori."

"Because why?" she persisted.

"Because we're not married, that's what," he said patiently. "And if I remember right, you never did say you'd remarry me after my proposal earlier this evening."

"No I didn't, did I?" Lori teased.

"Well?" Brad pressed. "Will you remarry me?"

Before Lori could answerer, the two of them were interrupted by a familiar voice. "Aye, and this does me heart good to be seein' the two of ye together like this. It's happy I be the angel Sam signed on for this tour of duty, says I."

"Blake," Brad laughed. "You always were good at picking the most opportune times to show up. You're not planning on spending the honeymoon with us, are you?"

"Ah no, matey. That I be not plannin' to do. I be here to bid ye me final good-bye. I'll not be poppin' in on ye again. Me time has come to be castin' anchor in the final harbor, says I. At least so far as me assignment with the two of ye be concerned."

A lump filled Lori's throat. "I want to thank you, Captain Blake," she said. "Not only for being an instrument in bringing Brad and me back together, but also for looking out for him all those years on the island. I look forward to the time I can meet your Angela Marie. She's a very lucky woman, having a man like you. And you can tell her I said so."

"I be thankin' ye for your kind words, lassie, and will be passin' yer message along to me Angela Marie when I sees her."

"So this is it then?" Brad asked. "I won't be seeing you again?"

"Aye, matey. Ye'll be seein' me again when yer time on this here mortal sea is spent. And when that time comes, I'll be takin' ye sailin' on a cruise over seas like ye can't even conjure in yer mind for now, says I. And I'll show ye islands that stagger yer imagination. Aye, ye and me will stand on a magnificent beach and talk of Lori and Angela Marie. And I promise ye, matey, there'll never be another lonesome night like the ones we spent together on the shores of me Caribbean island. Them be me words, and me word be me bond."

"I know Brad will miss you, Captain Blake, and so will I," Lori said. "You've been a good friend. I'm glad your haunting days are through."

"Well now, lassie," Blake smiled. "Me hauntin' days be not put to harbor just yet. I'll be hauntin' me old island, on a part-time basis, says I. You see, the angel Sam has appointed me watchkeeper over Howard while he be on me island. It be her plan to help the blackguard mend his ways, says she. Aye, and personally I be doubtin' the wisdom in such a plan. But who be Captain Blake to be arguin' with an angel as lovely as Sam?"

"You're going to be haunting Howard Placard?" Brad laughed. "Now that I would like to see. Give him a couple of scares for me, will you, old friend?"

"Aye, matey. I'll be glad to honor yer wishes." The captain stood tall and offered up a salute to Brad, who slowly pulled his own arm into a return salute. "I be wishin' ye calm seas, matey," Blake said triumphantly. Then with a wink at Brad and a warm smile for Lori, he simply vanished away.

"You are going to miss him, aren't you?" Lori asked after the two of them stared for several seconds of silence at where the captain had just been standing.

Brad swallowed away the lump in his throat. "Yeah, I'm going to miss him. But," he said taking Lori in his arms once more, "I have someone who can amply fill the void." Pressing their lips together, they kissed for a very long time. Afterward, Brad sighed. "You know what I wish," he said, looking up at the sky filled with diamond-like stars. "I wish I could do something spontaneous for once in my life."

"Spontaneous?" Lori laughed. "You? What, for heaven's sake, Brad?"

"Well, I was just reminiscing about how our troubles all started. It was when I caught a plane bound for Acapulco with you staying behind to teach at Sanderson's College. I should never have agreed to leaving you behind. If you'd only gone to Acapulco with me, none of this would ever have happened," Brad sighed in regret.

"But what's the point, Brad?" Lori asked practically. "I did stay behind, and it did all happen. I don't understand what you're trying to tell me."

"I'm just saying I wish we could begin our lives over again where we left off all those years ago," Brad explained. "I wish I could set this yacht on a course for Acapulco right now, and that the two of us could spend a new honeymoon where we should have spent our time together ten years ago."

Lori was elated. "I love it, Brad! Let's do it!"

"Lori, we can't. Not until after our wedding."

Lori reached out and pinched Brad's cheek. "There's not going to be any wedding," she said.

"No wedding?" Brad gasped. "But—I don't understand. I thought you loved me and still wanted me?"

"I do love you, Brad. But I can't marry you. I'm already married."

Brad's face went completely red. "Already married?" he choked. "But how—that is who?"

Lori kissed him. "To you, silly. Do you really think I could have ever divorced you?"

"You didn't divorce me? But I thought . . ."

Lori lay her fingers over his lips. "I know what you thought, Brad. And I know what Howard thought, too. I just let him believe what he wanted. That way he stopped pestering me about it. I never went through with the divorce because I kept praying you would come home to me someday. I was just sure you would. And I was right, wasn't I?"

Reaching behind her neck, Lori released the latch on the gold chain she was wearing. Very slowly she removed the chain, revealing two rings looped through it that had been hidden inside her blouse. "Do you remember giving me these?" she asked.

Brad's eyes opened wide at the sight of the rings. "Those are your wedding and engagement rings, Lori. You've kept them all these years?"

"I have. Right here on the end of this chain, just as close to my heart as I could get them. Now, will you kindly place these rings back on my aching finger so we can be on our way to Acapulco?"

Lori watched a very confused Brad Douglas take the rings and slide them back to their rightful place on her finger. "And by the way," she whispered through a mixture of sobs and laughter. "I do expect you to carry me over the threshold to our cabin, tonight. Are you up to it?"

"Am I up to it?" Brad laughed happily. "What do you think, pretty lady?" Having said this, he lifted her in his arms and whirled her round and round until he was too dizzy to stand. Falling to his knees, he lay her gently on the wooden deck. He then leaned down and kissed her.

Lori let her arms slide around his strong shoulders, and there in the moonlight they kissed away the loneliness of a thousand nights. She felt warm and alive in his arms. It was a feeling that came ten years late—but one well worth waiting for.

EPILOGUE

Lying on the warm Acapulco beach, Lori looked up at the beautiful night sky overhead. Brad lay half asleep on the blanket next to her. They had been back together a week now, and life couldn't be better. How could she ever have been so blind as to allow the likes of Howard Placard to make her doubt her love for Brad? All of those things that had seemed so exciting about Howard now seemed so empty. She once thought spending a week with Howard at Carmel by the Sea had added icing to the cake of an exciting new adventure. She had even supposed, at the time, that she had somehow missed out on much of what life had to offer by dating no one other than Brad. How she had dreaded the sound of the alarm clock that would wake her, bringing her back into Brad's drab world. Now, after all the wasted years, the alarm had finally sounded and she found herself in a world so beautiful it defied all description.

Lori glanced lovingly at Brad. Leaning over, she kissed him on the back of the neck. "Brad," she whispered while ruffing up his hair. "Are you awake?"

A smile crossed his lips as he rolled over, pausing with his face just inches below hers. "Yeah, I'm awake, you cute little imp. What else could I be with you trying to rub the hair off my head? What's on your mind, lady?"

Lori kissed him. "I was just wondering," she asked seductively. "Would you be terribly upset with me if I changed my mind about keeping the candy-apple red Porsche?"

ABOUT THE AUTHOR

Dan Yates has always loved being thought of as one who spins an interesting tale. Retired now, he can look back at a career that includes some fifteen years as a professional classroom instructor. "My favorite teaching tool," says Dan, "has always been a good story. Once you get someone's attention with a good story, you've left them wide open to be taught."

Dan continues to say he learned this principle from the greatest teacher who ever lived. "I never mention that teacher's name in any of my stories," Dan explains. "But this doesn't mean He isn't there. He sits in the presiding chair of the group of higher authorities often spoken of in my stories."

Dan adds that having his stories published, and made available for so many to read, "is one of the most humbling and one of the most exciting things ever to happen to me. I'd like to thank Covenant Communications, and especially my editor, Valerie Holladay, for all their help in making this possible."

Dan's previous writing efforts have resulted in Church productions and local publications as well as four previous best-selling novels in the Angels series: *Angels Don't Knock, Just Call Me an Angel, Angels to the Rescue,* and *An Angel in the Family.*

A former bishop and high counselor, Dan now lives in Phoenix with his wife, Shelby Jean. They have six children and eighteen grandchildren.

He still loves hearing from his readers, who have contacted him from such distant places as Hong Kong, Holland, and the Ukraine. He can be reached at yates@swlink.net.